Artania IV: Portal Rift

Artania IV

Portal Rift

Laurie Woodward

For Nicholas and Jessica

Chapter 1

Bartholomew Borax III staggered back and bounced off something hard. He thrust out his hands but still tumbled over, landing on all fours. Gasping for breath, he dug his fingers into the ground and clung to the grassy soil.

Please stay this time.

Arching his back, he gulped in a lungful of fresh air and choked on the ash in his throat. His body spasmed and he sputtered, coughing up dark phlegm. He spat twice.

Dew soaked through his silk pajamas to his knees. The boy leaned back on his haunches and tried to calm his breathing. He closed his eyes and began a silent count. *One... ten... thirty-one... thirty-three.* Once his chest rose and fell without spluttering, he opened them.

The shining moon broke through the clouds illuminating the Spanish-style building beyond. The school was still standing?

But he had just watched it melt away.

A breeze blew back his blonde hair. Slowly, he stood, bare feet slipping on the wet grass. He leaned against the flagpole and brushed his cheek against metal. Cool as the dark sky above. No hint of that fiery furnace now.

That Bartholomew was back in the real world.

The fourteen-year-old had traveled into the mystical Artania three times before, and while each journey was unique, he'd never experienced anything quite like this. Every other crossing had been with Alex by his side, knowing full-well that something magical was about to happen—he was about to breach an enchanted doorway.

Not this time.

This time he'd plodded into Mother's office to dutifully say goodnight and submit to inspection. After taking his third bath and patting his head to tame the cowlick that refused to stay down, Bartholomew had applied hand sanitizer, deodorant, and cologne. Since Hygenette Borax's sense of smell was stronger than a Mudlark elephant, he doubled each application before descending the winding staircase to make his way down the long hall toward her office.

As his footsteps echoed down the lonely hallway, he considered asking to return to school. Maybe the months of being extra clean were enough for her to say yes. It had been almost two years since the incident.

When he saw her from the doorway, he knew it wouldn't do any good. The monitor light shone on her pale skin as she mumbled something about cleansers. As she stared at her laptop on the Plexiglas desk, he felt a pang of pity. Those diamond blue eyes used to cut him to the core, but not anymore. Now, Bartholomew understood her cool glances were simply a mask protecting her from the world. A world where a husband can drown in inches of water and leave you to raise a child on your own.

"I'm ready to rest, Mother."

Her gaze stayed fixed on the computer screen. Mother must have been preoccupied, because for once, she didn't beckon him closer to look for dirt under his nails or specks of dust on his monogrammed robe.

He stepped up behind her. "Mother?"

"What?" She closed the laptop and set a hand over it, protectively.

That was strange. She usually reveled in sharing articles about how germs live everywhere, or a new cleanser. What was she looking at?

"I-I, uhh, have bathed."

"Hmm." She sniffed, raising her nose in the air. "Hand sanitizer?"

He held up his hands for inspection.

"Fine. Good night." She waved him away with a flick of her wrist, but waited until he was back at the doorway before returning to whatever was on the computer screen.

Back inside his room, Bartholomew pondered her strange behavior. Hygenette Borax was many things—controlling, fearful, and of course, obsessed with cleanliness. One thing she had never been, though, was secretive. All his life, Bartholomew had heard her tell stories of the horrors that waited just outside. How if he weren't careful, he could end up just like his father, drowning in mud.

For many years he'd believed her, but over time came to realize that it was all lies. Lies she told herself to explain Father's death.

He shook his head and had just hung up his robe, when the humming started. Then there was a flash.

And that crazy night began.

Chapter 2

Alexander Devinci had trouble falling asleep that night. Tossing. Turning. Getting tangled in the sheets. So much on his mind. Starting high school. Wondering if Gwen would go back to giving him that soft-eyed look, or keep smiling at Jose every time he walked by. Worrying if there'd be a relapse of Mom's heart condition.

Not to mention the nightmares.

Even painting in the garage studio, his fluffy-eared Australian Shepherd, Rembrandt, at his feet had brought little relief. When Alex settled onto the paint-splattered stool and faced the easel, savage images flashed in his mind.

He tried to fight them by painting something familiar, like a skater grinding a curb or one of the Olympian gods in Artania. But his hand would turn them into a gunner trying to kill freakin' terrorists.

"What's going on, boy?" He set the brush down and rubbed Rembrandt's black-and-gray-striped head.

Rembrandt didn't snuggle up against his knees, but cringed as if expecting a beating. This made no sense. The Devincis barely raised their voices at their dog, much less hit or kicked him. Gwen often said that his mom was so gentle you expected fairy dust to come out of her mouth instead of words.

Then Alex noticed a breeze rattle the garage window.

He wasn't exactly the superstitious type. More logical, a doer kind of kid. But after three trips into another dimension where opposing forces battled for control, he'd learned to take heed of signs. Some might indicate that Artania was about to call upon him, whereas others had a more sinister meaning.

Either way, he couldn't create that night.

After smearing a blotch over the whole canvas, he threw his brushes in the garage sink and rinsed them off. Swirls of color blended to gray and then brown as they circled the drain and disappeared down the pipes. He wiped his hands on the towel hanging over the sink and called Rembrandt inside.

Dad was sitting at the kitchen table with papers strewn in every direction, mumbling about some new equation he was working on. Alex smiled. Dad got as lost in mathematical theorems as he and Bartholomew did in their art. But where Dad's scribblings ended up in college journals or in front of the students at the University of Santa Barbara, Alex and his bud's created living beings.

When first there'd been hints of something supernatural, back when he was eleven, Alex had thought Bartholomew was messing with his mind. Then they passed through a painted doorway and ended up in a magical world where all art was alive. He didn't have long to gape at the wonders of Artania before discovering that it was in grave danger and he and Bartholomew were the only ones that could save it.

A heavy responsibility for a kid. One that continually weighed upon him.

So whenever he created, he tried to imagine what sort of creature he was unleashing in that world. And when malevolent images came from his fingertips, he painted over them. Like tonight.

Alex rolled over again. Punched his pillow. Slowly breathed in and out. "…ninety-seven, ninety-six, ninety-five…" By the time he reached twenty-one, the fog of sleep had finally drifted over him.

Restful? That's another story.

Chapter 3

Captain Sludge emerged from a sewage drain and held up his battle axe. As the glint of steel reflected moonlight into his yellow eyes, he smiled. Now that he had his weapon back from Crone, he could truly wreak havoc in those idiot boys' lives.

He sniffed and his piggish nostrils flared. "No Knights yet. Good."

Even if he did meet one of those painted protectors, he wasn't worried. He'd just recharged his axe's shielding, making it virtually undefeatable.

He faced the dull house that looked like every other one on the street, except Alexander's had a stupid little flower garden under the front window.

He sneered. "Blooms, soon to wilt in Devinci dreams."

The hunchbacked monster ran a palm over his slime-covered face, spreading viscous gel over his spiked hair. He began to morph and shrink, until a few moments later he was small enough to snake his way under the front door. When Sludge took shape inside, he opened and closed his claw-tipped fingers in bone crunching pops, so quiet only his bat-like ears could discern them. Narrowing his eyes, he scanned the entry and hall. All was still.

He took a deep breath through rattling nostrils and skulked down the hallway toward a closed door. There, he scratched sharp nails over the wood.

"Be ready to suffer, Deliverer." He slithered inside.

Alexander lie halfway out of the bunched-up graffiti-art comforter, sweat beading across his forehead.

Sludge ran a tongue over his bulbous lips, tasting the boy's discomfort. *The human's dreams will be easy to twist tonight.*

The captain of Lord Sickhert's army bent forward as curling wisps of smoke rose from his cavernous mouth and crept through the cracks of his shark-like teeth. These dark clouds floated over the bed and poured into Alex's right ear. The boy was still trapped in a sleep fantasy when he gasped and sat upright. Sludge reached into the vision to twist the stupid dream. His dream connection strengthened, causing the child to stir.

"No…no," Alex mumbled.

Inside Alex's dream, Sludge saw the mother jogging on the high school's track, her smile widening with every stride. It was a sunny day, with the sky a nauseatingly bright blue, and Alex was skateboarding in the lane next to her.

Well, he'd change that.

Sludge raised his arms, turning the dream sky dark and the track field into an undulating wave. Then he twisted a finger and the ground rose like a great tsunami poised to swallow both boy and mother. He smiled when the weak Cyndi Devinci fell to her knees and Alex bent down to help her.

"Stop or destroyed!" the Painted Knight commanded.

Sludge glanced away from the dream long enough to notice the robot painting train its binocular eyes on his long cloak. He had tangled with this Knight before and lost. But not this time.

This time he had the magic of a trapped unicorn.

Instead of running, Sludge turned to fight. He reached inside his cloak and raised a jet-black arm, curling his other hand into a fist.

From his perch at the foot of the bed, Sir Cyan pointed his binocular lenses at him. "I am warning you."

"Go back to your canvas, Creation!" Sludge growled, holding his axe up like a shield.

Sir Cyan twisted his lenses and his eyes magnified, brightening the glass for several seconds. Then, in a burst, dual beams of light shot out.

When the rays hit his axe, Sludge stumbled back and almost lost his footing. He teetered, only managing to stay upright by widening his stance. He'd show that Knight!

He grabbed the axe handle in both hands and tilted it until the blade was perpendicular to the assaulting rays. He crouched lower. A hum filled his bat-like ears as the Knight's lasers bounced off his axe. Sludge nodded.

Flapping his wings just like he had years before, Sir Cyan rose a few inches to lock onto his foe by narrowing each beam. He puffed up his robotic chest and flew nearer, eyes trained on the grinning captain.

Come closer, Knight.

With a sneer, Sludge swung his battle axe, knocking the Knight off balance. Sir Cyan's rays flickered and he fell onto the ground.

Without hesitation, the captain swung again, hurling Cyan against the wall. The crumpled Knight's lasers shot in crazy directions before he leaped to his feet and jabbed, fists meeting air. Then came a desperate kick. Sludge sidestepped it with an easy guffaw.

The captain would have loved nothing more than to destroy this Painted Knight right then and there. But Sir Cyan had been created before the Deliverers had journeyed into Artania, and he was strong. It would take all his unicorn magic to defeat him.

Anyhow, his work was nearly done.

After tucking his axe back inside his coat, Sludge once again spread slime over his spiked hair and began to shrink. With a final grin, the monster brought his hands together in a thunderous clap, sending another horrific vision into Alex's mind. One worthy of war.

Hand extended, the struggling boy crawled over the buckling ground, toward his mother. When his fingertips reached hers, the ground exploded, leaving the pair in a slow motion nightmare of ripping flesh.

As he watched the boy twitch and tremble, Captain Sludge began to cackle and howl, filling Alex's ears with nightmare sounds.

Chapter 4

Heart pounding, Alex leaped off the bed and rubbed his shivering arms. While trying to slow his panting breath, he looked around, confused. Stared at the crumpled sheets. That nightmare...was so real.

He had to know.

He swallowed hard and tiptoed down the hall toward his parents' room. Afraid of what he might find, he stuck his head through their open doorway. Both were sleeping soundly, Dad snoring away. Still, Alex couldn't stop shaking.

Something was wrong, and he needed to check it out. Now.

After throwing a sweatshirt and a pair of jeans on over his shorts, he shoved his pillows under the graffiti-art covers, in a boy shaped lump. It was a hurried form, but he wasn't concerned with making it perfect. Even if an earthquake dropped California into the ocean, his parents would keep on sleeping. And they weren't the paranoid, I-gotta-check-on-my-kid type. *The Dr. Bock Guide to Parenting* said to give teenagers space.

Rembrandt, who'd been sleeping on a rug at the foot of the bed, leaned against Alex's legs and whimpered.

"Shush. I'll be back soon." He caressed the dog's floppy ears.

Tennies in hand, Alex tiptoed over to the door and slowly turned the handle. Then he crept down the hall to the front entry, where his skateboard leaned against the wall. After tucking it under his arm, he stole out the front door, donned his shoes, and jogged across the front lawn.

As soon as he was out of earshot, Alex threw his board down and kicked off. Even though the misty summer evening was warm, he shivered, unable to shake the vision.

The stars twinkled above the streetlamps in the midnight sky. Porch lanterns glimmered through the fog. A lone car's headlights shone in the distance.

While the nightmare darkened every beam.

He thought focusing on the whirring wheels would calm him. If he willed himself to think of other things, maybe that horrific image would fade. But Mom's shocked face appeared in every shadow, turning what should have been a been a beautiful ride into a phantasm's trek.

Palm trees swayed in the low light, their sharp fronds cutting macabre shapes in the night air. Homes and store fronts seemed to inhale and exhale fetid breath. Clouds wisped by like wraiths assaulting the sky.

Alex skated faster. He tried closing his eyes against the violence assailing his psyche. But the back of his lids displayed images even worse than Santa Barbara shadows. Breathing hard, he kicked. Up one street. Down another. Dreading what he would find.

But when he turned the corner and saw the Spanish tiles resting below inky air, Alex let his skateboard drift.

The high school was still there?

Gaping, he almost forgot the deck below him as he coasted ever slower. He blinked repeatedly before realizing he'd glided to a stop. Then, shaking his head, he turned and pushed off toward the school.

In the center of the circular driveway stood the flagpole. The base looked odd. Lumpy. Alex squinted at the ghostly figure leaning against it, rubbing a cheek against the steel.

Alex inched toward it. "Bartholomew?"

When his best friend turned his head, Alex staggered. Even in the low light, he could see Bartholomew's agony. Disheveled hair. Clenched jaw. Quivering shoulders. The shadows beneath his eyes said, *I've just been through hell.*

B-3 tilted his head and spoke slowly. "Alex, what are you doing here?"

"I could ask you the same thing."

"I don't know. One minute I was getting ready for bed, the next I was in little garret in Artania—"

"What? Artania? Without me?"

Bartholomew nodded.

"But there've been no signs."

He nodded again. Stared off into space. "It was surreal. Of course, so was every trip we've taken there. But then, we had a beckoning doorway."

"The rainbow."

"But not this time. This time I had just hung up my robe, when I heard a sound like a balloon popping. Then I was in a dark attic. Alone."

That's when Alex noticed the silk pajamas and bare feet. He took off his sweatshirt and placed it over Bartholomew's shoulders.

"Dude, sorry. You okay?"

Nodding repeatedly, B-3 went on to explain that he'd ended up in a Parisian loft. Everything was soft and muted, an Impressionist painting. Here he met a morose artist who kept saying that he didn't have enough money to support his little baby. Bartholomew had talked with him for a few hours, hoping that sharing his own loneliness would comfort the depressed man. He thought he was making headway, when he found himself transported to a new land, as realistic as photos on a smartphone.

"I knew I was in the Photography District by the way black and white creations passed freely among full-fleshed Artanians.

Then I was in a film of Santa Barbara High. The school was empty. It was burning."

"Did you hear an explosion?" Alex recalled the nightmare that had driven him here.

"Yes. Then it all began to melt and you were there with your mom. It was…"

"I know, I dreamt it. Why do you think I skateboarded here in the middle of the freaking night?"

"That's never happened before. The nightmares and Artania have always been separate. Do you suppose that the Shadow Swine have some new power?"

Alex thought for a moment. There'd been a period the year before when every canvas he painted and every sculpture B-3 formed was altered into some macabre horror overnight. After some experimenting, they realized that the only creations which remained unchanged were the ones he and his bud made together. So for months they created as one to make Knights of Painted Light. But when they got back from their last journey into Artania, they'd tested it out and things had returned to normal.

"Maybe, like last year," Alex said.

"Sludge," Bartholomew spat.

Alex clenched his jaw, remembering that vile monster. If the Shadow Swine were learning to twist dreams into Artanian realities, they were in trouble.

Big trouble.

Chapter 5

Gwen Obranovich grinded her skateboard against the curb and brought her arm down in a fist pump.

"Yes!" she crowed popping back onto the concrete.

"You're improving," said Jose Hamlin, his hands clasped in front of him like a sexy yoga instructor.

"Cha, I know." Gwen tried to keep from shaking her head at him.

Even though he was easy on the eyes, with that long black ponytail, dimpled chin, and copper skin, her boyfriend could be annoying. Ever since he'd won the Volcom Games the year before, his ego had gotten bigger than a vert ramp.

But he did make up for it. In some pretty nice ways.

Gwen heard whirring wheels and turned to see Alex rolling up, lips pressed together in concentration as he kick-turned back and forth. Gaining speed, he crossed in front of Jose and skidded to a halt.

Jose stepped back and arched an eyebrow at Alex. "Brother, you're a hurricane when a breeze would do just fine."

"I like it that way. No wasting time."

Jose kept his gaze fixed on Gwen. "Grace and beauty are no waste."

Blushing, Gwen looked at her skater shoes.

"I know what's beautiful just fine," Alex said.

"Really. Is that so?"

"So dude, what's up?" Gwen interrupted, before the conversation got too awkward.

"I was wondering if we could talk. Umm, alone?"

Gwen tilted her head and narrowed her green eyes. After they'd returned from Artania in eighth grade, she'd thought he'd ask her out for sure. Expected him to. Yet weeks passed, then months. All he did was skateboard around her until she gave up and started dating Jose.

She put her hands on her hips. "Why?"

Alex opened and closed his mouth, jerked his head at Jose and raised his eyebrows.

"Perhaps she'd rather practice with me," Jose said.

Alex ignored him. "It won't take long. Promise."

Gwen considered giving him the cold shoulder. After all, he'd said he liked her a whole year before, but still hadn't done anything about it. She knew there were other considerations. Mr. Clean, that freaky painted world—keeping art true to fight those dream-invading monsters.

She turned to Jose. "Let's practice 50-50's later, 'kay?"

Jose undid his ponytail, shook out his long hair, and faced West Beach.

Gwen couldn't help but stare. Man, with the ocean breeze blowing it back, he looked like a friggin' model on the cover of a romance novel or something. *Gorgeous.*

Turning back with a knowing look, Jose placed one foot on his skateboard and kicked off into a long graceful curve around the skate park.

Why is such a hottie with me? She watched his buff bod cruise up and down concrete hills.

"Gwen? Hello?"

"Coming." She tried not to groan as she turned away from that vision.

Head down, Alex led her out the gate, toward the grassy strip between the sidewalk and the beach. Board under her arm, she followed him to the shade of a tall palm tree.

"So?" she asked.

Alex got straight to the point, like boringly usual. "I was wondering if anything strange had been happening to you. Like, at night?"

"What? What have you heard?" she blurted, afraid that the moonlit meeting with Jose had gotten around school.

"Not heard. Seen."

"Seen?" Gwen gulped.

"Yeah, it was horrible. Mom and I walking at the high school. Explosions…"

"Oh, nightmares." Gwen sighed. Alex had not been spying on her and Jose.

"Of course. What else?"

Yeah, what else? How about a kiss so soft it makes your stomach do flip flops? That's what else., she thought but said, "Nothing."

Alex explained how a couple nights before, he'd had this dream about their new high school exploding. It was so realistic he had to check it out, only to find B-3 there in his pajamas.

"PJ's?" Gwen said.

"Yeah, somehow he'd been transported from his bedroom. He said—"

"No blue jewel? No flash? No rainbow friggin' rollercoaster?"

"He just popped there. In the blink of an eye."

Alex went on to explain how Mr. Clean had spent a couple days with a French artist, then had gone to the Photography District, where pictures of their high school morphed and melted.

"No way."

"I know. It's never been like this before. The last few times, we could tell we were about to go."

"That crazy doorway."

"Yeah, B-3 is freaked out. I mean, if we can be transported to that other dimension any time, how can we prepare? And why our school? And my mom?" Alex's tan face turned pale.

"Hey, hey, chill. It'll be okay. You two just need to keep doing your art, and things'll get better."

Alex looked at her as if she were an idiot. "I don't think it's that simple."

Gwen shrugged. "So aside from needing to save a magical world, how are ya doing? Haven't seen you out in weeks."

"Okay." He paused. "Not really. B-3's been MIA."

"What's up with him?"

"I don't know. Maybe Mrs. Borax has him locked down taking baths or something."

"She is full-on obsessed. Poor dude."

"I know. Parents..." He paused for moment and got a pained look on his face. "My mom has been sleeping all the time. Looks tired."

Gwen knew Alex's mother had a heart condition which the doctors were still watching. Even had a gnarly heart attack three years before. But Cyndi Devinci had seemed better all through junior high, even jogging and stuff.

"Hope she's okay. I like your mom."

"Thanks. Means a lot. Anyhow, your dreams?"

More kisses from a ponytailed skater boy. Gwen smiled slightly at her private joke. "I'm fine. No nightmares for a year."

"One less thing to worry about." Alex raised his gaze to her. "You know, Gwen, I..."

"Yeah?" She tried not to look into those big honey-colored eyes.

She did have a boyfriend, after all. Who happened to slam the skate park gate just then, making both of them turn. With a confidant wave, Jose headed toward them.

Alex stepped back, glanced at her skateboard. "Uh, saw your grind. Good job."

Gwen sighed. "Thanks."

Even though Jose was full-on hot, she still felt a twinge of disappointment. It seemed like she and Alex were forever destined for the friend zone.

But after all they'd been through, traversing crazy worlds, fighting pirates and riding dragons, she had his back. Even if it meant slapping the slime off one of those disgusting monsters.

Again.

Chapter 6

Bartholomew tiptoed down the stairs toward the front entry, planning to steal out to the hidden studio under the conservatory, and sculpt. But when he reached the bottom tread, he heaved a tired sigh. *I'll probably just sit there, creating nothing. Never mind.*

He was about to go lay back down, when he overheard hushed voices down the hall. He ignored them at first, but when he heard his own name, curiosity got the better of him.

Slinking along the wall, he crept toward Mother's office.

"He hardly rises," Mr. White said. "In bed for hours."

What's the point? Nothing ever changes.

"But he's clean."

"Yes, but during his studies he's detached."

"He's always been easily distracted."

Bartholomew almost turned away. It seemed like his tutor was constantly sharing some concern with Mother. And he used to care. But now he was tired of trying. From the cleaning army shooing him from one room to another, faking focus during Mr. White's boring lessons, to Mother's panic attacks, it all wore him out.

"I know, but this is different, ma'am. For weeks there's been a sadness about him."

Mother's voice lowered until it was barely audible. "He hasn't been doing you-know-what?"

"Of course not. We keep all lessons most practical."

And boring.

"Which will continue, if you value your job."

"Yes ma'am."

"Paintings! Filth splashed across canvas."

"Yes, Mrs. Borax."

Most of their mansion had bare walls, with the exception of a few framed mirrors, a handful of family photos, and the Cleanliness is Next to Godliness poster glaring at him in the schoolroom.

I hate that stupid poster. Leaning back, Bartholomew hit his head on the wall.

"Did you hear something?" Mother asked.

"Shoot!" Bartholomew whispered, turning toward the stairs.

"Master Borax, what are you doing?" his British tutor said, before Bartholomew could take a step.

Dust bunnies! He'd hoped bolting down the hall would make it look like he had just arrived, but his tutor was too quick. Keeping his back turned, Bartholomew tried to think of some reason for lurking outside Mother's office.

"Bartholomew?" Mother said.

He pivoted slowly. "Hello, Mother."

"Don't *hello Mother* me. Mr. White asked you a question. Now answer it."

"I was just coming to ask you...to ask you..." He chewed on his lower lip.

Mother thrust her pale hands onto her slim hips. "Well?"

Just ask her what you always do, even though you know the answer. "I was wondering if I might be able to go back to school again. Alex says that Santa Barbara High is amazing. All kinds of interesting classes. Like—"

"Absolutely not! We have had this discussion multiple times. You are not to associate with those hooligans."

"But…"

She glowered at him through diamond blue eyes.

He hung his head. "All right, Mother."

"Now why don't you be a good boy and go take a bath. Mr. White and I have business to discuss."

Bartholomew shrugged. "Whatever," he mumbled, as he plodded to the stairs.

Chapter 7

Gwen rushed through the halls on her way to first period. She was tardy. Again. She didn't know what was up with her. In junior high she'd only been late once, and that was because Dad had a flat tire. And even then, he'd called an Uber and she got there right after the bell.

Dad was a time freak. He timed everything, from her morning jog on the treadmill in the exercise room to how long it took her to brush her teeth. Mr. Time Management said punctuality equaled responsibility. And boy did he have a lot of that, rushing around to manage his California Dreamin' gyms with the slogan *Where the dreams of a California body come true.* Gwen remembered Mom coming up with the phrase back when she and Dad were still married. Dad didn't like it at first, saying it put too much pressure on people to be movie star perfect. They'd argued for weeks, until one day he threw his hands in the air and said, "Fine, have it your way."

Mom always got what she wanted, in the end. Gwen just wished that included spending time with her daughter. She hadn't even called in, what was it now? Fifteen months? And then it was just to rag on Dad about money.

After years of this, Gwen was used to it being just the two of them. Sort of. I mean, she was fourteen and a freshman in high school, she should be too grown up to worry about stupid stuff like a mom who took off for Europe to model when Gwen was nine and hadn't visited since. Gwen was tough. A skater. A gym rat. She didn't need Mom's beautiful voice singing silly lullabies.

Gwen flashed on a memory of being really little, maybe two or three, and snuggling under the covers while Rochelle sang about a mockingbird that wouldn't sing, so she'd buy her a ring, or a goat, or a dog, or something. She'd looked up at Mom's pouty lips, thinking they were saying, *"I love you so much, I'd give you the world."*

"Yeah, right." Gwen muttered readjusting her backpack as she turned the corner.

The halls were nearly empty, just a few stragglers like herself rushing to get to class. Quiet with just enough morning breeze to pick up a math sheet someone must have dropped and swirl it past her vision. She paused and watched it rise and fall before gliding out of sight. Then, taking a deep breath, she clutched her hall pass and faced the door.

She knocked.

It seemed to take hours, but was only a few seconds before it opened. Gwen wasn't usually the get-embarrassed type, but being late to first period for the third time in a month gave her pause.

Keeping her gaze averted from the audience ready to snigger at the slightest hint of awkwardness, Gwen dropped her late pass on Ms. Leed's desk and took her seat. She expected her algebra teacher to say something snide about tardiness, but she must have been tired or something, because instead she just sighed and tossed the note in the trash before saying, "Page fifty-three, problems two through seven."

That's when Gwen noticed how quiet everyone was. She glanced over at Alex, who was curled around a piece of paper, face screwed up in concentration. Zach was chewing on his lower lip, looking at his paper as if it were Chinese. Even Lacey Zamora, who usually sat cross-legged, dangling a stiletto from one swaying toe, had both feet tucked under her desk as she copied the equations down in neat little rows.

Then Gwen remembered—Ms. Leed was famous for pop quizzes. At random times she'd assign a few problems and tell the class they were having a test that day. Oh, of course today would be one of those.

Pirate poop!

It's not that she never did her homework. Gwen wasn't a tweaker sneaking out to the parking lot to vape, or a populo like Lacey and her gang, who studied in spurts between shopping trips and parties. And she wasn't the type to study all the time like the Book Arms, who seemed to have a book growing from their bodies like one of those weird creatures in Artania. She was somewhere in the middle. She took a Goldilocks approach to school. Not too hard or too soft, studying just enough, kind of like Baby Bear's chair.

Anyhow, there were other things in life. Like nailing a fakie or looking into the dark eyes of dreamy skater boy while he brushed back a lock of hair that'd escaped one of her braids.

Gwen opened her book and read the directions. Just five problems. Did she remember how?

* * *

Forty minutes later she was slumping out the door with the other frustrated freshmen, when she caught up with Alex and Zachary Van Gromin, who we were commiserating about how tough the test was.

"Cha," she said. "Why does Ms. Leed do that? I mean, with no time to prepare?"

"Well, maybe if you got to school on time for once, you'd be ready." Alex flashed a patronizing look, which didn't escape Gwen.

"What? Can I help it if Dad's gotta leave early and can't give me a ride?"

"You managed last year."

"Hey, my mom could give you a ride," Zach said. "She loves doing carpools. Acts like they're as exciting as buying Volcom Games merch." He flicked his wrists toward his Carhartt chore coat, unbuttoned to show off a print tee.

That dude loved his clothes and usually rocked the skater boy look. Shopping all the time. So it made sense his Mom would be into the whole transport thing.

"Thanks, but I'll just skate. I like to, you know?"

Alex and Zach nodded their heads sympathetically as they moved down the hall.

A few doors down, Zach jerked a thumb at a classroom and said, "My stop," before entering.

Now Gwen and Alex were alone. She turned to ask him how things were going, but he wasn't there.

"Huh?" She looked around. *Where'd he go?*

But then she thought about his holier than thou attitude and got pissed. *Ditches me as some sort of lesson. Who does he think he is? My dad?*

Shaking her head, she tightened a backpack strap and stomped off toward second period.

"Jerk, jerk, jerk."

Chapter 8

While clutching his backpack, Alex glanced around. Five minutes ago, he'd been in the school halls chatting with Gwen. Then his body began tingling and he'd found himself in a cartoon-like park.

He knew he was in Artania—painted trees, cotton clouds, origami birds flying overhead, and clay-like grass under his feet.

A few yards away, a mustached man on top of a soap box was giving a speech.

"Another village has been swallowed! The third this month!" He punctuated each word with an index finger. "And what does our leader do? Nothing! It's time for change."

After pushing through a few men in berets to get closer, Alex cocked an ear to listen. Then the tingling started up again, and the next thing he knew, he was at his front door.

The shaking boy entered and headed for the kitchen. There was Dad, a jumble of papers strewn about on the farmhouse style table they'd had ever since Alex could remember. When he was little, Mom used to cover it in blankets to make a fort, or with a plastic tablecloth so he could work in play dough. Later, when her cookbooks took off, it became the backdrop for photo shoots of amazing dishes from around the world. And of course, it was the place they gathered nightly to talk about the day, share stories, and for Dad to impart wisdom from Dr. Bock's *How to be a Perfect Parent.*

Until lately.

Lately, Mom was more often in bed than experimenting with cool recipes, like Ziggurat Pancakes or Acorn Pudding. Lately, no exotic spices filled the kitchen with pungent aromas. Lately, her camera stayed in the case. I mean, who wants to photograph gooey, boxed mac and cheese or pizza from Dominoes? Recently her olive skin, so often rosy from a recent jog or bending over a warm oven, had taken on a greenish tint, and it worried Alex.

"Alex, what are you doing home?"

What could he say? *Oh, some magical planet seems to have gone haywire and transported me here.*

"Umm, I forgot an important essay. It's in my room."

"Shh. Keep your voice down. Mom's resting."

Alex swallowed hard. "Again?"

"She needs to."

"It's not—" Alex couldn't bear to finish the sentence.

A heart attack had nearly killed her when he was eleven.

"No, no, no. Not that." Dad gave him a reassuring smile.

"But it's been a lot lately."

"It's just her, *ahem*, tummy. Don't worry, kiddo." He turned back to his papers.

Dad was being so vague. Alex narrowed his eyes. What was the big secret?

He started to imagine something terrible and had just reached in his back pocket to Google it on his phone, when Dad slapped the table.

"Yes!"

"What?"

"I think I found a proof. Not complete yet, but if I keep the requirement of invariance of the joint probability density of all entries, I just might be able to arrive at a broader class of…" He began scribbling notes.

Alex shook his head. If Dad could get into Random Matrix Theory, then maybe Mom was okay.

He felt better. For about two seconds. But then this other part of his brain, which was just as mathematical as Dad's, began counting back. Mom had been resting for weeks now, and a cold usually only lasted a week at most. Even for a forty-four-year-old lady.

Actually, she'd started to look bad about the same time Bartholomew had returned from Artania. Could there be a connection? Might that crazy appear-disappear experience be causing illness? It'd been almost two months since that horrific night, and he still didn't know what was going on.

"Can Swineys make people sick?"

"Hmm?" Dad glanced up.

"Nothing, just thinking."

Pulling out his phone, Alex walked towards his room and googled, *What stomach problems lead to weeks of weakness?* One hundred forty-five things popped up on Webdoctor.

Lack of exercise, hypocalcemia, and multiple sclerosis.

He dismissed the first one since she did exercise, but as he read about the symptoms of the other two a pit grew in his gut. She might have muscle spasms, confusion, or weakness, like they described online.

He scrolled down further. *Anemia, hypothyroidism, lupus, hepatitis.* He scanned each disease and its description. She could have one of those. Or... *mononucleosis, pancreatitis, peptic ulcer, tropical parasites, heart rhythm disorder, diabetes, toxic shock, histoplasmosis, kidney stones, radiation sickness, typhoid fever, appendicitis, lead poisoning, shingles, atrial fibrillation, tuberculosis, gallstones, bird flu, stomach cancer, OR cat scratch disease!*

She had markers for every single one. She was tired, said she felt nauseous, and was in the bathroom a lot. Both colitis and diverticulosis caused intestinal cramping and diarrhea, along with about ten others. Including cancer. Oh, man. Anything on that list could cause increased sleep.

Alex gripped his phone tighter, tempted to just friggin' go knock on her door and ask. But if Dad said she needed rest, bugging her would make her sicker.

Shaking his head, Alex tore his gaze away from the phone. Some of his creations hung on the wall, next to his skater posters and Andy Warhol prints.

Dad had framed them a couple years back, saying, "Dr. Bock believes that one must display the fruits of a child's labor."

If Dad knew that each was a Knight of Painted Light protecting children's dreams from a slimy race of creatures, he would have had put them behind bullet proof glass.

Alex glanced back.

Intestinal ileus. Aortic regurgitation. Hypoparathyroidism.

Cursing, he tossed his phone on the bed, its neon handprint case blending in with the graffiti-art bedding and curtains. He'd picked out the patterns because their fat dayglo words splashed over a black canvas inspired him. They reminded him of the cool walls he'd seen in in L.A., where taggers marked their territory with one-of-a-kind images.

One day, while the family was on the way to the La Brea Tar Pits to check out all the ice age displays, Dad took a wrong turn and ended up in a rundown neighborhood. While he tried to figure out the navigation system on their new Honda, Mom pointed and shook her head.

"We don't do enough to take care of our own. Other countries make sure the poor are cared for," she'd said, once again railing against the cruel government, as Dad drove in circles up one alley and down another. "Europe, Canada, Australia, New Zealand all spend more. In fact, a smaller percentage of our economy goes to help needy individuals like the elderly and unemployed than twenty-six other developed countries…"

Alex had barely heard. He'd been too blown away by all the sprayed images on walls and fences, wondering if he'd ever have the chance to create something so big and bold. Some were just gang symbols and numbers, but man, others had such detail he was sure there must be a land in Artania just for graffiti.

Alex picked up his phone again. Over a hundred different diseases. Over a hundred sicknesses that could cause Mom real pain. Make her suffer again. Over a hundred things he was powerless against.

Like having nightmares where Mom's heart slowed to silence that seemed so real he woke in a cold sweat. Or being yanked into another world at any moment and ending up miles from where you started.

He stared at the long list in his phone. "What the frick is going on?"

Chapter 9

Bartholomew was lying in bed picking at a hangnail, when he heard a soft knock.

"Master Borax?" the maid, Yvette, called through the door. "You have a telephone call. It's young Alexander calling again."

Sighing, the boy slowly rose and said, "Coming," before shuffling down the long hallway toward the white telephone atop a glass table.

After handing him the receiver, Yvette curtsied and hurried down toward the hall.

"Hello?"

"What's up with you?"

"Huh?"

"I've been trying to call for hours and all I get is, 'He's resting.' How much can a dude rest?"

"I just haven't felt that good."

"Sick?"

"I don't know, maybe."

"Oh, I know. It's one of your pity parties. Poor me." Alex huffed. "Have you ever thought that other people are dealing with stuff, too?"

Bartholomew didn't know what to say. "I...I...I, yes."

"So ask."

"How are you?"

"I don't know. Mom's been sick for a while. Keeps resting but doesn't seem all down in the dumps like you. Dad says it's her stomach. But I think it could be something worse."

"Her heart?" Bartholomew gulped.

"God, I hope not. She's been better for three years now."

Bartholomew remembered how Alex had come in late to their sixth-grade class, his eyes hollow sockets. Later he shared how Mrs. Devinci had a heart attack and almost died.

"Me, too," Bartholomew whispered.

"You read a lot. Why don't you come over and see what you think?"

Bartholomew felt tired again. "I don't know. It's so hard."

"Getting a limo to drop you off is so hard?"

"I'm tired..."

"Oh, I get it, too tired to be a friend. Fine, I'll figure this out on my own. Baby." Alex hung up.

Bartholomew stared into the receiver and thought about calling back. Then he heard Mother's bell ringing from her boudoir. He knew what that meant. More maids would soon descend, and he'd be surrounded by whirring vacuum cleaners, feather dusters, and sponges.

It was too much.

He went back to bed, wishing he could sleep this stupid life away.

Chapter 10

Captain Sludge leaned back against his granite chair molded into the cave wall, and twirled his claw-tipped thumbs. Stench and Gunge sat across from him on boulders, expectant looks on their faces. But his minions knew enough to keep quiet until spoken to.

Crone, what are you playing at?

They'd been allies for years, with Crone including him in her every scheme. But lately she'd been shutting him out. What were these secrets she kept talking about? And she said she wanted to protect him?

"Bah! I don't need protection."

"Of course not, sir."

As he rolled his eyes at Stench, Sludge tapped his thumbs together. While the idea of the Deliverers popping in and out of Artania was as sweet as a dance with the Mud Princess, there still was this nagging feeling at the back of his mind. He couldn't help but think that this was part of a power play. One he'd either need to be included in, or thwart before Lord Sickhert found out.

"Hmm."

"Sir?" Stench straightened his hunched back.

"No, no, don't think so," the captain murmured.

Stench sunk back onto his rock, squirming from one perched butt cheek to the other. Beside him, Gunge scraped a jackboot on the dirt floor.

"Would you two stop with that infernal fidgeting? You're corporals, not nymphs!"

"Sorry, sir," Gunge said.

"Is that all you have to say? How about some new ideas for invading the Impressionist Republic? How about a way to keep those Deliverers from protecting Paris? Or perhaps a new dream-draining scheme. Have you even tried to make your nightmares more terrifying, you useless waste of space?"

"I-we-um…"

Sludge stood and pointed a bony finger at Stench. "And you? My second-in-command, whose intelligence should exceed all those in Subterranea. Do you have anything for me?"

"A dream of filth for the Deliverer's mother. Where dirt—"

"She's already a germaphobe, idiot! How about the other mother or the father?"

Stench blinked his yellow eyes, opened and closed his square jaw. "Attempts were blocked by a strange energy."

"Blocked, by a Knight?"

"No, not one of the Painted Knights. This was as if another Shadow Swine had started invading her mind but was keeping the nightmare to himself."

Or herself. Sludge thought. Then instead said, "And you could not join in?"

Stench shook his head.

"I had the same block," Gunge added.

"So what did you do? Give up and enjoy a cup of worm tea?"

Beads of viscous sweat popped up on Gunge's dark forehead. "No, sir, I tried three, four times before moving on to another human."

Sludge paced from one end of the cave cut into Subterranea's wall, to the other. "Did Lord Sickhert send you this dream, or did you actually show some initiative?"

"Our great leader sent it from his stalagmite castle. I was proud—"

"And you?" Sludge turned to Stench.

"The image of the Devinci mother floated down over the River of Lies before I snatched her ghost face from the sulfuric mist."

"He transported you to Earth?"

Stench nodded. "As always, I oozed up near the home of captured dreamer. But when I tried to snake in the Deliverer's doorway, my hand was met by an invisible wall."

"Did you relay this information to our leader?"

Stench and Gunge hung their heads and said no. Both were too afraid of the consequences.

"Keep it that way. Or you may find yourselves in the Correction Chamber. Again."

Gunge's snake-like eyes widened as he readjusted his army coat. Sludge knew he bore the scars of that torture chamber, as did most Shadow Swine. All who displeased Lord Sickhert endured the scalding shower. There, hot droplets dripped from an obsidian pipe and singed naked backs, burning their gelatinous hide until it cracked and peeled.

Only once, when those idiot Deliverers defeated him, had Captain Sludge watched sheets of his charred skin slide down the drain.

And he never wanted to repeat that excruciating experience.

"The next time either of you idiots encounter this blockage, report it to me immediately. Or I will deliver you to Lord Sickhert's Correction Chamber myself."

Chapter 11

Alex took a bite of his burrito and glanced around the Quad to see if any of his buds were there. None of the skatepark crew in sight, until Zachary Van Gromin made his usual strutting entrance, turning right and left as if expecting the rest of the teens to snap photos of his designer duds. Even though Zach was a good friend, he was totally conceited. Of course, when your mom has credit cards for every Rodeo Drive boutique, and a few designers on speed dial, your clothes do earn bragging rights.

Shaking his head, Alex waved him over. "Dude, how goes it?"

Zach put one foot on the bench and arched one arm as if posing for his Instagram account. "All right, for a Wednesday."

Alex raised his brows. "Leg tired?"

Ignoring Alex, Zach glanced over his shoulder. "Naw. Just stretching."

Alex smirked at him. "Sure?"

Tossing his pizza box on the table, Zach winked before sitting down.

"What can I say?" He brushed a hand over his denim shirt with the rolled-up sleeves.

They both chuckled. The dude might be vain, but he was cool enough to get the message when he was overdoing it.

Alex slapped him with the back of his hand. "But I get ya. Mid-week. Mid-semester. Piles of homework." *Still better than being jerked from one world to another.*

"So been to the Point lately? After last year, thought you'd be working on your skills for a rematch."

Zach was referring to the skateboarding competition he'd lost the year before.

Alex shrugged. How could he explain that when things like dragons appear in the sky, it makes it hard to compete?

"Nah. No more comps for me. Not my thing."

"And one red-headed lady has nothing to do with it?"

"I don't know. Maybe."

"Speak of the devil." Zach pointed to Jose and Gwen strolling toward them, arm in arm.

As soon as Alex saw them, all the blood drained from his face. It'd been months and he should have gotten used to them dating by now, but every time he saw them together he got a pit right in his gut.

"Hi, guys!" Gwen said, too brightly.

"Hey," Zach said, while Alex jerked his chin hello and pretended to enjoy his burrito.

"What?" Alex said. "Still not talking to me? Being all judgey?"

"Huh?"

"Your disappearing act last week after your *Tardiness is Next to Delinquency* lecture." She shook her head. "As if you've never been late."

Alex thought back. He'd forgotten that he'd been talking to Gwen when Artania had jerked him away. He guessed disappearing in the middle of a conversation *would* tick her off.

"Oh, that. Sorry, I had an emergency." he lied.

Gwen gave him a quizzical look as if not sure whether to believe him or not.

"You're choosing health, I see." Jose tilted his head at the lunch table.

Zach opened his mouth wide and took a huge bite of his slice. Then with his mouth full of food, mumbled, "Yep."

Still cracking up, Gwen and Jose sat down opposite. Alex sighed, glad to have her watching Zach's goofy antics instead of trying to exchange some sort of meaningful glance with him.

After a few minutes of catching up on who was dating who, how epic Lacey Zamora's fourteenth party had been, and Jose's latest victory at a recent skating competition, Gwen pulled out her phone and started sharing couple pics.

"Ahh, babe, you look adorable here." Jose draped an arm over her shoulder.

Can I vomit now? Alex thought.

"Thanks." Gwen snuggled into the crook of his arm. "You guys should have been there. Malibu. Skaters from all over the world. Even saw…"

Gwen's words barely registered. Alex was too engrossed in the dark mist coming from under her racerback tank. It twirled in tendrils behind her shoulders, rising toward the trees overhead.

"And then Jose said…"

Jaw dropping, Alex raised a pointing finger. The swirling smoke thickened, but Gwen went right on talking. He reached across the table and tried to wave it away, but it kept slithering out like a freshly upset nest of snakes. He extended the other hand and began flapping it faster and faster, hoping to stop whatever it was.

"Hey, dude, what's your trip?" Jose shoved Alex back.

The black fog twisted around Gwen multiple times like a boa constrictor around its prey. Her face paled.

Arms raised, Alex vaulted over the table and leaped behind her. "Get it off!" he cried, as more smoke encircled her.

"What the—!" Jose rushed at Alex.

Alex tried to cover Gwen's body with his own. "Hurry!"

Jose grabbed him by the throat and began tugging backwards. "Leave her alone."

"Jose, no!" Gwen cried.

But Jose only squeezed tighter. Gwen came up behind him and tried to pry his hands loose, while Zach grabbed him around the waist. Meanwhile, Alex went from grabbing at the elusive smoke to trying to wave it away. He didn't notice his increasing light-headedness until near to passing out.

Then Jose relaxed his grip and they all fell back in a tangled heap on the grass.

"Moron!" Jose jerked his body to the side.

Rolling away, he stood and helped Gwen to her feet. Alex sat up and blinked at them. The mist had disappeared and Gwen looked normal. Sort of. If a grass- and leaf-covered girl inside a circle of gaping teens could be called normal.

"What is wrong with you?" Gwen accused.

"I saw... it was... dark... and you..." He glanced around at the silent faces and shook his head. "Crap."

"Alex?" Zach whispered. "You okay?"

"Sorry." Alex waved and bolted out of there.

Chapter 12

Far away, in a magical art-created land, the sculpted Thinker gazed into his steely hand as sparks fizzled down his bronze arm. The images of Alex flickered in his palm and faded.

How could this be? Alexander shouldn't be seeing visions, nor traveling to Artania and back. Never had one Deliverer traversed their worlds without his knowledge, much less two.

He thought back. For millennia, every time a human lifted a paint brush or dipped hands in clay, a wondrous being, like himself, had been born. Over time, Artania's population grew into a perfect blend of watercolor, collage, and mosaics—a mix of multi-hued lives.

As art changed, separate countries emerged. From the Renaissance Nation, where the competing Michelangelo and Leonardo watched over Mona Lisa to the Land of Antiquities, where Greek, Roman, and Egyptian gods raced over sands to Gothia, where medieval knights fought dragons. He had watched his world expand.

Until the time of danger.

Shadow Swine horrors were becoming all too common. The new millennium brought constant tales of Sickhert's army attacking from their underground lair. With increasing frequency, they pulled his brethren below to become mindless slaves. Or at chosen times they opened their horrible mouths, and with great slurps, swallowed brilliant chunks of this land's beauty.

Like a fading photo, every bite turned the earth whiter, causing the Blank Canvas to grow. Now they were attacking the Impressionist Republic, that place where muted light and color capture a moment in time.

Closing his bronze fist, Thinker lifted his gaze to the man in the bushy beard and linen suit in the wooden chair opposite. His words echoed in the nearly empty cafe as he spoke.

"The Shadow Swine seem to have some new power. I fear for the soft hues of this land."

Claude Monet took a long draught on the stub of a cigar and blew a wisp of smoke over Thinker's head.

"As do I."

"The Blank Canvas grows."

"*Oui.* There have been reports of new areas bleached white. The sinking village of the Alps."

"When you ceased dipping brush in paint."

Monet looked at his feet and nodded sadly. "I was immersed in depression."

"Do not berate yourself, friend. It was he who painted you. His poverty got the best of him, and no one, not even I, could have altered that."

"Gauguin would argue otherwise."

"Is he spouting more talk of revolution?"

"Larger crowds come to listen. Many say you are growing old and are unable to lead us."

"My strength does not wane with age, but with the belief in the power of creation."

"I know that, but others do not."

Thinker shook his head. "It seems that no matter how hard we try, it is never enough. The Shadow Swine capture more and more of our kind."

"We are weighed down every moment by the sensation of Time. And there are but two means of escaping this nightmare—pleasure and work. Work strengthens us."

"True. I only hope Bartholomew realizes this before it's too late." The Thinker shook his head.

"Yet now he struggles."

"Leaving ripples of despair here. If he'd just—"

Thinker heard a buzz. Then a whine. The gaslights in the café began to flicker. Tilting his head, the sculpted man glanced up. Every glass lampshade was quivering and expanding as if the god Vulcan was filling each with superheated magma. As the sound amplified into a din, Monet dug his boots into the floor and scooted his chair back. Although a painting, Thinker knew his friend could be injured as easily as any human, and rose to protect his ally.

Diving over the table, he extended his bronze arms and tackled the gaping painter to cover the creation's body with his own. A moment later, the crystal globes exploded in a deafening blast, shooting glass in all directions. Streaming shards sharp as knives rained down.

Thinker pushed Monet beneath the table. Strong back heaving, he glanced to the side at the blinking barkeep, now dusted with glass shards. A few slivers jutting from the painted man's balding scalp began to bleed.

"Help me," he said, lip quivering.

Artania's leader had just begun to stand, when a hissing sound from under the floorboards stopped him mid-crouch.

A stunned Monet angled a finger at the ground, where rotten steam rose from cracks in the wood.

"Shadow Swine, here?"

White tendrils twisted upward, filling the café with sulfuric fumes. Then, as if someone were using a crowbar to pry them open, the floorboards next to the bar began to part and a dark arm slithered from the opening.

The barkeep gasped, stepping back. Opened and closed his mouth in silent screams. The arm grasped him by the ankle and the painted man stumbled and fell against the wall. The crack in the floor widened, swallowing half his leg, then a thigh, and soon his hips.

Arms outstretched, Thinker vaulted toward the barkeep, crossing the room in two strides.

He reached out, clutching at air.

It was too late. The injured barman was gone. Another water-colored being taken below to become a mindless slave in Subterranea.

"No!" he cried as the floorboards closed.

Chapter 13

Bartholomew closed the hatch to the underground studio before settling into a chair across from Alex. Ever since he'd shown Alex the secret room beneath the conservatory and how to circumvent security at the front gate, they'd often met here to catch up, make plans, and talk in private.

Although Mother had ordered most of the estate bulldozed when they'd inherited the Santa Barbara property, one corner remained as wild and glorious as when Grandfather Borax was alive. Grandfather's will required that the area near the glass conservatory remain untouched. So today, lush vines, vibrant flowers, and moss-covered fountains graced every corner, in place of the plastic ones Mother commanded for every square foot of the estate.

Bartholomew had first discovered the hidden space when he was eleven. One day, while exploring the glass greenhouse, a trap door opened and dropped him into the underground room. There, a message from Grandfather explained how he'd designed a studio with enough art supplies to last years.

"Is Gwen okay?" Bartholomew asked when Alex told him the story of mist rising from her body.

He nodded. "Yeah. Ticked off at me, of course. I did freak out when I saw that smoke. When I explained later, she said she hadn't seen or dreamt anything strange…Artania wise, at least."

Bartholomew cocked his head. "Other odd happenings?"

"Oh, you know. Jose doing his usual I'm-this-champion-skater-ready-to-impart-wisdom bull."

"I do feel bad for you. But you know Alex, it's time to face facts. They are together."

Alex's tan face clouded over. "Yeah, I know. I know. They're an item. Him with his puffed-up chest, and her looking up with doe eyes. Well, if she'd rather listen to Buddha Jr. talk about his greatness, there's nothing I can do about it."

Bartholomew knew Alex had had a crush on Gwen for more than a year, but hadn't asked her out. He'd planned to lots of times, but at the last minute he'd lose his nerve, saying stuff like, *there was plenty of time*. Now the clock had run out and she'd found someone else.

"It's comforting to know that she's safe," Bartholomew said. "After last year..."

"Cha."

"And your mom?"

"I don't know what's up. She keeps sleeping, but Dad says it's fine." Alex paused and threw Bartholomew a dirty look. "You know, you could try to answer your phone once in a while. I know the *phone police* screen your calls, but jeesh, you're not the only one trying to deal here."

"Sorry. It's been quite challenging lately. Mother..." Bartholomew shrugged, pretending that Hygenette's compulsive cleaning was why he hadn't answered Alex's calls.

There was no way he could tell his best friend what he'd been going through. Alex would just judge his depression and make him feel guilty for trying to escape in sleep.

After a few uncomfortable silent seconds, Alex changed the subject.

"Are you creating new work? With things so freaky, we need to keep making the true art." He jerked a thumb toward the potter's wheel next to the kiln.

Bartholomew walked over to the art supply cabinet and pulled a cloth off one of the small sculptures drying there. He'd made the sad creature when Mother was in one of her cleaning frenzies and he was feeling lonely. It'd been near impossible to get out, and he'd needed some company that didn't speak in a clipped British accent like his uptight tutor, Mr. White, or carry a mop and dust cloth like the army of maids on the estate.

"This is the last thing I made, two weeks ago."

"Two weeks? That's not like you. You're usually sculpting every day. If your mom isn't on a cleaning binge."

Bartholomew shrugged. "What's the point?"

"You seriously have to ask?"

"Nothing ever changes. I'm still trapped here."

Alex gave him a pitying look. "She still won't listen, huh?"

Bartholomew shook his head. "No matter how many times I ask. Now I've just given up. She'll never let me go back to school."

"Sorry, B-3." Alex fixed him with an even stare. "But that's no reason for you to stop creating."

Bartholomew didn't tell Alex how bad it had been. How some days he'd lain in bed until his middle-aged tutor forced him to get up. How he'd shuffle into the shower and stand there, uncaring, until the water turned cold. Then half-wet he'd crawl back under the covers, letting the blackness of sleep take him.

"Well, at least I made this little guy." He forced a smile. "Part dragon. Part puppy. I imagine him flying around Gothia with Princess Rhea and our friends."

Bartholomew sighed, remembering last year's journey into Artania when he and Alex had stood side by side to make creations to save a land. When life had been more than an endless sea of bleach and lonely lessons with Mr. White.

"Maybe he is hanging with Wade and Erantha," Alex said.

"Perhaps, and maybe keeping them safe." Bartholomew caressed the sculpture's head with an index finger and thought back to their dragon friends in Artania.

Alex crossed his arms. "Maybe nothing. They need all the help they can get. You know what the Prophecy says—it's up to us."

"I know. But I've just been so tired."

"*Our world will be saved if their art is true.* Stop wussing out."

"Okay! You don't have to quote ancient—"

A distant rumbling cut his words short. Cocking his head to one side, Bartholomew turned toward the humming sound.

The ground began to shake and he teetered, afraid his underground studio might collapse. Just when he was about to shout, *Duck, earthquake*!, he heard a pop.

And turned back to watch Alex disappear into thin air.

Chapter 14

Arms akimbo, Alex stumbled back. He wobbled a few steps, then his heel caught on something, lobbing him backwards to land on his rear with a thud. He opened and closed his eyes.

Bartholomew and the studio were gone.

Heart pounding, he glanced around. Alex no longer sat in a chair facing his bud, but was plopped between wood-paneled brick buildings in the middle of a cobblestone street. It was night, with the distant *clip-clap* of a horse-drawn carriage replacing B-3's whirring washing machine.

"What the—?" He stared at the gas-lit road that looked like a watercolor painting.

He heard a slamming sound and turned to see two figures hobbling out of a cafe doorway. He'd never seen the painted man that could barely stand, but the metallic sculpture supporting him was all too familiar.

Thinker. Artania's leader. The bronze icon that guided Bartholomew and his every journey.

Alex gaped. The limping statue half-dragged, half-carried the man into the cobbled street. At the same time, a strange odor wafted over the sidewalk. He sniffed, smelling rotten eggs and sulfur.

And knew.

The doorway to the Subterranea was open. From Sludge, or one of his Shadow Swine minions. The pair were under attack!

Springing to his feet, Alex rushed over to Thinker.

"Sir!" He reached out to grab Artania's leader by the elbow.

Thinker raised his bronze head. The furrowed metal in his brow rippled in confusion.

"You? But…"

"I know. But right now let's get you to safety." Alex kept one eye on the open doorway.

Nodding, Thinker adjusted his grip on the man in the long coat and began shuffling across the street.

Alex barely had a moment to relax, when a new smell joined the rotten egg one. Breathing in something acrid, he halted and tilted his head.

A spark appeared in the corner of his eye and he glanced back. The café had become clouded in mist and a strange red glow emanated from the first floor.

The painted man's eyebrows drew together. "Smoke?"

Alex stared, confused. Tried to pull Thinker forward.

Pointing, the bronze leader jerked away. "Fire!"

That's when Alex saw the flames. They were whipping from one window to another like a multi-headed snake trying to escape. He tugged harder on Thinker's arm.

Thinker wrenched out of his grasp. "No."

"But sir—"

"Many Artanians populate these structures."

Alex stopped arguing. There was no point. The bronze man would risk life, limb, or even death to keep his people safe.

But they were only three. Alex glanced around this quiet-as-midnight street. He had no idea where he was, if there were firemen nearby, or how to call for any. It's not like there were crowds scrambling to the rescue, and even if he had his cellphone it wouldn't work here.

The fiery snakes grew as more heads undulated through the broken glass. Alex swallowed hard. What he wouldn't give for a garden hose right then.

When he heard a crackling sound, he turned toward the café to see part of the windowsill break off and fall onto the front patio. Meanwhile, sparks erupted from another window, sending a shower of embers in their direction.

Seeming to find some strength from within, the wounded 3D painting stood to his full height, put two fingers between his lips, and blew a piercing whistle.

"Pompier! Pompier," he cried, in what sounded like French, then crumpled into Thinker's arms again.

With nobody around, Alex doubted it would do any good. He started to jog down the street in search of a well, when he heard a distant horse's whinnying, followed by hooves clattering. As a bell clanged, a pair of dark geldings pulling a wooden cart with a strange seesaw type of apparatus appeared. Behind this wagon clomped a crowd of firemen in old-fashioned clothes. The man on the raised seat shouted orders to them, while his painted partner steered the horses their way.

"Over here!" Alex waved the firemen toward the burning café.

The driver reined the horses to a halt, while a trio of men grabbed the brass end of a long leather hose and aimed it at the burning building. Pairs of firemen positioned themselves on either side of the wooden seesaw contraption and began to pump it up and down.

In a few seconds, a blast of water sprayed from the brass end. The firefighters tried to hold their ground, but the water's force drove them back. One released his end and fell to his knees while his partners struggled to hold on to the pulsing hose. No luck. The free tube whipped to and fro, knocking the others down.

Thinker lowered the 3D photo onto the ground on the opposite side of the street. With the long-coated man safely out of the way, he shuffled back to help the slipping and sliding firefighters battle to grab hold of the snaking hose.

Worries clouded Alex's judgement as he watched the bronze man draw closer to the blaze. His heart pounded. *What if he's caught inside? The flames could turn him into a burned-out hull.*

Artania would be lost without their leader.

Clenching his fists, Alex took a step toward the man who had guided several journeys into this mystical land. More smoke billowed from the windows, leaving a terrible taste in the back of his throat. How had the fire grown so quickly?

Closer to the café, sweltering air assaulted his face and the hot rush of cinders peppered his skin. He watched, horrified as Thinker stepped closer to the building to grab the end of the thrashing hose. His strong back rippled in the fire's glow as he moved in on the raging inferno.

"Thinker, no!"

"Fear not, Deliverer. I have the true art protecting me," the sculpted man called over his shoulder.

Fighting all instinct, Alex ran toward the bronze man, closing the distance even as Thinker crossed the patio. More spray attacked the flames thickening the smoke. Placing his hands behind his mentor's to help guide the hose, Alex shuffled forward closer to the flames.

The firemen pumped the seesaw levers and water blasted from the brass end. Alex stumbled on the slippery sidewalk, nearly fell, but got his footing and tugged on the leather hose as they stepped closer to the blaze.

Ten feet...

Alex's eyes burned. Squinting, he blinked away smoke-stained tears. Flames licked at the walls as he moved in.

Seven...

Another step. A burning timber fell from the roof. Crashed next to them. The ground shuddered.

Alex jerked. Froze.

"Closer, young one!"

He forced his legs to move.

Five feet…

Crossing the threshold, a monster flame met them. Its crackling roar filled his ears.

Thinker tugged him through the doorway barely a yard from the fiery beast.

"Ready yourself!" Thinker aimed the firehose at the center of the red-hot wall.

The smoke was so thick all Alex could see was black clouds tinged with red. Readjusting his grip, he leaned back.

Thinker stumbled and began to fall headfirst into the blaze.

Alex reached out.

Heard a crackling pop.

And was right back in Bartholomew's studio. His friend standing over him, mouth agape.

Chapter 15

"No!" Alex cried when he reappeared in the studio.

Clutching the tiny dragon sculpture, Bartholomew watched his friend turn round and round.

"No, no, no," Alex said.

When Bartholomew was thrown back into the real world so abruptly, he'd been just as distressed.

He set the dragon down. "Alex, it's all right."

"Fire everywhere. Thinker…"

"Alex."

"Where's a doorway?" Alex paced to one end of the hidden studio and tapped on the wall.

He moved a few inches down and knocked again.

"Hey. It's okay."

Alex shook his head. "I have to save him."

Almost joining the panic, Bartholomew started to see his own terrifying journey in and out of worlds. The suicidal man grappling with depression. Explosions throughout the high school. Alex's mom…

With shaking hands, Bartholomew picked up a bottle of hand sanitizer and rubbed a dollop in.

"Take me back, damnit!" Alex pounded harder on the wall.

Bartholomew held his breath a moment and counted silently, trying to slow his racing heart. If he could return Alex to that art-created world, he would. But like everything else in his life, Artanian journeys were out of his control.

The only thing he had control over was his art.

That's when familiar words came to mind. *Of course.*

He grabbed Alex by the shoulders. "But hope will lie in the hands of twins."

"Shut up and help me get back."

"That's not an option. You know that as well as I do. *On the eleventh year of their lives, they will join together like single forged knives.*"

Alex began to protest, but Bartholomew cut him off. "But our world will be saved if their art is true."

"Are you messing with me?" Alex shoved him away. "Throwing my words back at me now? You don't get it. Thinker was inside a burning building and stuff was collapsing. I have to get back, help him."

"Then stop panicking like Mother near dirt, and do something."

"Like what? Call on forces I still don't understand and ask them to transport me?"

"You know full well that our only power comes from creating. *Our world will be saved if their art is true.*"

Shaking his head, Bartholomew went over to the cabinet and opened the door. He pulled out a pound of molding clay and tossed it at his friend.

"Ouch!" Alex cried rubbing his head.

"Unwrap it, dummy."

"Who you calling dummy?"

"You. Come on. If he's in that much danger, he needs our protection."

"I doubt it'll help." Alex stared at the package at his feet.

"Well, we'll never know if we don't try." Bartholomew unwrapped the white clay and placed it on the cloth-covered table in front of Alex.

"You're the sculptor."

"And?" Bartholomew asked, frustrated.

"It won't be fast like in Artania. There's no magic."

"Then we better get started." Tired of arguing, Bartholomew turned away and picked up the aluminum foil armature he often used as a framework for human like figures.

He imagined Thinker's strong form as he bent the x-shaped foil into a half-sized figure sitting in a hunched over position. Then he tore off another few pieces from the roll and looped and twisted the new sections around each other to make the torso and head. Next, he reached for the clay, hoping his best friend would follow suit.

But Alex kept standing there, arms crossed.

Bartholomew exhaled loudly and raised both arms. "Seriously?"

"All right, you don't have to be a grouch about it." Alex positioned himself on the other side of the table. "What do you want me to do?"

"We need to cover this aluminum foil guy with several layers of clay."

Envisioning the figure he was about to form, Bartholomew dug in and pinched off an apple-sized piece. He handed it to Alex, who stretched out the chunk and flattened it with his palm.

"Good. I have some practice sketches I've used. I'll get them." Bartholomew remembered that a good sculptor needs to check both front and side angles for good proportion.

Alex nodded while repeating the pinch-off-roll-out process with a new piece. He handed these to Bartholomew, who flattened them next to the growing figure and got back to work.

For the next two hours they applied layer after layer, standing back to compare their progress to the sketches. Alex suggested new ways to smooth the clay, while a nodding Bartholomew showed how to attach it to the armature.

As they worked side by side, Bartholomew forgot about that lonely mansion with bleach white hallways leading to empty rooms. For a while he forgot about how it all kept him apart from the world. He didn't even think about Father and how different life would have been had he lived.

He was creating.

Bartholomew pointed at a place where Alex was struggling. "No, not like that. You aren't starting in the correct location."

Alex closed one eye and leaned back, holding up a thumb. He waved it back and forth in front of the sculpture.

"Like this, Mr. Professor?"

"Better. Now use your fingertips to make the musculature more realistic."

"O-kay." Alex jumped up, fingers stretched out like a clumsy giant.

He reached ridiculously wide hands toward the sculpture.

"No!"

Alex held his arms millimeters above the figure, immobile. Then he pivoted his head toward Bartholomew and winked.

"Gotcha."

Bartholomew curled a lip and punched his shoulder. "Glad you feel better."

"Still don't know if it's going to work. But you gotta admit, this is a pretty good copy of Rodin's masterpiece." Alex smoothed the clay around the arms.

"Yes, it is."

But whether this version of Thinker would help Artania's leader to battle flames in that world, Bartholomew could only hope.

Chapter 16

"Yeah, B-3 is okay," Alex replied to Mom, about his visit to the Borax estate. "Sort of. But I think being trapped with a fingernail-obsessed tutor and a germaphobe mother is getting to—"

Mid-sentence Cyndi Devinci covered her mouth and rushed towards the hallway bathroom. Slammed the door, and a second later Alex could hear retching and coughing sounds.

While pacing the room, Alex ran his hands through his hair.

"Mom? Are you okay?" he called through the door.

More retching. Soon followed by a flush. Then he heard the faucet being turned on and splashing. Mom emerged a few seconds later, her face flushed. Alex was surprised that she had a sheepish smile, as if hiding a special secret, instead of the pained expression he was expecting.

"I'm fine, sweetheart."

Narrowing his gaze, Alex shook his head. "But you just threw up again."

"It's a good thing. Believe me. Now, about you. It's Saturday. Why'd you come home when you could've been skateboarding?"

"I needed to know why you've been so sick. It's been weeks now."

"Oh, you came home to check on me? That's so sweet. What a lucky mom I am." She patted his arm. "Don't worry, I'm fine. You go skate now."

Alex crossed his arms. "I am not leaving until you tell me what's going on!"

Cyndi bobbed her head up and down several times as if thinking.

"I wanted your father here when I told you."

"Told me what?" Alex asked, in exasperation.

"You might want to sit down."

Gripping the back of the couch, he swallowed hard. "Tell me."

"Alex, my stomach has not been upset because I'm sick."

"O-kay. That's good. Then why?"

"You know how you've always wanted a little brother or sister?"

"Yeah."

Alex had begged for years, but Mom always said that it was out of her hands. That God would give her a baby if He saw fit.

"Well, it's going to happen. In about five and a half months."

"What?" Alex fell forward against the couch.

"I'm pregnant."

"No way."

"In your lingo, *way*." Mom smirked.

A smile crept up the corners of Alex's mouth, but stopped halfway before turning upside down.

"But your heart…can it take it?"

"That's why we were waiting to tell you. The specialists say this is risky for both me and the baby. Things could go wrong…"

Mom had always called Alex *her miracle*. After years of trying to get pregnant and losing one baby early on, she'd finally been able to carry him to term. She'd told him that it wasn't easy. Lots of bed rest and trips to the doctor. But it all had been worth it just to see his adorable face scrunched up like a little monkey. Time and again she said it was the most beautiful moment of her life.

He nodded.

"In case something bad happened like before, we didn't want to burden you."

"You should have told me. I've been so worried. Thinking you had cancer, or your heart had gotten worse or something."

"We thought it best to keep it to ourselves. Sorry." She came around the couch and rubbed his back. "But they're monitoring me closely, so don't you worry."

"Sure?"

"Yes. Now you go have some fun. We'll talk more when Dad gets home."

Chapter 17

Bartholomew pressed his face to the limo's privacy glass, as palms, sycamores, and oaks blurred past. Outside, brick side-walks led up to white adobe buildings under Spanish-style roofs.

He nodded. Soon he'd be in one of his favorite places. A place he could dream and where every corner said *welcome*. A place without sloshing mops or whirring vacuum cleaners. A place with portals that could take him anywhere.

The library.

As they drew closer, Bartholomew shifted his weight and ripped the paper seat cover.

"Shush, Bartholomew! I'm on the phone," Mother scolded from the seat opposite.

Pressing his lips together, he nodded. Maybe if she hadn't ordered the headrests removed and replaced with rolls of exam-ining room paper, he could be quiet. But with every seat covered in crinkling sheets, moving the slightest inch caused the paper to crackle and tear.

Mother had designed the limousine herself. There were three built-in hand sanitizers—one on the front dash for the chauffeur, and two behind the front seats. A scented air purifier hummed from the floor. Of course, this wasn't enough for Hygenette

Borax, so behind the second privacy screen a bubbling bathtub was always ready.

"As I was saying," Mother said, into the phone.

Then she lowered her voice and turned away.

For the next few moments, Bartholomew strained to listen in on yet another of Mother's secretive conversations. Though he only heard snatches, he thought he could make out the word *son*. He bent closer but couldn't get much else. *Is she talking about me?* He began to wonder.

They pulled up outside the building with the tiered fountain in front. Bartholomew grabbed the door handle, ready to leap from the car.

"Just a moment, Bartholomew."

He sighed, knowing what was coming. The stay-clean-stay safe-the-limo-will-soon-return lecture. If he so much as brushed against filth, he was supposed to dash out to the parked limousine for a bath and a change of clothes.

Yeah, right.

"...immediately. Do you understand?" Mother said.

"Yes, I understand. You need not worry. I'll see you at dinner."

A few minutes later he was running a finger over all of the glorious spines, looking for his favorite author's newest release. He bent down and had just found it, when he felt a tap on his shoulder.

"Alex," he whispered, standing back up.

"Hey, Mr. Clean." Alex beckoned him outside.

Once they'd passed the doors, Alex led him under a tree. He broke off a leaf and started to twirl it in his hands.

"It's not every day you get past the *phone police*," Bartholmew said. "What's up?"

He knew how hard it was to get a call through. Mother didn't allow him a cell phone, and the landline was always manned by butlers, who grilled any caller about their intentions before passing on the call.

"Cha. And I thought you were going to do something about that. Took me saying it was an emergency. It'd been easier to talk to the president." Alex shook his head. "But there was something I needed to talk to you about."

Had Alex seen something? Bartholomew swallowed hard, trying not to imagine what might have happened to Thinker.

"Yes?"

"You know how my mom has been so sick."

"It's been a constant worry."

"Understatement. Well, after I left your studio a couple days ago, I went straight home and called her on it. Refused to budge until she told me what the heck was going on."

Bartholomew rolled his hand. "And?"

"It wasn't bad news at all." Alex grinned.

"Okay. What is it?"

"It's actually good. Really good."

"And it is?"

"Amazingly good."

Bartholomew stomped a foot. "Then tell me! The suspense is killing me."

"I'm going to be a brother. Mom's pregnant."

"But isn't she like forty, with a heart condition?"

"I know, my exact reaction. But I guess she's got all these specialists monitoring her. So far so good."

"Wow. A little brother or sister." Bartholomew reached out to shake Alex's hand. "Congratulations."

"Thanks." Alex started to chatter about Halloween and all the things he was going to do with the new baby.

As he listened to all the plans, Bartholomew couldn't help but wonder where he'd fit in. Alex was pretty much his only friend. Yeah, Gwen, Jose, and Zach put up with him if he were around, might even ask him a question or two, but Alex was the one who understood. Alex knew about art, about creating, about the pressure of being a Deliverer, and how desolate life in the Borax mansion could be.

A new baby would take up all his time. Then Bartholomew would truly be alone.

Chapter 18

"I look ridiculous. I should just go home." Bartholomew touched the rubber wound on his painted face.

"No way, Mr. I-can't-go-anywhere-for-weeks," Alex said. "I worked too friggin' hard on your costume."

"But if Mother—"

"It was Halloween, and the hills of Santa Barbara were as warm as the look a dame gives you when she wants a rock the size of Gibraltar on her finger. Two private eyes scanned the party perimeter, deciding it *would be* fun." Alex dropped into his imitation of an old-time detective.

"I still don't see how you do that." Bartholomew marveled at Alex's ability to impersonate all kinds of voices.

Bugging out sunken eyes, Alex barred his rotten fake teeth.

"Nice." Curling a dead grey lip, Bartholomew adjusted the top of his hound's tooth cap.

He wished he could join in with Alex's enthusiasm, but parties just made him nervous, even if he'd been allowed to go instead of pretending to be asleep and sneaking out. And this being at Gwen's house didn't help, especially after everything Alex had told him about the strange mist appearing under her shirt.

Giving Bartholomew a playful punch, Alex started up the long driveway that lead to Gwen's multilevel home set into the hillside. Flickering jack-o-lanterns, fake tombstones, and giant spiders skirted the path, while plastic skeletons and grim reapers leered from the yard.

When he heard the sound of thunder and rain, Bartholomew stopped and glanced up. "Huh?"

"Just sound effects." Alex explained before continuing to act like a detective. He flipped up the collar of his trench coat and adjusted the fedora on his head. "The party goers shivered as they heard the distant sounds of eerie recordings."

Bartholomew tried to smile through all the fake wounds attached to his face. "And I was afraid it might be the start of another crazy journey."

"No way. Not tonight." Alex lifted his putrid yellow face to the sky. "You hear me, Artania? No doorways tonight! This night is for fun."

"You really think that's going to work?"

"Worth a try. Now let's case this joint to make our entry."

As long as Bartholomew had known him, Alex raved about Halloween. It was his favorite holiday. Every year he spent weeks planning, designing, and creating a costume so elaborate it could have been used in a Broadway play. And as soon as he put it on, he became that character.

Their costumes were right out of Hollywood, with zombified clothes grimed up with dirt and mold. Once he'd decided on a detective theme, Alex had scoured thrift stores for the right slacks, caps, and trench coats. He would be that old 1940's detective Phillip Marlowe, with Bartholomew as the famous Sherlock Holmes.

Next came getting the fabric to look tattered by cutting and snipping random places with a serrated knife before he ran a lighter over the edges to singe off a few parts. To make sure they still fit after alterations, Bartholomew stopped by every week or so to try them on.

The only times he'd been out of the house.

Alex even made all kinds of dyes from tea and household materials to simulate blood, sweat, and mildew. These he mixed up in spray bottles, misting the costumes several times before rubbing them in the dirt. Then he started in on making mold by mixing liquid latex and oatmeal which he applied to select places to simulate a rotting corpse.

"I have to admit, we do look pretty authentic," Bartholomew said, then added under his breath, "maybe this party will be okay."

"Not just okay. This is going to be amazing. The best night of the year."

Bartholomew nodded. With their classic detective theme, who knew? Perhaps they'd even win the costume contest Alex had been chattering about. He glanced up ready to echo Alex's eager words.

And froze.

Like a great claw dripping blood, the crescent moon had turned deep red.

He grabbed his friend by the lapel. "You see that?"

"What?"

"That?" He pointed at the sky.

"Nice." Alex nodded appreciatively at the shining silver moon. "Sets a cool mood for Halloween."

"No, a second ago it was…different." Bartholomew shook his head.

Alex crossed his arms. "You aren't trying to bail on me, are you?"

"It's just I thought I saw…" Bartholomew paused wondering if it was just his imagination.

"Saw what?"

"Oh, never mind." He decided that even if he did see something, he should pretend he didn't.

Although they'd gotten together a few times to try on the costumes, Alex had been so preoccupied with his mom's pregnancy that they'd barely hung out. And Bartholomew had been so lonely…

"Good." Alex returned to his detective voice. "Because this seems like a nice neighborhood to have bad habits in."

Joining in with the pater, Bartholomew said, "Elementary, my dear Marlowe."

He approached the doorway as a cold wind blew. Ominous shapes and shadowy figures lurked in windows beneath strings of orange and black lights. The howling wind and werewolf recording grew louder with every step, turning his veins to ice.

Suddenly, he wanted to run as fast as he could away from there. He'd dash back down the hill, around the corner, and through downtown, not stopping until he was at his back gate where he'd disabled the security camera earlier. Then he'd steal inside the Borax mansion and up the long staircase to his private bathroom. In that peaceful place, he'd rip off these itchy prosthetics, throw this musty smelling costume in the trash, and slide under the soothing waters of his rainwater shower.

There, he'd dream of creating with his buddy by his side, instead of trying to fit in with a bunch of teenagers he barely knew.

Alex jerked a thumb at the door draped in fake spiderwebs. "With my brains and your bad looks, we'll go down mean streets where everything is tarnished." He rang the bell.

It gonged, and a creepy voice toned, "Enter at your own risk. Ha. Ha. Ha."

Bartholomew lifted his leaden feet and stepped over the threshold.

Chapter 19

Giggling, Gwen grabbed the doorknob and flattened herself against the wall before slowly opening the door. Two zombies waded through hanging cheesecloth into her dimly lit entryway.

"Hello?" Bartholomew's quivering voice called through the mist-filled doorway.

This is going to be good. Gwen leapt out from her hiding place. "Ahh!" She waved her satin-gloved hands.

The one dressed like a dead Sherlock Holmes jumped back.

But the boy in the trench coat crossed his arms and said, in a movie detective voice, "Is that any way to greet a couple of private eyes?"

Gwen leaned closer until the homemade crescent moon wrapped around her head almost touched a fake wound on his cheek.

She squinted at the zombie-faced boy. "Alex?"

"You got it, moon doll." Alex winked.

"Wow, I didn't recognize you." She turned to B-3 as Holmes. "And if it weren't for that Richie voice, I wouldn't have recognized you either."

Bartholomew pointed at the Styrofoam moon headpiece she'd painted silver earlier.

Alex, still in character, said, "Nice costume, doll face."

Gwen furrowed her brow. "Hey, I'm no…"

She started to rail against his sexist comments, then remembered how much Alex loved Halloween. In sixth grade he'd been Rembrandt, his Australian Shepherd, and had been so into it she was surprised he didn't lift his leg and pee on the trees as they trick-or-treated in his neighborhood.

She shook her head, smiling. "Come on in."

As she led them toward the living room, she asked about Alex's mom. Then they chatted a bit about how she was feeling, if she was starting to show, and how excited Alex was about becoming a brother.

"So tell me about this case. Any suspects?" Alex asked a moment later.

Gwen cocked her head. Which wasn't easy with the crescent moon wrapped around under her chin.

"Huh?"

Alex lifted a dead hand and pointed around the room.

"Ahh. Who's here?" Now Gwen caught on to Alex's detective lingo. "The usual crew. And before you start ragging on me, yes, I invited Lacey, Coco, and some of the Populos. They should be here soon. She finally apologized about last year, and well, when they go to a party, everybody goes."

"I'm just a humble private eye trying figure out who did this to me," Alex said indicating his body.

"Umm, elementary, my dear Marlowe." Bartholomew stuck a plastic pipe in his mouth.

"You guys." Gwen chuckled. "Come on, I'll show you the grub table. It came out pretty cool." She led them toward the buffet she and Dad had worked on all afternoon.

Dad's old jeans and dress shirt were laid out like a body on a blood-stained white tablecloth. They'd cut open the pant legs and placed trays of buffalo wings there to look like muscles. Inside the shirt were trays of sausages and slices of steak where the guts and heart would be. Pretty gross, if she did say so.

Dressed as the sun, her boyfriend strolled up in a gold spandex unitard. He started to lean in for a kiss, but she leaned back, afraid those protruding rays on his shiny mask would poke her. Jose slowly lifted it, gave her that soft smile, and then brushed his lips across hers. Gwen almost stumbled in her strappy heels. Those lips knocked her out.

"*Turn your face to the sun and the shadows fall behind you,*" he said.

Gwen stared at him blankly.

"The shadows fall behind you" Jose repeated and raised his eyebrows.

Gwen scrunched up her face, trying to remember the quote from Percy Shelley that Jose had made her memorize.

"As in the soft…'" he rolled his hand in a circle.

"Oh, yeah." She took a deep breath. "*As in the soft and sweet eclipse, when soul meets soul on lover's lips.*"

Jose fit his mask back on. Then, pretending to be an eclipse, he picked up his inflated earth and slowly circled Gwen.

Snickering under his breath, Alex grabbed a plastic cup and ladled up some Witch's Brew from the toy cauldron Dad had lined with dry ice. As he lifted his hand, the grey mist rising from the punch bowl turned a shade darker, to a freaky red.

In spite of just finishing a drink, Gwen's mouth went dry. Her tongue stuck to the roof of her mouth as her jaw fell open.

The mist thickened into a gel-like mass.

Blinking, Gwen detected a faint malodor, metallic, like iron or blood. She sniffed and was about to take a step closer, when Zach, dressed as a styling vampire, slid in front of her.

Doing his signature gun-hand, he said, "I want to suck yer blood, pardner."

"Dude, Bella Lugosi was Hungarian, not Texan," Alex said.

"With Saint Laurent ankle boots, who cares?" Zach brushed the back of his curled hand tipped with long black fingernails, over his tailored sports coat.

When he stepped aside to admire Alex and B-3's costumes, Gwen could see the punch bowl. Grey mist again.

Swallowing the rock in her dry throat, she forced herself to check out Zach's costume. Mr. GQ had on black skinny pants and a grey satin shirt complete with a cravat attached with a red jeweled pendant. He'd even side combed his dirty blonde hair with peaked bangs for a greased look like Barnabas in that Johnny Wep movie.

"Stylin'," she said.

Zach started to tell them about designer this and designer that, while Gwen joined the guys in party chatter. Her lips moved, but if you asked her later what she'd said, she wouldn't remember. She was too focused on what the heck that was. *If* it was anything.

Alex had seen something a while back and freaked out. Almost lost Jose's friendship until Gwen told him a made-up story about a big spider crawling on her back.

But neither he nor B-3 seemed to notice anything just then. Or were they hiding the fact? She couldn't tell behind all that makeup.

She didn't have long to think about it, because the doorbell rang again. And again. For the next hour, she greeted ghosts, witches, mummies, along with Lacey and her crew dressed as hot pirates.

Alex and Bartholomew were a real hit, going from guest to guest questioning them while writing down notes in clue books. B-3 kept chewing on his plastic pipe and actually looked like he was having some fun—a pretty friggin' rare occurrence.

Now it was time to crank up the tunes and hopefully get a few kids on the dance floor she and Dad had created that morning. They'd spent an hour making enough space for kids to do the L.A Shake and Danky Leg, moving furniture around until it looked just right. Double checking her playlist, Gwen grabbed the remote and turned up the volume.

A few ghosts started waving their sheet arms to "Mash Zombie," while Lacey and the populos started to affect their ask-me-to-dance-hip-thrust poses. Gwen smiled, watching Alex take a break from his detective game to ladle up another cup of Witch's Brew.

The dry ice mist turned from grey to red as soon as the dipper touched the punch. Veils of red steam floated in the air. Then tendrils of scarlet smoke rose around Alex and morphed into a mass of macabre twisting organs.

Zach led Lacey onto the dance floor, opening and closing his black-tipped fingers into snaky shapes. As soon as Lacey had an audience, she raised both arms and did a slow sensuous turn.

Grinning, Alex turned toward the dancers as a ruby haze of condensation coalesced over his head. A heart and intestines appeared, their pulsing veins drip-drip-dripping into the punch bowl.

Gwen dropped the stereo remote and dashed over to the buffet table. She took three long breaths and gaped. Then, forcing herself to reach for the eerie image, she extended a shaking hand. But as soon as her fingertips touched the vision, it turned back into mist.

As more dancers joined Lacey and Zach, Gwen stood trembling near the punch bowl.

Just back from the restroom, Jose slipped an arm around her waist. It didn't comfort her. She gave the punch bowl a sideways glance and shivered.

"Babe, I'm going to make sure Dad has the extra grub ready." She patted his shoulder. Waving to Alex and Bartholomew, she called, "Detective zombies, come here and help me." She gave them a meaningful look before leading them towards the kitchen.

"But I thought—" Jose said to her back.

Gwen walked faster. She didn't have time for boyfriend maintenance right then. She had to know if someone had poured something besides root beer in that Witch's Brew.

Or that mist really was turning to blood.

Chapter 20

After following the River of Lies upstream to Swallow Hole Swamp, where the young ones hatched and grew, Captain Sludge approached the shack beyond its banks. The dwelling was unique in his underground home. Whereas all other Shadow Swine of Subterranea lived inside stony walls, Crone alone dwelled among wood. The hut appeared small and dilapidated from the outside, but Captain Sludge had discovered long ago that this was an illusion.

The untold rooms inside held oddly shaped cauldrons. From perfect ovals to warped and twisted metal to huge vessels of iron, each unique pot boiled a magical brew, full of answers.

Most Shadow Swine shied away from Crone. But from the time Sludge was a pupa wading through the waters of Swallow Hole Swamp, he'd watched her from the waters. When he morphed into a nymph, he braved the swamp's shore to seek answers from the wizened woman.

Of course, each reply came with a heavy price. The hardest one was his height. He would have been just as tall as any other Shadow Swine had she not given him the knowledge, helping to mold his natural intelligence into cunning stratagems as a master dream drainer.

So he gave her a few inches of his height and spiked his hair to reach his underlings' shoulders. It was all worth it. It made him the most powerful Shadow Swine of them all. Save Lord Sickhert, of course.

Sludge glanced back at Swallow Hole Swamp, where he'd crawled over pupae and nymph alike to gain notice. Even before he'd bowed before Lord Sickhert on the banks of the River of Lies, he'd practiced dream draining on his peers.

Not that they liked it much, but he didn't care.

"I see you have returned," a woman's shaky voice noted.

Looking up, he nodded at Crone who had appeared on her rickety porch, inviting him to sit in the rocking chair beside her.

"I said I would." He plunked down, keeping both jackbooted feet on the floor.

The dwarfed woman gave him a snaggle-toothed grin as she rocked. "Ahh, but you have said many things over the years, haven't you, Pupae?"

Sludge gripped his knees. He hated this infant name and would have slapped most to the ground for such insolence. But there was something strangely comforting in this wrinkled witch's presence. She had helped him defeat the Deliverers so many times.

So he rocked once. "It is recharged."

She raised her hairless eyebrows. "Ahh. You have come again to play."

Captain Sludge reached under his coat and pulled out his battle axe, its steel blade shining in the lava glow. With the unicorn magic, it had helped him defeat many Knights of Painted Light in recent months, *and* mess with a couple of Deliverers.

"More unexpected journeys for the humans." Crone pointed.

Sludge caressed the glinting steel. "Even Lord Sickhert is perplexed."

"You didn't—"

"Do you take me for an idiot? After all that has occurred, you should know more than anyone the care I take."

"Good. For if he knew our new power—"

"Yes, he'd take it for himself. I know. Now are you ready for some sport?"

"Let the games begin." Crone led him inside.

At the end of a long hallway they came to a round door, where she waved a knobby hand. It opened, revealing a fire pit and a warped cauldron with a long ladle inside. The boiling concoction popped and steamed as the little woman waddled up on her stunted legs.

Crone stirred the bubbling brew while misty images of Thinker, Alexander and Bartholomew, and Gwen appeared. Once they took shape, Crone beckoned him closer.

"Hold your axe aloft," she said.

Sludge stepped up. This was new. Every other time, she had simply stirred while he gripped the axe.

He narrowed his hairless brows. "Why?"

"For a game unlike any other" She stirred the pot once more.

Sludge did not trust this old witch. Over the years she'd tricked him too many times, often making him feel the fool. He still wondered why she kept him in her confidence, whether he was a pawn or a true ally.

Still, without her, he'd never have gained such power.

He raised the axe. "Like so?"

"Closer." She rested her free hand on the blade to draw it toward the steam.

The captain eased his hatchet nearer as Crone raised a ladleful in her gnarled hands. Once his blade was directly under the wooden spoon, she tilted it and steaming potion dribbled over the metal. There was a hissing sound and the images began a slow turn.

"What now?" Sludge said.

"Watch."

Thinker's misty form morphed and shrunk while Alex and Bartholomew reached toward him with melting fingers. The red-headed girl rotated twice more, then huddled down as if cringing in terror. Sludge chuckled.

Crone poured more brew on his blade and the images began to spin wildly. Her face twisted and contorted in pleasure as the apparitions faded in and out of sight, until finally they disappeared.

Knowing they were launching a new series of upsets for the Artania-Earth connection, Sludge felt a shiver of excitement roll down his hunched back. Somewhere, a human or a Deliverer was being thrust into nightmare. And in turn, panicking.

Glorious.

Lowering his axe, Sludge leaned over the oddly shaped cauldron and gazed into the simmering potion. A sick sweet smell filled his piggish nostrils. The concoction bubbled and swelled in peaks and valleys, but he didn't see anything special.

He turned toward Crone. "Now what?"

"Just watch." She dropped the ladle back into the pot.

The tiny woman threw her head back and began to cackle ever louder as Sludge shrunk and the room faded from view.

Chapter 21

"So why would a dame who obviously has everything under control, need a couple private eyes?" Alex asked when Gwen led him around the corner, to the hallway behind the kitchen.

"Alex would you stop that stupid voice and get serious? I'm freaking out here!"

"Hey, what's wrong?" Bartholomew set his black plastic plate on the side table.

"I saw something and need to know if you saw it, too," Gwen said.

Stumbling, Bartholomew grabbed the table edge.

Alex stared at him before switching to his normal voice. "What was it?"

"The dry ice fog around the punch...changed. Darkened to this eerie color. But only when *you* were getting a drink. Every time you ladled up some punch, it turned red."

"Red?" Bartholomew squeaked. "Are you putting us on? A Halloween joke?"

"No, I swear. It even started bleeding. Like guts or veins or something. And it reminded me of when Alex went all superhero on me in the quad. Remember?"

"Yeah, smoke was billowing out of your shirt. I thought you were on fire." Alex shuddered at the memory.

The table shook when Bartholomew gripped it tighter. "Oh, no."

"What?" Alex said.

"I saw red, too. In the moon. And there." B-3 pointed at Gwen's headpiece.

A plaiting chill wove into Alex. "Why didn't you say anything?"

"I tried to, but you were so excited I didn't want to bug you. Then it occurred to me that perhaps I'd imagined it. This has been such an odd year."

"Hello? Transporting in and out of Artania with no warning, ending up God knows where. Thinker being attacked. Freaky visions unlike any we've seen. I'd say so."

While Alex and Bartholomew had shared strange glimpses of Artania when they'd first met before sixth grade, they didn't look dangerous. They weirded him out, sure, but back then it seemed like the painted faces were cheering them on—not hinting at treacherous threats.

"I'm sure that the Shadow Swine have a new kind of power," B-3 said.

"Something that even Thinker is powerless against?" Alex said.

Bartholomew nodded.

"But he's like Ironman of the Avengers," Gwen said, "Charles Xavier of the X-Men, Batman of the Justice League." Her voice grew shriller with each listed superhero.

"We're trying to fight it," Alex said.

"You dudes making enough art for that Prophecy?"

Even through the zombie makeup, Alex could see Bartholomew blush.

"Mr. Clean! You have to."

"I know. I just haven't felt up to it."

"Haven't felt up to it? There've been times I've had a fever of a hundred and Dad still had me in the gym. No excuse."

"I'm sorry. Life has become…I can't explain." B-3 started to pick at one of the fake sores on his face.

Alex brushed his hand away. "You'll mess up your makeup." Then to Gwen, he said, "B-3 deals with stuff you and I have no clue about. Let's give him a break."

"Whatever. So you didn't see it?"

Alex shook his head. "But that doesn't mean it wasn't there. Or that it wasn't an omen."

"A sign that we are about to be transported through the portal again," Bartholomew said.

"Don't tell me that." Gwen shivered and rubbed her bare arms. "You know, I was glad to have your back and all, but I think two trips into that crazy world is enough, don't you?"

Alex flashed back to the previous year when the doorway to Artania dumped them in separate locations, leading to long fretful days searching for Gwen. All alone, she'd gone through hell, but what he wouldn't have done to take that all on himself.

"Not exactly trips to Disneyland," he said. Then in a quieter voice said, "Sorry."

"Understatement." Gwen crossed her arms. "And what are you two zombies going to do about it?"

Alex exchanged a glance with Bartholomew, who raised his eyebrows and shrugged.

"Seriously? You've fought dragons, pirates, bat-turd crazy nightmares, and you can't figure out how to keep me from seeing freaking horrors?"

Alex tapped his chin, thinking. "Let me check out a few things. I'll start with the punchbowl." He returned to his detective imitation. "We'll follow the clues and get to the bottom of this, doll face."

Back in the living room, the party was now in full swing. About fifty teens mingled among hanging ghosts, fake spiderwebs, waving skeletons, and leering jack-o-lanterns. The spooky sounds that had greeted them outside had been replaced with a Halloween playlist, while "Monster" by Reyonce had Lacey and her crew, in identical pirate costumes from the latest movie, bobbing and swaying to the music.

Ignoring a waving invite from Coco to join him on the dance floor, Alex made a beeline for the grub table. Here, just the slightest bit of fog wafted from the Witch's Brew, but that was dissipating. He supposed Gwen's dad hadn't added more hot water to the dry ice in a while.

Alex leaned over the bowl and peered in. The licorice scent of root beer and allspice filled his nostrils with a pleasant sensation, reminding him of being in the kitchen when Mom experimented with one of her dessert recipes. Or at Jose's where Mrs. Hamlin burned cinnamon incense. He waited for it to morph, but the dark brown liquid was as still as Santa Barbara Bay at dawn.

Nothing remotely resembled blood.

He straightened his back and had begun to shrug when he found Lacey Zamora looking him up and down. Her usual crew of Populos stood behind her in their lusty pirate get-ups.

"And what are you supposed to be? A zombie pervert?" she asked, one hand on her hip.

"He just so happens to be Phillip Marlowe," Bartholomew said.

"And who is that? Some cronk friend of yours?"

Alex didn't really feel like educating little-miss-I'm-so-cool-I-don't-read, just then. But at the same time was relieved to have a distraction from this crazy mystery.

"No, he was a hard-boiled detective, from the old-time movies," he said.

"You would choose something so old no one knows about it."

After taking a sip from her plastic cup, her friend Coco said, "I know those films. Bogie and Bacall. Sooo romantic." She sighed and then affected a pose that Alex figured she imagined was sexy. "You know how to whistle, don't you? You just put your lips together and blow."

With these words the front door slammed open and a howling breeze rustled through the cheesecloth spiderwebs. The murmuring voices ceased, as if everyone had suddenly been muzzled. The music paused and the room grew supernaturally silent. Alex watched and waited.

For whatever was coming.

Chapter 22

Sludge's claw-tipped fingers cracked as he curled them into a fist.

"Crone!" he groused, punching the moonlit sky.

The captain of the Shadow Swine glanced around. He had materialized in front of an open door that looked vaguely familiar except for the orange lights and draping spiderwebs.

Sludge loved spiders. They stirred fear in most humans. A wondrous image for building nightmares.

Beyond the open door came pounding music. This he did not like. He abhorred anything that made children smile.

Sludge flicked out his tongue to test the air. Santa Barbara, California, a house filled with optimistic youth.

Ahh. The Deliverers are near. Crone, you sneaky old witch, sending me to Earth without a word. But I will enjoy playing, nonetheless.

Affecting a sneer, Sludge stepped over the threshold and waited for the screams. The glorious shrieks of terror and inevitable feet scrambling for an exit.

But that didn't happen.

Instead a roomful of oddly dressed teens gaped at him.

Sludge blinked, unable to register their reaction. They should be running for the nearest doorway by now. After all, he was the most frightening Shadow Swine in all of Subterranea, save Lord Sickhert of course.

"Oooh, awesome costume," gushed one scantily clad girl.

A boy made a gun with his hand and pointed a black fingernail at him. "Bullseye."

The next thing he knew, Sludge was surrounded by the strangest group of humans he'd ever seen, all chattering about his appearance. He started to curl his hunched back into what he thought would be an intimidating pose, when he noticed one youth wearing a mask.

He cocked his slime-covered head to the side. Then he saw three more masks, a sheet draped child, and flickering jack-o-lanterns. As he scanned the room, the realization hit him.

All Hallow's Eve. That ancient celebration to remember the dead. Now a secular holiday for children.

The Crone was genius. Here was the one night a Shadow Swine could pass unnoticed among human beings. He could walk among them, listen in on conversations, and gather rumors that he'd later use in dream draining.

Here was power.

"You look just like an Orc in *Lord of the Rings*," said one of the girls dressed as a pirate.

"For once, Coco, you're right," said her taller companion, before looking Sludge up and down. "Who are you, anyhow? I thought I knew everybody here. I usually do."

Sludge blinked, pondering what to say. Shadow Swine never had gatherings such as this one and were unpracticed at conversation. Sure, they'd used flattery to turn Artanians to their side, and the captain had barked orders at underlings, but disgusting party banter?

Never.

He curled a thick lip up and barred his sharp teeth. "I am one to be feared."

The kids all burst into laughter.

Sludge staggered back. Such insolence! He would cut down every single one of those sniggering children, silencing their ridiculous guffaws with each magnificent swipe.

After reaching inside his ankle-length coat, Sludge pulled out a battle axe. He gripped the handle with both hands and squeezed while visions of choking each brazen throat filled his mind. *Which impudent brat should I strike first?*

His gaze rested on the dark-haired beauty with one smug hand on her hip. Her arrogance would soon be twisted to terror. He leaned back on one leg and raised the weapon overhead.

Chapter 23

Bartholomew barely registered the unfolding scene across the room. Sludge, here? With everyone awake? It couldn't be.

Thinker would never allow it.

He gripped Alex's arm. His friend's zombie face paled his to a deader shade of green. If that was possible.

Bartholomew viewed Captain Sludge with a mixture of horror and anger. In battle after battle he had watched this hunch-backed creature torture many of his friends, dropping more than he could count.

Then there were the nightmares. That guttural voice had invaded Bartholomew's dreams, twisting happy scenes of painting with his father into horrific images that continued to haunt his mind.

Watch as he drowns, that voice said, while he watched Father struggling toward a muddy surface. Bartholomew woke to sheets wrapped like a noose around his throat. He often lay shivering until Mr. White came in ordering him to rise.

Frozen to that spot near the punch bowl, he squeezed Alex's arm tighter. If Sludge had this kind of power, he shuddered to imagine what he could do. To all of them.

Then he saw the glint of steel raised over Lacey. Bartholomew's legs bent, springing into a ten-yard dash that had him across the room in three strides.

"There you are, Sam!" he said slapping the Swiney on the back.

Turning, the monster raised his hairless brows at him and snarled.

Meanwhile, Alex moved in, reaching for Sludge's weapon. "Wow, that looks so real. Let me see it." he said, his detective voice replaced by bad acting.

"Don't touch it!" Jerking the axe back, Sludge glared with those pit viper eyes.

"Sor-ry." Alex raised both hands.

Sludge waved his glittering axe, ready to strike.

Bartholomew felt around in his pockets. He didn't think his magnifying glass would be much of a shield against that battle axe, and throwing the toy plastic pipe would only anger Captain Sludge. He chewed his lip, wishing Alex's costume at least included a toy gun to bluff with.

With no weapons and no way to make them, Bartholomew was afraid that everyone would soon look deader than any zombie mask.

Chapter 24

Shivering, Gwen rubbed her bare arms. Her rocking party was quickly devolving into a horrible dream, reminding her of the horrors those monsters had sent to her last year.

The nightmares—*streaming powder rained down. Sandy granules pooled in her nose and mouth, scratching her throat and raking her eyes. Suffocating, she sputtered and choked, drowning in a dust she fought to dig free from.*

She'd woken clawing at air.

If Sludge on Earth was anything like he was in Artania, everyone was in buko danger.

Well, Mitch Obranovich had not raised her to let a nightmare-maker threaten her friends. Gwen picked up one corner of her long satin gown and marched…well tiptoed—*stupid stilet-toes*—through the crowd to the Swiney.

"Hey, Sam," she said picking up on Alex and B-3's invented name. "So glad you could make it."

"You." He narrowed his yellow eyes.

"Yep, me." She put on a weak smile. Then, in an effort to get the monster away from her friends, suggested, "Hey, I bet you're hungry. Why not check out the grub table?"

"I agree," Bartholomew said, his deerstalker hat flaps bobbing up and down. "There are all kinds of treats to choose from."

"Who are you?" Sludge leaned toward the Sherlock-Holmes-dressed B-3.

"He's a guy from the mean streets of London." Alex dropped back into his detective voice. "Holmes is his name, and solving crime is his game."

If Gwen hadn't been so terrified, she would have razzed Alex, saying that rhyme was totally lame. She tucked the zinger away, planning to tease him later. *If* they survived that long.

Still, it was a relief that the Shadow Swine captain hadn't recognized her buds yet.

"How about some Witch's Brew and buffalo wings?" Gwen suggested.

Sludge looked at her as if she were an idiot. "Buffalo do not have wings."

The room filled with more laughter. When it died down, Lacey Zamora turned her deep red lips into that pout Gwen had been nauseated by all too many times.

"He was hanging out with us. *We'll* get him some goodies."

Sludge glanced from Lacey to Gwen and back as if deciding what to do.

"Come on." Pivoting on a red-ribboned black boot, Lacey shook her butt toward the food table.

Gwen was shocked to see Sludge follow, while the selfie-shooting Coco, Zach, and the Populos trailed behind. It seemed that even monsters weren't immune to Lacey's charms.

Disgusting.

"That didn't work. Now what do we do?" Gwen whispered to Alex.

Chapter 25

Alex wanted to jump out of his skin. The room had warmed by several degrees in the last few moments, and a trench coat over the detective suit was so hot his makeup had started to run. He took off his fedora and started fanning his face with it.

But he didn't remove his coat. Once Sludge realized who he was dealing with, Alex would lose the element of surprise and he needed to delay that moment until he and Bartholomew came up with a plan.

Still surrounded by a crowd of teens, Sludge seemed to be enjoying the attention. His sneer had warped into something that resembled a Komodo dragon grin, and he stood taller with every gushing word about his *costume.*

Alex knew it wouldn't last. Any second now he might lift that battle axe and strike.

Sweat trickled down his back. "We have to get him out of here," he muttered.

"Cha! But how?" Gwen looked to B-3. "Any ideas, Mr. Clean?"

"In Artania we can create weapons at light speed, but not here."

"But they do become a Knight of Painted Light," Alex said hopefully.

"Which work only when we're asleep. Knights can't battle Shadow Swine now."

"Vulture vomit." Alex shook his head, trying to think. "Well, I'm not going to stand around waiting to see what Sludge does. That axe is friggin' sharp."

"What we need is a distraction to get him away from our friends," Gwen said.

"I believe that the only way we are going to do that is if we reveal ourselves," Bartholomew said.

Alex agreed. If Sludge saw two Deliverers, he'd be sure to give chase. He hated Alex and B-3 for every sculpture, painting, or sketch they'd ever made. Add to it that these creations had helped to beat him at his own game a time or two definitely fueled his rage.

Alex tried to keep the disappointment out of his voice. "Okay, then, you know what to do, B-3?"

Barely begun, the best night of the year would soon end.

With a nod, Bartholomew strode over to the front door. He placed a hand, which Alex had painted zombie green, on the handle.

"Ready."

After ordering Gwen to shut down the music on cue, Alex joined him.

When the room was plunged into silence, he shouted at the top of his lungs, "Hey, slime monster, have you been looking for me?"

Alex ripped off his trench coat and fedora, tossed them aside and waved. Then he removed a latex wound and ruffled his hair so Sludge would recognize his distinct curls. B-3 followed suit, stripping down until a mound of British detective clothes were piled up near the front door.

Alex's heart ticked like the pendulum clock at his grandmother's house in Boulder. Time seemed to stop as everyone except Sludge stared at him as if he were absolutely bonkers.

Then the monster twitched, his reptile grin replaced with an angry scowl. Growling, the Swiney moved in on them like a crocodile rushing a water buffalo.

Both boys shot through the front door, scuttling down the long walk toward the steep drive. The jack-o-lanterns leered from the concrete path as they rushed past.

"Run, B-3!"

Arms circling ridiculously, his friend galloped down the steps, his feet slapping against the pavement like war drum mallets. Bartholomew stumbled but didn't fall before making a hard right turn at the drive.

Alex was sure they'd be safe from there, but those jackboots were quicker than he realized. The captain rounded the corner three seconds behind Bartholomew.

After pausing near the head of canyon where the road turned left and carved a winding path through the hills, Alex clenched his fists.

Bartholomew's bicycling legs barely touched the ground, spinning like the Roadrunner in cartoons. He hurtled toward the road, rounded the bend and glanced back, forgetting that there was a felled log at the bottom of the drive.

"Watch out, B-3!"

Bartholomew glanced back, leaping a moment too late, and one foot caught on a jutting branch. He fell forward, flat on his chest.

Shivers colder than melting ice trickled down Alex's spine.

Bartholomew's head rolled back and forth, and he groaned. He rose on one knee a second before Captain Sludge marched to a halt at his feet. The slimy monster stood over him, serrated teeth glinting in the moonlight.

Brain numb, Alex picked up a handful of gravel and hurled it. The stones peppered the road but fell short by yards.

Sludge reached out a clawed hand and grabbed B-3 by the collar.

"No, stop!" Alex's cry was cut short when the ground began to shake.

He held out his arms for balance and heard a familiar pop as Santa Barbara disappeared.

Chapter 26

Sludge reached toward that stupid Deliverer's collar. *Now I have you, idiot.* He curled his nails to tug at the fabric, but fell back against the wooden fence instead.

"Huh?" The captain blinked at his empty hand.

When he realized what had happened, he shook his fist at the sky. "Crone, I am sick of your games!"

No breeze blew back his long trench coat. No irritating bird song met his bat-like ears. He glanced up and knew that both Deliverers were in Artania, and that meant that time was frozen on Earth. What trickery could he get up to in a frozen world? He couldn't create nightmares. With time halted, all minds would be impermeable to dream draining.

He tapped his long claw-tipped fingers together. The unmoving clouds had just parted, leaving the crescent moon cutting into a wisp. He'd love to be like that sharp edge and pierce a few dreams.

Short of that, maybe he could wreak some havoc. The house up the hill was still filled with humans.

Sludge strode up the drive, trying to think of ways to mess with those insolent teens. Laugh at his power, would they? Well, he'd show them.

He passed through the open doorway, scanning the party's immobile guests. The discarded costumes that had fooled him were still piled up near the entry. He considered bending down and ripping them to shreds. But that would terrify no one and he didn't know how long he had before the Crone would yank him back to Subterranea.

Reflected light caught his gaze. Gwen's shimmery gown bounced light beams that humans probably thought were beautiful. Not to him. Each shining ray filled Sludge with disgust. And that headpiece she had on? A glittery moon brought one thought to mind.

Destroy.

"Gwendolyn Obranovich. I have terrified you before, and I will again."

He stepped up next to the girl, whose open mouth appeared to be in mid-shout.

He circled her like a butcher about to make the first cut into a slab of beef. Appraising her weaknesses, his yellow eyes slanted as visions of terror filled his mind. He'd give her something horrifying to awake to.

Sludge rubbed his hands together and licked his bulbous lips. Curling his long-nailed hands into claws, he reached up toward her crescent moon headpiece and tried to scratch horrific words into the glitter.

It was as if his hands had met stone. Not a single glitter grain moved.

He flexed his biceps, and rolling his shoulders, swiped at her mask. Nothing.

He knew the world froze when the Deliverers were in Artania, but he had no idea that this also made everything as hard as stone.

Then he remembered. His battle axe had been strengthened with fear magic. The week before, the dragon, Lucretia, had terrorized the trapped unicorn by surrounding it in fire. While the nickering creature screeched in terror, the dragon inserted the axe's blade into the flames.

And later the Crone had ladled some of her brew on the sharp edge, giving it even more power. Maybe that's what she'd planned for this journey. Although, why she'd failed to tell him was still a mystery.

Sludge pulled the battle axe from the folds of his long coat and rubbed the steel lovingly against his slimy cheek.

"Terrify, dear blade. Terrify."

Choking up on the handle, he grasped the moon around Gwen's head in one hand and began to etch words with the other.

He had just finished the last letter when he felt his strength waning. In moments he'd be home. Where he'd seek out a couple of infuriating Deliverers.

And do battle.

Chapter 27

Expecting imminent pain, Bartholomew braced himself. He closed his eyes and waited for Captain Sludge's sharp fingernails to burrow into his neck. But the grip loosened, sending him careening forward.

Into space.

For a moment all was stars as he rocketed beyond Santa Barbara, and then Earth, but two blinks later he was suspended in the painted skies of Artania. He floated above cotton and paper clouds as tiny people and animals scurried in the forested area below. Below a long river snaked past a multicolored woodland so beautiful it would be wonderful to sketch.

If he made it through the trees.

Knowing that this balloon-like bobbing wouldn't last, Bartholomew thrust out his arms to slow his descent. His stomach lurched and he tucked in his legs. God, he hoped he'd land on something soft. He plummeted toward the canopy, falling ever faster in a blur of clouds and sky.

When the treetops rose up to meet him, he jerked left. His feet struck a branch and broke it in half. Then another. He bounced like a kid off a trampoline, right toward a group of people seated in a meadow.

"Watch out!" he cried, curling into a ball.

Too late. His feet plunged into something squishy. He rocked twice, teetered and fell forward, face down in a three-tiered cake.

Sputtering, he rose to his knees and wiped frosting from his eyes. He definitely got the soft landing he wanted. Through the icing he could see a group of picnickers in nineteenth-century attire. They gaped at him. Then the ladies picked up their long full skirts and backed away while a couple of the men brushed off some of the crumbs Bartholomew had sent flying when he'd landed in the middle of their picnic blanket.

"Sorry, I didn't mean to—oh, I ruined your party. But I was falling so fast I couldn't stop." he stammered.

Bartholomew stood, trying not to upset any more of their beautiful spread. Although he tiptoed, he still upended two teacups, four plates, and a wine bottle before hopping onto the grass.

"Quite an entrance," Alex said, from the birch tree he was leaning against on the opposite side of the picnickers.

"I tried to aim away, but…"

"It's okay, Bartholomew."

Alex turned to the company and began to say hello, when the man in a boater hat interrupted him.

"Back, you undead beast," the man warned, brandishing a fork. "We want none of your kind here."

A mustached guy with a hooked nose came up to his side and raised his fists. "Return to whichever horrendous place birthed you."

Meanwhile, the ladies scurried toward the underbrush as two more painted men marched in front of them. They linked arms and thrust their fists into their hips, glaring at the boys.

Looking at Alex, Bartholomew shrugged. "What are they talking about?"

Alex tilted his head and then burst into laughter. "Ha! No, we're not monsters. This is just makeup. See?" He ripped off one of the latex scars from his face and held it up. "We were at a costume party."

Keeping his fork aloft, the man in the hat stepped closer and examined Alex's face with intense eyes that seemed to have no whites. Bartholomew noticed that his dark brown irises were so large that both the upper and the lower lids hid the edges.

The man tilted his head, showing just a hint of white in the corner of each eye. "But you have no mask. And your attire is so grotesque. *Pourquoi*?"

"It's a tradition. Long story." Bartholomew picked up a cloth napkin and began to rub the frosting off of his hands. "Umm, would you mind telling us where we are?"

"Fontainebleau Forest," the man said. "Of corze." He clapped a hand to his boater hat, looked from Alex to Bartholomew. "You are not monsters yet came from zee sky. While zee Impressionist Republic has hot air balloons, I see none. Who or *what* are you?"

Alex draped an arm over Bartholomew's shoulder. "Alexander Devinci and Bartholomew Borax."

"The third," Bartholomew added.

"Oh, can't forget that. The third." Alex winked.

Scattered gasps came from the company.

"You are *not* the chosen ones from the Prophecy." The man with the bulging nose crossed his arms.

"Yep. In the flesh."

"The Deliverers would never dress in such attire. I do not believe you."

Bartholomew had experienced this before, so instead of arguing he ignored the doubting man and extended a hand toward the one who'd lowered his fork. He had a kinder face anyhow.

"Nice to meet you, "Mister…?"

"Monsieur Renoir," he said, shaking Bartholomew's hand. It sounded like Miss-zhur Ren-wah. "And my skeptical companion is Paul, Paul Gauguin."

"Why are you being so trusting? Do they have proof, Auguste?"

"I doubt that Shadow Swine would be so clumsy, Paul."

Bartholomew felt his cheeks redden. He opened his mouth to defend himself, but clamped is shut again.

"Just like The Thinker, you're trusting that everything is fine."

"Oh, here we go again. Would you stop zat infernal nonsense?"

"Just because I believe that Artania's leadership is wanting, does not make my arguments less valid. You yourself have seen the signs."

"The Blank Canvas," whispered on of the ladies.

"Yes, the growing white," Renoir said. "It keeps swallowing huge chunks of our land while Thinker does nothing!"

"Hey!" Alex interrupted. "Watch what you say."

"What? Is your life easier today? Has The Thinker brought calm to your existence? Because I've heard tell of humans popping in and out of Artania with no warning."

Bartholomew had to admit that Gauguin had a point. Things had been crazy lately. He never knew when he'd end up in Artania.

But Alex shook a finger at the mustached artist. "That's not his fault. It's the Shadow Swine."

"Naïve."

Alex's face clouded over. "I don't think someone who has saved your land three times is friggin' naive. What the heck have you done?"

"Painted that which breathes faith, suffering, and nature with its scream. He who birthed me was a revolutionary of the sublime. Never once settling for the mediocre, the middling, the average."

"Oh, give me a break. I've met lots of Artanians who can say the same thing," Alex argued. "And that is still no reason to diss Thinker."

"He barely guides, much less inspires." Gauguin leaned closer, his bulging nose almost tip to tip with Alex's. "Look at you, what have you created of late?"

"Lots."

"Is that so? And you Bartholomew Borax the Third, what have your hands wrought in clay?"

Bartholomew's face reddened. "I-uh…umm…well, you see, I…"

Chapter 28

Alex was getting really ticked off at this Gauguin. Not only was he treating B-3 like a baby, but he also was the same guy who'd spouted crap about The Thinker in that Artanian park he'd popped into a few weeks back. Even though the day had ended up a happy one when Alex realized he was going to be a big brother, that jerk's speech really stuck in his craw.

Who was he to demand answers? Just another Impressionist painter. Had he led armies to face scores of Shadow Swine on skateboard? Or suffered capture from traitorous pirates, like Bartholomew? No, he was just some complainer that seemed to think he was better than the rest of them.

When Gauguin gave B-3 a superior look while flaring the nostrils of his huge hooked nose, Alex curled his hands into fists. What he wouldn't give to punch him right in the middle of that schnozzle. Then Mr. I-have-all-the-answers-for-you-idiots would have a new bump to match the first.

But he was a Deliverer. One chosen at birth to create the true art that would save Artania from destruction. And he had a job to do. So he swallowed his anger and turned away from Gauguin to face Renoir.

"Sir, every other time we've come to Artania, there was a task, like the seven foretold in the Prophecy. Pharaohs captured.

Mona Lisa kidnapped. The Golden Dragon gone? Do you know what it is now, why we're here?"

Auguste Renoir tilted his head and his boater hat wobbled. "Earthquakes shake the Impressionist Republic as the Blank Canvas grows. More villages have been swallowed by the growing white."

"Not to mention, the fires of Paris" Gauguin added, shaking his head. "That our so-called leader put out only after losing three buildings, a café, and two homes."

Alex swallowed hard. *Had the sculpture they'd made kept Thinker safe?* He crossed his fingers before asking, "Is he okay?"

"Oui," Renoir said, his rosy cheeks rounding. "Both he and Monet escaped."

Sighing, Alex patted Bartholomew on the back. "We did it, B-3."

Bartholomew nodded. "But tell us more about these earthquakes. Have you noticed anything happening around the same time?"

"Not I," Renoir replied.

"There is much that affects Artania, young man," Gauguin said with a sniff. "The events on Earth also can cause ripples of destruction. And if you'd been paying attention to your duties as a Deliverer, you'd know that."

Bartholomew got a funny look on his face. "I've been trying—"

"It's okay B-3."

"No, it is not," Gauguin said. "The two of you have responsibilities. Which if shirked could lead to our destruction."

"Dude, we know. And we're creating."

"But does Thinker send inspiration your way? Keeping your hands moving?"

"Like how?" asked Bartholomew.

"Oh, you do not want to get Paul started," Renoir said.

"What's that supposed to mean?" Gauguin said.

"You are always preaching dissent, fueling zee fires of revolution."

"And revolution is what we need if we are ever to defeat the Shadow Swine. Sickhert's army invaded Paris!"

"And Thinker dealt with it."

"He did not. He let a fire break out."

"He doused it, risking life and limb."

"Excuse me," Bartholomew said. "But that still doesn't tell us what Artania needs us to do."

"Of corze. Of corze. My apologies." Renoir placed a hand over his heart. "Politics get me, how do you say, enraged."

Gauguin's tone changed. Now his voice was as smooth as the yellow fabric on the taller lady's dress.

"Yes, Deliverers. This is an old argument. One you need not worry your creative heads over. How can we help you?"

Alex eyed him suspiciously before tapping his chin. "Maybe we should go to the last place that was swallowed by the Blank Canvas. Mr. Renoir, can you show us?"

"But of corze. It is not far from here."

"Okay. Let's go."

Bartholomew cleared his throat. "I do not think that's going to work."

"Why?"

B-3 raised his eyebrows and ran a hand up and down his body. "Huh?"

"Look at us, Alex. If a small group were ready to attack us with forks, can you imagine how a crowd might react?"

"What? Get smacked with a spoon?"

"No, worse."

Alex didn't want to stop teasing B-3 just yet.

He chuckled before asking with fake seriousness, "Or walloped with a napkin?"

"Alex!"

He winked, then turning to Renoir, asked for help to remove their makeup.

Turning, the Impressionist artists led them off to the River Seine to bathe.

Chapter 29

Inside the little wooden changing house next to the River Seine, Bartholomew crinkled his face. He couldn't wait to get that gunk off. The beating sun had baked the frosting onto his face, hardening it atop the zombie makeup until it felt like he had dipped his whole head in mud.

Yuck.

He shed his clothes and folded them before setting them atop the wooden bench. Renoir said it was fine to swim in his undies—many Frenchmen did—but there was no way Bartholomew was going to do that! Instead, he opted for the old-fashioned bathing suit that was hanging on a peg attached to the weatherboard siding.

He wriggled into the short pants and pulled the woolen shirt over his head. Another ridiculous costume. Alex would probably burst out laughing the minute he stepped outside. He could just hear him, *"Oh, no, people can see your ankles, Richie!"*

"Better covered than nearly naked," Bartholomew said.

"What iz zat? Monsieur Borax?" Renoir called, from the other side of the door.

"Nothing. I'm coming out." Bartholomew pushed open the door.

Too hard. It banged against the wall, and scores of bathing, laughing, and painted people stopped splashing and stared.

Bartholomew waved weakly.

"Come on in B-3! The water's great," Alex called, from a roped-off area between two short docks about thirty feet away.

At Renoir's urging, Bartholomew tiptoed toward the river-bank, where women in puffed sleeve tops with sailor collars strolled between men dressed in a variety of costumes. Some of them wore bathing suits like Bartholomew's, whereas others were in striped shorts.

As soon as Bartholomew reached the water's edge, he scoped out an empty spot and bent his knees for a long racing dive. Gliding underwater, he blew a few tiny bubbles and twisted back and forth. He emerged smiling before rubbing his face to get that yucky stuff off.

He glanced back at the row of playhouse-sized changing sheds. Each was brightly painted, but the orange one on the end had a few rotten timbers and appeared to be under repair. The carpenter obviously wasn't very neat, because hammers, saws, and other tools were strewn all over the sandy ground.

"Hey, B-3," Alex called, from behind him.

He turned, but his friend disappeared. Bartholomew leaned over and thought he saw a shadowy form beneath the gentle currents. He lowered his face toward the river surface and squinted.

"Alex?" The name barely escaped his lips before a spout sprayed water up his nose.

Sputtering, Bartholomew fell back while Alex chortled how he'd got him good. Raising one eyebrow, Bartholomew dove under and began to kick his feet on the surface to drench the guffawing Alex.

"Get zee Deliverers!" Renoir called from the dock, before cannonballing next to them with an enormous splash.

Within moments, scores of ladies in long black stockings under bloomers, boys in shorts, and a couple rowers had jumped in and were splattering the two of them with glee.

Bartholomew was beginning to like these Impressionists. They knew how to have fun. All except Gauguin, who stood on the riverbank rolling his eyes like Bartholomew's tutor, Mr. White, did whenever the boy got silly.

What a stuck-up prig.

After interlacing his fingers and widening his hands to fill the hollow between, Bartholomew began to spray Renoir with his makeshift squirt gun. He was in the middle of unleashing a gushing fountain, when he heard a rumbling.

He glanced around, thinking maybe one of the paddleboats he'd seen upriver was approaching. But those steam-powered ships were nowhere in sight.

The ground shuddered again. On the short dock, one man's top hat teetered and he raised a hand to right it. The lady in the long-hooped skirt next to him stumbled on the planks and dropped her parasol.

The umbrella fluttered toward the river, landing handle up. Ripples radiated, and its bowl shape rocked, taking on more water with every listing tilt. The ribbing filled until finally the parasol went under, its curved handle clutching at the surface before it sunk.

A chill filled the air.

Overhead, a swaying birch tree threatened. A cool wind picked up, whistling through the trees. Shivering, Bartholomew gaped at looming branches quiver and lean toward them.

Then a white hole opened right next to the bathhouse he'd just come out of.

"The Blank Canvas, here?" Renoir grabbed Bartholomew's slippery arm. "No!"

But the sinking building told them that it was.

"To the boats! Everyone!" Gauguin cried running up the dock.

He untied one of the moored skiffs and held out his hand so the lady who'd lost her umbrella could step into it.

Bartholomew dove under the water toward another rocking rowboat. He grabbed the line at the bow and towed it toward shore. There, he lifted a little boy and set him down in the hull before helping two dripping ladies and their babies over the gunnels.

"I'll take it from here, Deliverer," said a woman dressed in a man's suit, as she hopped in and put the oars in the oarlocks.

Nodding, Bartholomew gave the stern a shove before the strong woman rowed downstream.

The bleached pit grew, swallowing chairs and fallen logs in its wake. Another bathhouse wobbled, ready to topple over. It hit a birch tree and menacing limbs stretched towards them.

"Hurry!" Gauguin dashed down the dock, toward a moored sailboat.

He called for qualified sailors as the terrified bathers scrambled over each other to escape.

Alex raised his hands. "No, slow down. You'll hurt each other!"

The panicking crowd didn't listen.

The joyful splashes were now whirling eddies from a maelstrom of arms and legs. Bartholomew was about to swim out to grab another rowboat, when someone kicked him in the gut. He doubled over, gasping for breath.

Painful waves throbbed through his stomach. He struggled to stand, but clawing fingers scratched his face and knocked him back. Sharp cries filled the air as the matted horde swarmed the waters. Instinct told him to escape and he looked for somewhere to run, knowing all the while that it was pointless because he would stay to help them. He was honor bound as a Deliverer.

Alex's breath—he heard it in short, gasping bursts. He felt it, too.

"There aren't enough boats," his friend whispered.

"I know." Bartholomew gaped at the surrounding mayhem. "What do we do?"

Panic had given way to anarchy as people fought for the few boats that remained. One man pushed another's head under as he scrabbled up a sailboat's hull. He began to climb over the gunnels, when the second one grabbed him by the shorts and climbed over his body. As soon as he pulled himself on deck, the first man was on him. He threw a punch, and a moment later both were back in the water in a whirling battle.

"We need the friggin' Titanic!" Alex said.

Glancing up the River Seine, Bartholomew almost expected to see a rescue ship. *If only one of those paddle boats would return.* But he knew there was no way any Artanian would come near the deafening sound of crashing trees and crushing rocks.

Chewing on his lower lip, he chanced his gaze upon the orange bathhouse and tools. He tilted his head, blinking. Something about that shape gave him hope.

His mind began bending, forming, cutting. And he knew.

Chapter 30

B-3 pointed. "Come on."

Alex glanced toward the bathhouses and nodded, envisioning exactly what Bartholomew was planning. It was weird that way in Artania. If one had an idea for creating, the other picked up on it right away.

Pushing through the surging waters, he leapt over another panicked man to the dry bank and dashed up the slope toward the overturned building. Many of the rotten panels had now split, leaving a gap in one side, which would make a workable hull.

Bartholomew jogged up beside him, holding a long oar. "Do you see it?"

Nodding, Alex bent over and began to yank on a loose board. He lifted it and set it against a tree before karate kicking the center to split it in two. While he repeated the process, Bartholomew dug into the ground with the oar and piled up two mounds of soil on either side of the broken bath house.

Now to turn a changing house into a paddle boat.

As time slowed around him, Alex picked up the short saw and hewed four planks into pieces. Then he grabbed the hammer and raised an arm. *Clang!* Board met board. Pound. A bow and stern emerged. *Bang!* A ship took shape.

His arm rose and fell as the creation force cursed through his veins. Lumber became a paddle wheel, and nails a steam box. A long thin smokestack appeared.

"I'll make the engine. I studied its basic design last year," Bartholomew said as he began twisting the earth into a boiler with attached cylinders, rods, and pistons.

That dude was into engineering, always reading about one invention or another. Fascinated by the Industrial Revolution, B-3 had even memorized how to make a steam engine. Sometimes his factoid reciting could be annoying, but not today. Today his knowledge guided their creation magic.

Mirror images flashing in their minds, the boys worked as one, molding, forming, and hewing. Faster they went as their sculpture grew, approaching the speed of sound. Surpassing it. Soon, their arms were moving at 186,000 miles a second.

A moment later, it was done.

Alex stood back, waiting for the Creation Magic to morph it into a working steamship. When nothing happened after long moments, he shrugged, palms up.

"What do you—"

More rumbling. The ground heaved and rolled, nearly knocking him over as the white swallowed two more bath houses.

A woman on shore screamed.

B-3 dropped to his knees and grabbed two handfuls of soil. "Maybe if we fill in the gaps" he said pressing mud into the spaces between the boards.

Alex glanced over at the growing chasm. He had watched the Creation Magic morph sculptures into tiny soldiers, weapons, a hydra, and even a dragon, but whether it would work next to the Blank Canvas was anyone's guess.

"Come on, help me," B-3 said.

When Alex plunged his hands into the ground, twigs and dirt plowed under his nails, one stick so sharp he jerked back. With clenched teeth, he brought his hands together in the shape of a shovel and lifted. As soon as his hands cleared the surface, Alex got up on one knee, heaving the mass at the hull.

Next, Bartholomew rubbed it into the chinks between the boards and sat back. He raised his eyebrows expectantly, but Alex wasn't about to wait and see if would work. He plowed his hands in again. And again.

Still no morphing. Just some weird contraption of planks and dirt sticking out in crazier directions than a toddler's mud pie.

"What's wrong?"

B-3 didn't answer, but rubbed harder at the hull as if greater pressure would force it to transform. Alex felt another shudder and held his breath.

No change.

He could hear Gauguin over on the short dock, cursing Artania's leader. That jerk acted as if it were all Thinker's fault that this was happening. The more Alex heard, the angrier he became. If that arrogant know-it-all didn't shut his trap soon, he'd take some of this mud and pummel him with it.

The pit grew. Now half of the buildings had disappeared beneath that white chasm. To where, Alex had no idea. No one knew what happened to things swallowed by the Blank Canvas. Did they just become nothing? The Thinker said they returned to the Before Time, whatever that was.

"If Thinker had only listened to me, zis would not have happened," Gauguin said, before continuing with his tirade against Artania's leader.

Alex curled his hands into fists and glared at the man.

"You are not helping." Renoir shook a finger at Gauguin before lifting another child into a rowboat.

The hook-nosed artist didn't miss a beat, but ranted on while waving the air with his superior sneer.

Alex couldn't take it anymore. "Shut up, you egotistical jerk! Can't you see we have a job to do here?"

Gauguin took a step back and gaped, his mouth opening and closing in silent protest.

Shaking his head, Alex turned back to the ship assemblage to apply more mud to the hull. He bent over to scoop up a fresh handful, when he noticed a gleam in the corner of his eye.

"Something's happening," Bartholomew said.

Sure enough, their sculpture was shimmering and morphing into a real paddle boat. In less than three seconds it stood complete with a boiler burning coal, whistling steam and smoke billowing out its stack.

Alex started to grin, when another building behind them teetered.

"Help us get it into the river," he cried. "Hurry!"

Jogging through the now-choppy waters, Renoir and a couple other swimmers dashed over to the back of the boat.

"Ready?" B-3 asked when Alex lined up at the stern.

Alex nodded and they all leaned forward. Pushing. Goading. Pressing against the unyielding ship.

"Come on, heave ho!" Alex cried. "Heave ho!"

Then he thought he felt the slightest nudge. Or was that the ground shuddering again?

"Iz working. Push harder," Renoir said.

While the earth trembled, the steamship began sliding toward the river. It hit the water with an enormous splash, and the people wading waist-deep scrambled aboard to safety.

Alex opened his mouth to cheer, but the shout he heard was not his own.

"My leg. Iz trapped!"

Alex turned back, horrified to see Auguste Renoir on his back, pressing against the side of a bathhouse. The lower half of his body was entombed in a building-shaped coffin, just yards from the white abyss.

Alex gasped. Renoir's face was deathly pale. The pain must have been excruciating.

The ground rumbled and the pit swallowed another patch of green as the white inched closer to the man.

Now on the verge of being sucked into the growing chasm, Renoir pounded against the wood, but the bathhouse did not move.

One of the swimmers dashed for the paddle boat. "Run! The white approaches!"

The other three looked to Alex.

"Go. We'll take care of this." He waved them toward the rescue boat, where Gauguin had already manned the ship's wheel.

While the others splashed to safety, Alex squatted next to Renoir and slipped his hands under the end of the fallen building.

"Don't worry. We'll get you out," he said to the grimacing painter, only-half believing his own words.

Alex planted his feet and leaned back. For long seconds, his arms strained as sweat began to bead on his brow.

The bathhouse didn't budge.

Chewing on his lower lip again, Bartholomew gave Alex a panicked glance before picking up a paddle and starting to dig under the buried man.

"Good idea," Alex said. He dug faster and faster until his arms became a high-speed tractor pulling a plow.

The growing chasm creaked and groaned.

B-3's paddle hoed and turned next to Alex's circling hands while dirt churned and flew. A moment later, they'd excavated a large hole under Renoir and Alex grabbed the building's edge again. He leaned back to raise the building, and the wall tilted slightly upward.

"Grab him. Now!" he ordered.

Bartholomew wrapped his arms around Renoir's torso and pulled.

There was a sucking sound and dust swirled in front of Alex's eyes. Sputtering, he clutched at air as he fell back into the cold emptiness.

Chapter 31

Bartholomew helped Renoir to his feet and patted his back. Letting out a long sigh, he turned to congratulate Alex, but cocked his head instead. He looked right and left, right again.

The bathhouse and his friend had disappeared.

His voice quivered when he called, "Alex?"

Renoir pointed toward the growing pit where four clutching fingers curled around the edge of that bone-white abyss. Bartholomew rushed over and gasped.

There hung Alex, arms stretched overhead and feet dangling into the ever-expanding fissure. The howling wind whipped at his friend's baggy jeans, twisting them like ropes around his limbs. A chilling gust coiled from below and Alex jerked, his body quivering.

"It has me," Alex cried. "Like quicksand. Help!"

With the wind's roar rising toward him, Bartholomew grit his teeth and kneeled. He leaned over and thrust out a hand to grasp Alex by the wrist. Bartholomew yanked, but something tugged back. Then cold barbs crept up his arm, prickling his skin with stinging needles.

He let go and his friend began to slip downward.

Alex clawed at soil and roots. "No!" he cried, sinking deeper into the void.

While Bartholomew made a fumbling lunge, Alex's hands and face burrowed into the cliff wall. As choking dirt filled his mouth, he sputtered, coughed, and then threw his head back. His body thrashed as kicked wildly for footing.

Meanwhile, Bartholomew dropped to his stomach and scooched forward, praying that the tree root overhead would be within Alex's grasp.

"There's a root right above your head! Grab it, Alex."

Seconds ticked slowly before Alex finally wrapped his dirt-encrusted fingers around the woody stem.

"Good." Then Bartholomew ordered Renoir to hold his legs.

Once the Impressionist painter had a firm grip around them, he extended a hand again.

But his fellow Deliverer was just out of reach.

"I can't move my feet," Alex murmured, with a weak cough. "They're going numb."

"Hold on, Alex. I'm almost there."

Bartholomew looked back to make sure Renoir had a firm grip, and wriggled over the unstable ground. Like a worm he inched forward, until his torso hung over the abyss. He extended an arm. His fingertips just touched Alex's.

The ground shook and a few more pebbles gave way. Most rolled past Alex, but a larger one hit the tree root he was grasping. It bent and began to crack, dropping Alex further down the cliff face.

Ignoring the possibility that they'd both end up at the bottom of that white pit, Bartholomew sprung after him. He dove downward, expecting a long plummet, but Renoir held fast.

All that was left between Alex and a drop into endless nothing was a tiny tree root.

Strange, but at that moment an image of Alex and Gwen celebrating the victory in the Renaissance Nation with him came to mind. He couldn't recall their exact words, only that they'd all started cracking up right after.

Bartholomew giggled.

The wind howled as Alex stared incredulously. "Seriously?"

"Remember, feelings are an illusion. You have the power to control them. Reach up." He fixed Alex with an even stare.

Alex shook his head and said, weakly, "This is different. I'm frozen, like something just turned me to stone."

"Come on, grab my hand. We'll work together."

"Don't you get it? I'm numb."

"No, you're not. Your arms are strong. With flexing muscles, like Gwen's dad. See it. Believe."

"I can't. It has me. And if you don't let go, it'll get you, too."

Even though Bartholomew was willing strength, the frost opposed his every attempt. It moved up his arms, deadening muscle after muscle until he, too, was frozen.

"Go, B-3. Save yourself."

"No! We are Deliverers."

Alex shook his head. "Renoir pull him away, please!"

"I cannot, Deliverer."

"I'm not strong enough," Alex said.

"Think of your mom. What would your disappearing do to her?"

Alex crinkled his brow and then looked into Bartholomew's eyes. "She'd be heartbroken."

"And that little brother or sister to come? Don't you want to meet them?"

"Of course." Alex slipped farther down.

"Then do something about it. You are a Deliverer. Say it. Help me!"

"I...am...a...Deliverer," Alex whispered, between labored breaths. "One chosen."

"Yes. Now louder!"

"I am a Deliverer. Born to create and keep a world safe. I have the power."

With these words, the feeling returned to Bartholomew's arms. He reached down.

"Come on, climb," he said.

Alex spat again. Then with a clenched jaw, he reached a hand upward. But like a dead talon, the curled fingers were fixed into a claw and unable to grasp.

Fighting through the cold, Bartholomew hooked his fingers under Alex's.

"Don't let go."

Alex nodded.

Muscles cramping and spasming, Bartholomew called over his shoulder, "Now, Mr. Renoir, pull!"

The painter winched them backwards. One step. Two.

Alex's forearm cleared the ridge...a shoulder, his head.

Now on solid ground, Bartholomew grasped Alex's collar. Renoir backed up two more steps. And then they were dragging his best friend over ferns and pebbles.

Bartholomew barely had a moment to ask Alex if he was all right, before more ground gave way.

Renoir gasped. "Get up, Deliverers. Run! N—"

Bartholomew didn't hear the rest, because the artist began to fade away.

The next thing he knew he was on the road near Gwen's house, in the exact place he'd escaped Sludge. He expected to feel claws digging into his neck, and ducked. But there was no sign of the monster.

Only a confused Alex turning in circles and gaping at the sky.

Chapter 32

"…don't go!" Gwen finished the sentence she'd begun when Jose started to follow Alex and B-3 out the door.

Jose turned back from the entryway. "Why?"

"It's…it's…just part of a show. Yeah, a show we planned. Thought it'd be funny." She waved at her friends. "Just a Halloween prank, guys."

A few of the party goers let out a collective sigh. Gwen could tell by the look on their faces that Sludge chasing her two buds out the door had freaked some of them out.

"And is that," Jose pointed at her moon headdress, "part of the show?"

"What?"

"Your moon."

"What? It's crooked?" Gwen reached up to right it.

Jose stepped up closer, picked up the remote and turned the music back on.

As soon as the kids began chattering amongst themselves, he whispered, "The words."

"Words?"

"I thought you and I were going to be the show. The poetry of Percy Shelly symbolizing our love. We were becoming an eclipse, soft, sweet, and full of light."

Gwen was confused. "We were. I said the line, *When soul meets soul on lover's lips.*"

"Yeah, but I don't think *Death Comes* and our poetry go together." Jose crossed his arms.

"*What* are you talking about?"

"Your freaking head dress, of course!"

"Huh?" Gwen walked over to the mirror in the dining area, and gasped.

Etched in the center of her glittery crescent moon were the words *Death Comes.* Her mouth went dry and she gulped. There was only one way it could have got there.

Sludge.

"See?" Jose sniffed. "You know, if you wanted to tell me we were breaking up, you could do it in a more mature way."

Gwen ripped the moon off and threw it on the ground. Stared, aghast. "No. I-I-"

Just then, there was the sound of applause. Gwen turned to see Alex and Bartholomew shuffling through the doorway. She expected to see the captain of the Shadow Swine behind them, but no slimy moon-etcher stepped over the threshold.

Blinking through his zombie makeup, Alex at least had the presence of mind to take a bow. Bartholomew stared, stupefied, with a dazed expression until Alex elbowed him, and he, too, bowed awkwardly.

"Epic." Zach walked over to high-five Alex.

Coco joined him. "Yes, like watching *Godzilla* or *King Kong.* If only I had some popcorn." She sighed.

Lacey strutted over and sniffed. "Your big butt doesn't need any more." She smiled coyly at Alex. "I guess I'm lucky that way."

"Yeah, whatever." Alex rolled his eyes and headed toward Gwen.

"So what happened to your friend Sam?" Jose asked.

"Sam? Oh, he had another party to go to. With a, umm, costume like that he's in high demand."

"Yes," Bartholomew said, from behind. "He graces many Halloween festivities."

"Wouldn't call *that* grace, dude." Jose pointed at the moon headdress still on the floor. "Whose idea was that, anyhow?" He turned to Alex. "Yours?"

While Jose's head was turned, Gwen gave Alex a pleading look and mouthed, *Say yes.*

"Yeah, thought it'd add to the uh, uh—"

"Show," Gwen said, helping him finish his thought. "He thought it'd be funny."

"I do not find the words *Death Comes* funny."

"Maybe not," Alex said.

"In fact, it's negative energy." Jose narrowed his eyes. "That's the second time you've done something weird around my girl. What are you trying to do, worm your way in?"

Alex held up a hand. "Jose, no. I'm just into Halloween. Awesome holiday. The costumes. Spooky decorations. Eerie music. Fun."

"Don't believe you. Ever since I won the Volcom Games, you've been jealous. And now you're trying to steal my girl with bizarre parlor tricks."

"Babe," Gwen said, "it's not like that, I swear."

"Oooh. Lovers' spat," Lacey cooed.

Gwen's heart raced. This situation was getting out of control. If she didn't do something soon, she was going to lose her boyfriend in front of the biggest gossip at Santa Barbara High, who just happened to be his ex.

She tried to take his hand. "Let's go in the other room, okay?"

Jose brushed it off. "This party's over for me. I'm out of here. Need some space. Time to think."

"But, honey—"

"So do you. During which you might think about how your choices effect our relationship. Try reflecting on your actions for once."

The pain in Jose's handsome face before he turned and marched out the door socked Gwen in the gut. She turned on Alex with a savage intensity.

Shaking with rage, she curled her hands into fists. "You and your, your, your—you-know-what! Why do you always ruin things?"

"I'm sorry, Gwen, I—"

"Leave me alone!" Gwen shoved him and rushed toward the stairs, which she took two at a time.

Eyes brimming with tears, she retreated down the hall toward her surfer-inspired bedroom. She slammed the door and looked at the curling wave painting on the far wall. It reminded her of all the times she and Jose had skated along the boardwalk, looking out at Santa Barbara Harbor. With gentle encouragement, he'd coached her, pointing out her foot placement on an ollie, or her body position for a tail flip.

Her throat tightened around a lump she couldn't swallow, *I will not cry. I won't.* Gwen fought to keep the tears from spilling over. She paced the room, trying to focus on something other than losing her boyfriend for good.

The pink lava lamp. Jose's long black hair. The hibiscus print comforter. His incense-filled home. The surfer poster. Him skating over concrete as graceful as air.

Everywhere she looked were memories.

Gwen stomped, then threw herself on the bed and buried her face in a pillow.

"Damned Artania!"

Chapter 33

If Alex had been next to a wall, he would have thrust a fist through it. Poor Gwen, all caught up in this crap. Maybe he should go after Jose and explain that his girlfriend wasn't trying to diss him. She had just been suspended in time when a monster decided to scratch scary words into her glitter moon.

But of course, that wouldn't fly.

He shrugged at Zach. "I guess that's my cue to go."

"Sorry, dude." Zach gave a weak imitation of his signature move.

Alex tried to smile. But even those black-tipped fingers bent into a gun shape couldn't coax his mouth upward. Gwen was slipping away like a rope drifting out to sea, and even stretching his arms as far as he could left her friendship beyond his reach.

He sighed. "Come on, B-3. It looks like Halloween is over."

They walked down the long drive in silence. Alex rubbed his forehead, questions twisting in his mind. *Popping in and out without notice? What the frick is going on?*

Once they turned onto the dimly lit street, Bartholomew broke the silence. "I know the party wasn't what you expected, but at least—"

"At least what?" Alex threw his hands up in exasperation. "At least I almost got swallowed by a white pit? At least Swineys can attack our friends when they're frozen in time? At least

Gauguin is promoting rebellion against The Thinker? I don't see an upside to all of this."

"Yes, but—"

"But what, Mister-I'm-too-depressed-to-create?"

"That's not fair. You don't know what it's like."

"Oh, yes, I do. I've met your mom plenty of times. It sucks."

"And lately."

"I know, I know, I know. She's been on cleaning binges and stuff. But damnit, Artania needs us. So instead of moaning, why don't you do something about it?"

"I'm trying."

Bartholomew's whiny voice made Alex want to hit him upside the head. "Yeah, right. I don't see you doing much."

"I'd welcome suggestions."

"Start creating more, for a start."

"But Mother—"

"If you can find ways to circumvent security to sneak out here, I'm sure you could get to your studio."

"Maybe."

"Not maybe. Try. Some deep friggin' crap is going on, and I don't know what it is. But I'm afraid that if we don't do something soon…" Alex stared at the setting moon.

"Gwen," Bartholomew whispered.

Alex swallowed hard and nodded. "And not just her. It looks like everyone we care about is in danger."

Chapter 34

Not bothering to see if the coast was clear, Bartholomew dragged his feet across the threshold and lumbered toward the stairs. Numb, he could barely put one foot in front of the other. With drooping eyes, he fixed his gaze on his scuffed shoes rising and falling on each tread. *Lift foot. Step up. Repeat.*

"Bartholomew Griffith Borax! Where have you been?" Mother screeched from the top of the stairs.

Bartholomew was expecting this.

Wearily, he glanced up. "I went to Alex's."

"Went out? Went out! And you didn't bother to tell anyone. Or ask permission? I've had the servants searching everywhere."

"Sorry."

"That's all you have to say? After hours of worry? I didn't know if you were alive or …or…trapped in some terrible pile of filth," she said referring to Father's accident years before.

Bartholomew was too tired to deal with paranoid delusions about drowning mud puddles.

"I'm fine. See?" He hobbled upward.

Mother gasped. "And what is all over your face?"

"Zombie makeup."

When he reached the landing, Hygenette Borax leaned forward and squinted at him.

"Halloween? You know how I feel about…about…"

Bartholomew kept his eyes cast down at the white carpet. "Yes."

With a whimper, Mother stumbled back. "My baby. Mr. White. Someone! Help him."

Here we go again.

His tutor, the butler, and three maids appeared all armed with sponges, mops, and bottles of cleanser. With feather dusters raised, the French maids surrounded the teen and began to brush the dirt off of his clothes.

"No! He is covered in filth. Look at him."

Mr. White stepped up closer. "Having a bit of fun, eh, chappy?"

"You call ripped clothing and funeral parlor makeup fun? He looks... looks... oh, the horror!"

Wishing his exhausted brain would work, Bartholomew tried to invent a lie. But he was so tired nothing came. So he decided he might as well tell the truth, or a version of it, and let the chips fall where they may.

"Mother, it's fine. Some friends had a Halloween party. I dressed up and went. End of story."

"Friends? You mean those hooligans that got you into trouble when I allowed you to attend school? Those filthy, germ-infested ruffians?" Hygenette's voice grew shriller when she turned on the servants. "And you all let him leave?"

"But ma'am, you never asked us to keep him here," said the oldest maid.

Hygenette gave her a diamond-cold stare. "Controlling filth is your job. And it lies in wait. Everywhere!"

The maid bowed her head and curtsied. "Sorry, ma'am."

Mother placed the back of her hand on her forehead. "Oh, the horrors. My poor baby. Why would you torture me like this?"

Bartholomew rolled his eyes. "How many times do I have to tell you I'm not a baby? I'm fourteen, for God's sake! And have you ever considered that perhaps it's not about you? That maybe, for once, I wanted to do things like a normal teen?"

Hygenette turned on Mr. White and held up a French-manicured finger. "This is your fault. If you'd been doing your job properly, this wouldn't have happened."

"I have tried."

"Have you? Look at him. Filth!"

"Worry not, ma'am." Mr. White waved the maids closer. "We'll have him clean as a whistle any moment."

Mother stared off into space, seeing things that weren't there. "Germs. Death. Filth. It's everywhere." She swooned, and two maids propped her up by the elbows.

"It's all right, mum," the older one said. "Come with us."

"Bathe, bathe, bathe," Hygenette mumbled, as they lead her off, the butler and other maid trailing behind, brushing feather dusters over the walls.

"Now look what you've done," Mr. White said. "Upset your mother."

"What else is new?"

"That is not a very good attitude, Master Borax."

"So. Who cares?"

"You should. Now the entire household will be thrust into a cleaning frenzy that may last weeks."

"And?"

"And it could be much better."

"No, it couldn't."

"Couldn't it?" Mr. White leaned closer. "What is going on with you?"

"Nothing."

"No, you've seemed different lately. And I found that book. About...sadness."

"You were snooping. Again." Bartholomew crossed his arms and glared at his tutor.

"It is my job to make sure that you are mentally fit. Recently, you seem to have less… what is the word? Ambition. Drive. Spirit."

"What's the point? It's always the same."

"Why, someday you will head an entire cleaning empire. Things will change greatly then."

Pivoting on one foot, Bartholomew held up a hand to cut him off. "I don't think they ever will. Now leave me be."

He trudged back up the stairs to the prison that was his life.

Chapter 35

While picking up speed at the skatepark for another grind, Alex heard Bartholomew's *whoop* ringtone on his phone. This was the call he'd been waiting for. He put his heel on the back of his board and tail dragged into a halt before reaching into his pocket and pushing *Accept.*

"Hi, Alex," his friend's morose voice droned.

"Finally, B-3. How's it going? Did you do like I asked?"

"Yes. I made two large sculptures of Thinker. I think they'll help."

"Hopefully."

Ever since Halloween, he and Bartholomew had been on a quest to discover why the cosmic connection between Artania and Earth had changed so much. As far as they knew, no Chosen Ones had ever popped in and out of Artania like they had all autumn.

Luckily, Halloween seemed to be the end of it, with no crazy trips for six months now. Christmas had come and gone without incident. Well, mostly. If he didn't count Gwen throwing his gift back in his face saying.

"I don't want anything from you! It'll just draw your freaky monsters to me!"

Alex understood. Mostly. And tried to tell himself that even though he missed her, at least Gwen was safe. Last time he asked, there'd been no dream invasions or etchings of *Death Comes,* or other spooky messages into her stuff.

"I could email you some pictures," B-3 said.

Hoping to lessen whatever power the Shadow Swine now had, the boys had started making more Thinker art pieces. They thought that creating lots of paintings and sculptures would strengthen Artania's leader, making him less vulnerable to Swiney attacks.

"Nah. Why don't you print copies and stop by? Mom'd love to see you."

Bartholomew sighed, just like he did during every conversation they'd had these past few months.

"Come on. You need to get out of the house. And Mom could use the company."

"I don't know."

"Stop being a freakin' baby. I need to talk to you about something. So suck it up and come on over. See you in twenty." Alex pressed *End* and glanced wistfully over at Gwen skating with Jose.

She'd finally convinced her boyfriend to forgive her for that *Death Comes* etching in her moon costume. Of course, she did this by blaming everything on Alex and promising to avoid him. And boy was Gwen true to her word. She had barely nodded hello to Alex ever since.

Not that he had a ton of time to notice. What, with Mom's high-risk pregnancy putting her on bed rest, trying to help the Richie with his whiney depression, keeping up with freshman English—boring!—and painting new creations he hoped would help Thinker in the Impressionist Republic, Alex barely had time to rest. Much less worry about whether an elfin-faced skater girl, who was practicing fakies a few yards away with Jose, would ever be his friend again.

Alex glanced down at his phone. 1:32. He had less than twenty to get home if we was to meet B-3. He crossed his fingers that his rouse would get Mr. Depression off his rear and out of the house, and then shot Gwen a sideways glance. She rolled up the concrete ramp and back. Then, bending her knees, she flipped the board into a 360. And fell. Alex turned to go to her, but then Buddha boyfriend bent down at her side with calming words and Alex stopped mid-step.

Leave her alone. She's safe with Jose.

With a sigh, he hopped over the short fence and threw his board onto the sidewalk before kicking off toward his rendezvous with Bartholomew.

Chapter 36

The bronze Thinker stood at the podium and looked out over the gathered company in the Parisian park. So many friends. From the rosy-cheeked Renoir to Monet and his lovely bride, Camille. Degas, surrounded by ballerinas in tutus, nodded and smiled from his perch on the grassy hillock. Of course, a sneering Paul Gauguin stood nearby, accompanied by a few men in long regency waistcoats and top hats. They would be his toughest audience.

"Friends," Thinker began in his deep, rich voice. "The Blank Canvas continues to grow, causing many of you great worry. But I am here to allay your fears. The Deliverers are creating daily, working long and hard to protect the Impressionist Republic."

"Still not enough," Gauguin heckled, from the crowd.

"Oui!" another called. "My friends were almost swallowed by zee white. And Renoir—"

"I am fine," Auguste Renoir shouted. The Deliverers saved me."

"Only because I wuz there." Gauguin stepped closer to the lectern. "It wuz I who thought to evacuate in zee boats. Where were you then?" He pointed at Thinker.

"Consulting the Soothsayer Stone. I needed its wisdom."

"Action is what we need now. Not reading an ancient stone!"

Several Artanians in the crowd mumbled their agreement.

"But the Prophecy says, *Hope will lie in the hands of twins*," Thinker said.

"It's not the Prophecy we question," Gauguin replied. "But how you carry out its words."

"Dear Artanians," Thinker said. "I live to lead you well. And the proof is in the paint. Have not three tasks been completed by the Deliverers?"

"Yes!" Renoir and Monet replied in unison.

"The Land of Antiquities has its pharaohs and monuments. The Smiling One continues to sustain the Renaissance Nation. And in Gothia, the golden dragons fill the skies. The Prophecy is being fulfilled."

"Those were not your doing, but the humans, young Alex and Bartholomew."

"Know you nothing, Gauguin?" Thinker said, quietly.

"More than you realize." Gauguin sneered.

"My steely palm sees into both worlds, helping to guide our salvation. Many times, I have called upon the Knights of Painted Light to keep dreams safe." Thinker paused and pointed into the crowd. "These actions ensured your safety."

Gauguin crossed his arms. "If that's the case, then prove it."

"Oui! Oui!" called several of his comrades.

"You know it is forbidden. The Soothsayer Stone says—"

"Lies! You will not show us because you are not acting. I should be the leader of Artania. Who's with me?"

Thinker was shocked to hear at least twenty Artanians shout, "I."

"Then let us leave this useless sculpture."

"Yes!"

"And go to a place where paint is fresh and no white chasms open." Gauguin held a fist high like a flag, and marched past the podium.

A score of painted Artanians trailing behind, their scowls striking fear into Thinker's heart.

Chapter 37

Panting, Bartholomew slowed to a stop on the faded smiley welcome mat. Mopping his brow with a monogrammed handkerchief, he wiped his feet before ringing the bell, and shifted his weight. In just a few moments, he'd get to share something he'd created.

Alex opened the door, looking disheveled and ticked off, but Bartholomew was used to that. It seemed he was a constant source of disappointment.

"What's up?" Bartholomew peered into his eyes.

"In a minute." Alex put a finger to his lips and then pointed behind his chest, into the living room.

A very pregnant Cyndi Devinci lie stretched out on the overstuffed beige couch, with a bright colored throw blanket wrapped around her legs.

When she saw Bartholomew, she waved. "Come on in, sweetheart."

"Oh, thank you, Mrs. Devinci." Bartholomew approached and put out his hand.

"Cyndi. How many times do I have to tell you?" She took his hand and patted it.

"You are looking well," Bartholomew cleared his throat, "Cyndi."

She smiled. "For a lounging hippopotamus."

"Mom's doing great. Doctor says everything is progressing just like it should."

"Just a few more weeks now." Cyndi went on to outline her last doctor visit, the baby's weight and size, the nursery decorations, and how helpful Alex had been with her on bed rest.

Bartholomew nodded, trying to listen and be polite. But he couldn't stop thinking about what Alex had said on the phone. What did he need to talk about? Had he discovered something?

Alex must have picked up on his impatience because he said, "Come on B-3, let me show you some of my new work."

As soon as they had privacy inside Alex's room, Bartholomew said, "So what's this all about?"

"Nothing really. Just wanted to get you out of the house."

"What?"

"I didn't think you'd come if I said *let's hang out,* so I pretended I had something big to share."

"You lied to me?"

"For your own good. The last few months, you've hardly gotten out. Been a wuss."

Bartholomew thought about sharing how hard it had been. How life was just one lonely moment after another. Even creating didn't give him that sense of hope it used to. That sleep was his only salvation.

But Alex already thought he was a wimp, so he said, "Mother's been more diligent since Halloween."

"So be sneaky. I could use someone to talk to once in a while, you know."

Bartholomew opened his mouth to protest, but Alex cut him off.

"And no arguments. You know full well that you can get out when you really want to. *If* you were a real friend."

Bartholomew's face blanched. "I am."

"Then freakin' start acting like it, instead of hiding out in that sterile hospital you call home."

"I can't help it if Father's death was hard on Mother."

"That was before you were born. Fourteen years ago."

"So? She acts like the same thing is waiting to happen to me at any moment."

"Have you ever thought of trying to do something about it instead of whining? Call a therapist or something."

"Oh, of course that would go over really well. I can just hear her now, *Filthy office.* Believe me I've tried. Nothing works but getting clean."

"Well, you do smell good." Alex guffawed.

Bartholomew smirked. "Yeah, there's that."

"So these new sculptures. You got photos?"

"Right here." Bartholomew pulled out the pictures he'd secretly printed out earlier, and handed them to Alex.

"That's weird." Alex held the photo up to his face.

"What?" Bartholomew asked stepping closer.

"Your face!" Alex cuffed his shoulder.

Smiling, Bartholomew shook his head, and the two of them began sharing their recent creations. And he forgot all about the loneliness.

For a while.

Chapter 38

Gwen was walking hand in hand with Jose between classes, when she saw Alex heading her way, his face scrunched up in concentration as he stared into his phone. She smiled remembering how he used to get that look whenever he was trying out a new skateboard trick. His lips would pucker into a duck face every time he was practicing backside ollies or fakies. She'd teased him about it lots of times, but secretly admired how he never grumbled when he messed up. No matter how many times he fell, Alex just brushed it off and tried again.

Jose followed her gaze and gave her hand a tug. "You agreed to stay away from him. Remember?"

Gwen's smile faded. "I know."

Images of Captain Sludge strutting into her house on Halloween came to mind, his huge arm holding that battle axe at the ready. Her friends had oohed and aahed, but to Gwen his heaving hunched back and slime-covered face was full-on freaky.

She was safer without Alex and B-3 in her life.

Hot anger boiled in Gwen's gut. Is that why she was avoiding her buds? Just to play it safe? That wasn't like her. She was tough, strong, could bench press two hundred. She'd battled monsters on skateboards in Venice, on dragonback in Gothia, and on sailing ships in stormy seas. She didn't let fear control her life.

Some friend you've been, hiding like a wuss. She shook her head.

And suddenly she decided.

"I need to hit the head. Catch you later," she said giving Jose a quick peck on the cheek.

He squeezed her shoulder and turned toward his algebra class in C-Pod.

As soon as Jose cleared the corner, Gwen dashed up to Alex. "Hey, hold up!"

Alex halted, glanced up from his phone. "Hi, Gwen." He looked around. "You sure this is cool? Will Jose get ticked?"

"I don't care. Miss you. Wondering how you're doing."

"Things have been crazy. You wouldn't believe..."

"Really?"

"Don't have a lot of time to share now."

"You okay? Any more freaky visitations or trips?"

"Not since Halloween. Thank God."

"And your mom?"

"Still on bed rest, but good. Only a couple of weeks now, and I'll be a big brother." Alex smiled.

"So cool."

Gwen hadn't noticed how the halls were thinning, until the bell rang.

"Rat farts! Late again." She glanced at the clock overhead.

She turned back to shrug at Alex, but he had disappeared. She knew this time that he wasn't yanking her chain. He had just been pulled into Artania.

Toward what, she had no idea.

Chapter 39

Arms akimbo, Alex swirled, twisted, and spiraled through the air. Cartwheeling through space, he reached out for something, anything to grab a hold of. There was nothing, just blackness in a sprinkling of stars. No school. No Gwen acting kissy face with Jose one second and then finally talking to him the next. Not even that rollercoaster rainbow he'd ridden so many times before.

Like a skater on a crazy loop the loop course, he hurtled through the emptiness, spinning and rolling on an invisible board. But this steed was relentless, jerking and flipping his body in wild directions with such force he was afraid it'd pull him apart.

He was tucking halfway into a forward roll, when everything froze and all was silence save the throbbing pulse in his ears. Now suspended between distant constellations, Alex sucked in a quick breath.

Cold darkness filled his lungs with a stale mixture that seemed...just wrong. Instead of a breathable tunnel, the healthy atmosphere had suddenly turned into a death gas, making him nauseous.

"What the—?" He exhaled, trying not to breathe another micro ounce of the sick miasma.

He hung there in the silent void, refusing to inhale. Interminable moments passed as his chest tightened. Alex covered his mouth. How long could he hold his breath? Five, six minutes?

Fighting the dizziness that was threatening to overcome him, he tried swimming his arms. Nothing happened. Kicked a leg. He stayed put.

Just when Alex's lungs began to spasm and force him to swallow that poison, he shot forth. Like an accelerating rocket with stars blurring in the abyss, he jetted through the blackness.

For several seconds, the force flattened his hair against his scalp and pressed his arms to his sides. Alex sputtered and coughed. Then the next thing he knew, he was bouncing off a cloud of cotton and somersaulting through the painted air of Artania.

This art world was one strange place. The living paintings and sculptures were like weather patterns rearranging the sky. One moment the heavens were dark and thick oil paintings, while next they became light and airy colored chalk. Yet each change edged in soft clouds was so gradual that it all fit together perfectly.

Except for a figure in the distance, arms splayed out like an "X." The form was familiar, so Alex squinted to confirm his suspicions. But his whirling body made it impossible to focus, so he tried extending his hands to slow the rotations. But he just spun more wildly.

Alex tucked into a ball, sped up, and tumbled closer to the whizzing figure.

"Watch out!" he cried.

Boom! He crashed headfirst into whoever or whatever it was, and everything went black.

Chapter 40

"Alex, Alex! Are you all right?" Bartholomew cried kneeling beside his unconscious friend.

No response.

Bartholomew grabbed him by the shoulder and shook him once. Twice. Three times. Alex lie there as pale as dandelion seeds, a round, red, bump growing in the center of his forehead. Bartholomew probed the top of his own scalp where he'd collided with his friend, and his hand recoiled. He felt a sharp pain, but wasn't lightheaded.

Kneeling closer, Bartholomew drew an ear close to Alex's face and listened. Nothing but silence.

Bartholomew clenched his fists, listening for some sign of life. *Please be okay.*

The seconds ticked by. Shaking, he placed two fingers on his friend's carotid artery and checked for a pulse.

Nothing.

Tears welled up in Bartholomew's eyes. Swallowing hard, he readjusted his fingers.

Then he heard a shallow breath.

"Thank God." He leaned back on his haunches.

He drew his brows together. Just a moment before, he'd been in his room wishing his life were different. Then he was spinning crazily through Artanian skies. He'd thrust his arms out, only to crash into Alex.

Before landing here.

The light was low, whether from morning or evening, he couldn't tell. But he knew he was in Artania because everything looked like a soft-focus painting.

Which country had he landed in this time? It didn't appear realistic like the Photography District, or ancient like the Land of Antiquities. No castles and fortresses jut out of a painted landscape like in Gothia or The Renaissance Nation. This place had the same feel as that forest when he'd landed in the middle of Renoir's picnic.

The Impressionist Republic.

Through the mist, Bartholomew saw two massive towers on the opposite shore. They flanked a central spire that must have been at least one-hundred-fifty-feet high, and as an avid reader, he recognized it at once—Notre Dame. The famous Paris cathedral from Victor Hugo's novel *The Hunchback of Notre Dame.*

Bartholomew was kneeling on a riverbank that was deserted except for one lone man facing the gothic cathedral. He was wearing a smock and had a bushy beard, but Bartholomew couldn't tell much about his hair since a French beret covered his head.

"Hey! Over here!" he cried, waving.

The bereted man turned, cocked his head. He looked familiar.

"I need some help!"

Slowly, the artist set his brushes down on the palette across his forearm, lay them next to his easel, and began strolling toward the boy.

Hands quivering, Bartholomew shook Alex again. No response. A deep pit grew in his gut. He tried to remember what he might have read about concussions, but drew a blank.

"I need help. Please hurry!"

"Bonjour." The artist drew close and clapped a hand to his beret. "You?"

Recognizing him as the same morose man he'd met in the little garret the first time he was thrust into Artania, Bartholomew nodded.

"With my friend. And he's hurt. I can't wake him up."

"He look bad. Perhapz gone?" the man said.

"No! I just checked. He's breathing. Please do something."

"Ahh. I zee." After bending down, the artist held the back of his hand an inch above Alex's mouth and began to count in French, "*Un, deux, trois, quatre, cinq...*" He stroked his bushy beard and gave Bartholomew a sad look, then stood. "I sink it iz a coma. We should take him to zee hospital. Over zhere beyond the River Seine."

Unable to speak, Bartholomew's gaze followed the pointing finger to the river, up the faded brick retaining walls, and past the huge building towering over the river like a looming giant.

Just beyond Notre Dame, he could see a five-story building with a rectangular roof and a bank of windows topped with dormers in the typical French style. A long way to carry an unconscious fourteen-year-old.

He'd dealt with lots of scary stuff in Artania, but this was the first time he truly feared for his friend's life. They were supposed to have powers that protected them from this sort of stuff, for God's sake!

The artist raised his eyebrows. "Well?"

With a dry swallow, Bartholomew bent at Alex's feet and nodded. "Ready."

The painted man slid both hands under Alex's shoulders and lifted as Bartholomew grasped the ankles and leaned into a stand. Then the two began a shuffling walk toward a stone bridge over the River Seine.

Back straining, Bartholomew doubted he could carry Alex fifty yards, much less the quarter mile it looked like they needed to go. He readjusted his grip, but it didn't help. He rolled his shoulders, even tightened his core like in that bodybuilding book he'd read, but it made his spine cramp so much he had to slow to a snail's pace.

Then he remembered what a goddess had told him on his first trip to Artania.

"You are creators," she'd said. "You have only to think of water, and your thirst will be quenched. Imagine coolness, and it is so."

He imagined Alex as light as feather. But it didn't work. Closed his eyes to envision it. Alex still weighed one hundred forty-three pounds. Six more than him. After Alex's growth spurt last fall, they'd compared heights and weights, and Bartholomew was bummed to realize Alex had surpassed him.

"What is your name, anyhow?" he asked stopping about halfway over the River Seine to readjust his grip.

"Oh, zat is right. I did not tell you when you were here before. My head was in a bad place."

"I remember. I hope you're not still thinking of..." Bartholomew pointed his chin toward the river but didn't finish the thought. He knew about depression. It'd been his constant companion this last year.

"No, no. But my namesake, zee artist that birthed me, did just such a thing."

"Who was?"

"Claude, Claude Monet." The man bowed his head slightly.

"Thought so. When I got home, I looked up artists of the Impressionist period, and that name was at the top," Bartholomew said feeling a twinge of pride for guessing right.

Then he glanced at Alex's pale face, and knots of guilt joined the worry ones in his stomach.

"Oui. Now we go zis way. To the Hôtel-Dieu de Paris," Monet said as he passed under Notre Dame's shadow.

"Hotel?" Bartholomew halted. "Alex needs a hospital."

"Zat is what we French call them these many centuries."

"Oh."

Monet led them past the cathedral with its massive Gothic towers and huge doors topped by a carved row of chattering kings. Bartholomew expected the sculpted men to jump down from their perch and offer help, but they were so engrossed in their conversation they didn't even glance his way.

Alex still hadn't stirred.

Bartholomew tried not to think of how serious it might be as they turned up a cobbled street and approached the block-long building with a steep roof that they'd seen from across the river.

Monet shouted, "Doctor!"

When no one emerged from the hospital, Bartholomew joined in. "Doctor! We need a doctor!"

Still no one came out. Bartholomew swallowed hard, ready to heft Alex up the stairs. Then shuffling feet echoed down the stone steps.

A woman in a long dress and white apron rushed to their aide and cradled the unconscious Alex in soothing arms.

Chapter 41

While washing her hands in the B-Pod restroom, Gwen glanced in the mirror and checked her hair. One of her braids was coming loose, so she yanked off her hair tie to re-plait the end. She was already late, so another minute wouldn't make much difference.

I hope Alex is okay. Disappearing like that. Full-on freaky.

She finished twisting the rubber band, trying not to imagine the horrors he might be facing. Then the mirror began to shimmer. Gwen blinked. Waves rippled over the glass and she stood back, confused.

"Huh?" she muttered looking around.

The restroom was empty since everyone else had gone to class.

Slowly, the red-headed skater girl in the mirror faded. Then it disappeared, replaced by the misty apparition of a big-nosed man with protruding eyes, whose mouth kept opening and closing in silent shouts.

"What?" She cocked an ear.

The foggy image reached out and Gwen leaped back, her green eyes wide. A hand emerged over the sink, followed by an arm and shoulder. Then a leg stepped through.

Five seconds later, a painted man stood at her side.

"Whoa, whoa, stay back," Gwen said, raising both hands.

The man barely noticed her, but turned his head right and left. "Zee Salon. Where did it go?"

Gwen was about to cry out, when she remembered what Alex had told her about Mr. Clean being jerked into Artania without warning. She looked this guy over. He didn't resemble those gross Shadow Swine creatures or their Mudlark slaves, but reminded her of the painted people they'd met on their last two journeys there.

"Are you, umm, from Artania?" she ventured.

"But of course. Where elze?"

"But I didn't think your kind ever came here."

"Here? Huh?"

"I thought you guys, like, stayed on your planet."

"I was in Paris a moment ago, then poof!" He glanced around. "Where am I? Photography District? Movie Pozter Land?"

"Dude, you are on Earth."

Gasping, the painted Frenchman stumbled back against the sink. "No."

"Yeah, and in the girl's restroom. Of my high school."

"No, iz not possible."

"Maybe not, but here you are." She paused. "Who are you, anyhow?"

I am Paul, Paul Gauguin." He smoothed his bushy moustache with one finger. "Not just an artist flaneur, a spectator of modern life, but a painter of ways new and impressionistic. I am a great artist. Surely you humans know my name?"

"Sorry. Most people aren't into the whole art history thing. Unless some boring teacher makes you study it for a test."

He reached out and clutched at Gwen's hoodie. "But don't you see? Art requires philosophy and study. Otherwise, what will become of beauty? And our world?"

Before she had a chance to push him away, there was a distant rumbling and the floor began to quiver. Gwen thrust out her arms for balance.

And the restroom disappeared.

Chapter 42

Bartholomew followed the nurse down a wide flight of stone steps that looked more like the entrance to a monastery than any hospital he'd ever seen. The curved entry lead to a central courtyard, like in an old church with a grassy square, a few scattered trees, and a marble man standing on a pedestal.

Pale arches of stone held up each of the first four floors of the tall building, the first one short and squat, while the second and third floors were taller and more ornate. Through multi-paned windows, Bartholomew glimpsed nurses skittering back and forth, basins and pitchers in hand.

"How far is the emergency room?" he asked. "Alex needs help, now."

Monet looked at him quizzically. "We approach the room that has space. With so many poor, hospitals are very crowded in Paris, yet the Hotel-Dieu is one of charity, the first of its kind."

"So there are lots of sick people here?" Bartholomew halted, imagining the diseases floating in the air.

"Oui. But none can affect the Deliverers."

"Of course." Bartholomew shook his head. "I wasn't thinking. Sorry."

"This way." The nurse turned inside one of the arched door-ways. Bartholomew followed her down a long tiled hallway, into a large room with a series of beds against the walls, filled with coughing, moaning, and crying people.

Bartholomew averted his gaze and helped carry Alex to an empty cot at the far side of the room. Here, a shelf that looked like a mantle topped with a mortar and pestle, a bottle, and a metal cup served as a headboard.

"Un, deux, trois," the nurse said, as Monet and Bartholomew swung Alex's limp body up onto the bed.

Bartholomew picked up Alex's flopping arm and folded it across his chest before pulling the blankets up and tucking them in.

"Where's the doctor?" he said.

"Zat is strange. I will look." With a curt bow of her head, the nurse exited.

Bartholomew watched her go and was just about to ask Monet something, when he heard a familiar humming. He glanced at a man huddled over the wood-burning stove in the center of the room, and then at Monet, who was staring out the window with his back to him.

Neither seemed to notice.

Then little electric shocks passed over his fingers and toes, and he knew.

"No!" he rasped, ferreting eyes hunting for something to cling to.

Head pivoting, Bartholomew darted from one end of the room to the other. His mind raced. Maybe if he held onto something, these random forces wouldn't rip him away.

Unconscious and alone, Alex will be Swiney prey for sure!

Bartholomew started for the cabinet, only to realize there were no knobs to grab a hold of. He turned toward the beds, but they lacked headboards.

"I can't leave him!"

After scurrying toward the exit, Bartholomew reached out with both hands, grasped a hold of the doorknob, and planted his feet firmly into the wooden floor. Gritting his teeth for a fight, he watched a shimmering apparition appear near Alex.

"Huh?"

A braided head appeared. Then a slim body. Ghostly arms waved like a rag doll in a windstorm.

"Gwen?" Blinking, he squeezed the door knob tighter.

Before she could answer, another figure emerged directly over her. A painted man whose mustached face grimaced as he slowly turned his head from right to left and right again.

"Gauguin?" Monet said. "Zis cannot be."

Bartholomew felt his form fading, a sign he was about to return to Earth. He had to do something. Anything.

Then he remembered that time some Shadow Swine had threatened Alex. They'd been in the Valley of the Kings and his best friend was hiding inside a sarcophagus, when several approached, battle axes raised. Just when all hope seemed lost, he had found some strength and acted.

Time to act again.

With a dry swallow, Bartholomew envisioned a bull charging at Gwen. He bent over and pushed off the door.

"Aargh!" Bartholomew cried as he headbutt her in the gut.

Green eyes wide, the still-misty skater girl shot upward, knocking the painter towards the plaster ceiling. As soon as his back hit the mottled grey surface, Gauguin vanished into the plaster, followed by Gwen a moment later.

"What was zat?" Monet asked his mouth agape.

Chest heaving, Bartholomew stared at his hands. Their tingling had stopped, and they appeared solid. Still, he wasn't taking any chances. He sat on the bed next to Alex and clutched the worn blanket, hoping it would keep him anchored to his friend.

"Deliverer Borax?" Monet said.

"I don't know what it was. Just who. Gauguin with a friend from Earth." Bartholomew wrapped the edge of the blanket around his hand and gripped it tightly.

"And you did not want zem here?"

"I didn't want them to take my place."

"*Hope will lie in the hands of twins.* Oui. I know zee Prophecy."

"It's more than that. I think I'm the only one that can help him." Bartholomew looked down at Alex's pale face.

Monet came around to the other side of the bed and nodded. "Iz possible. The Blank Canvas grows."

"Just like it did last year, and the year before." Bartholomew shook his head.

He'd seen that gaping hole too many times on his Artanian journeys. Every time he saw it, he was left feeling as empty as death.

"Iz hard to fight the blankness inside. I know."

Bartholomew nodded. Every day, the spotlessness of his existence reminded him of the void. That hole he usually filled with art had grown over the past year, and now he wondered if there really was any point to it all.

"Deliverer." Monet said, sometime later.

"Yes?" Bartholomew replied, without looking up.

"He has zee strength. Worry not."

"Maybe. But I've never seen him like this."

He barely glanced in Monet's direction before continuing to search Alex's face for some sign of consciousness.

Even hours later, his best friend refused to stir.

Chapter 43

Why can't I wake up? Alex thought, struggling to open his eyes, move a finger, or form a word with his dry lips.

He was motionless.

The dreams held him in a palette of colors that blended like an abstract painting. He saw his mother clutching at her blouse, jaw open wide. She sputtered and gasped, seeming to fight for breath.

Her hands shot to her throat. She mouthed his name. No sound came out. He wanted to go to her, but couldn't move. He was trapped, as if at the end of a long tunnel.

Mom desperately sucked for air. Then her head slumped.

Next, he was standing by her hospital bed, where breathing bellows rose and fell. The heart monitor beeped ever slower as holes grew in the ventilators. Her whistling breath thinned. Then every machine shut off, and there was silence.

He reached out to her, but the palette morphed and he was deep below Artania, in a dark cavern surrounded by axe-wielding monsters.

Bartholomew was kneeling at his side, staring at wounds burned into his palms.

"I can't heal them," his friend whispered.

Alex's dream-self tried to utter reassuring words, but Bartholomew only repeated, "I can't heal them."

Then the Shadow Swine advanced, descending upon him in a mist. That filled Alex's mind.

Chapter 44

"Deliverer, I need to examine him. Please move away," said a sketched man in a long black coat.

"About time," Bartholomew mumbled releasing the blanket he'd had a vice grip on all day.

He opened and closed his numb fingers. A sudden cramp made him clutch his forearm, and he rubbed at it.

"You are a welcome sight, Doctor" Monet said, stepping aside to give the man access to Alex.

"Are you injured as well?" the doctor said to Bartholomew.

"No, I'm fine. Just get to it."

When Claude Monet arched a brow at his abruptness, he quickly added, "I'm Bartholomew, Bartholomew Borax III, by the way."

"Doctor Rene Laennec, the hospital's resident physician. And here, all know your name. You needn't speak it."

Monet introduced himself and explained that Alex had been motionless all day.

"We collided mid-air before landing next to the River Seine," Bartholomew added.

"I see." Dr. Laennec ran a hand lightly over the goose egg on Alex's forehead before pulling out a wooden instrument that looked like a toy horn. He placed this on Alex's chest, then turned his head to the side and set his ear to it.

"What's that?" Bartholomew said.

"Shh." The doctor placed a finger to his lips.

He listened for several moments, and then pulled out a small notebook from his breast pocket. After scribbling a few notes, he listened again.

Bartholomew gave Dr. Laennec a questioning look.

When he didn't respond, Monet whispered, "That is his invention for listening. An early stethoscope."

"I call it the *cylinder,* and it mediates auscultation. That's why I need quiet."

Bartholomew swallowed hard. "How does he sound?"

"His heartbeat is weak, but steady. As is his breathing."

"Then why won't he wake up? It's been hours."

In response Rene Laennec picked up a handled object with curved glass on the end. He leaned over, using his thumb and forefinger to force Alex's right eye open. At the same time, he waved his optical instrument back and forth.

Alex still didn't stir.

"What's that?" Bartholomew asked, forgetting he was supposed to be quiet.

"This, young Deliverer, is an ophthalmoscope—a device for looking inside the eye. It tells me the state of consciousness of the patient."

Bartholomew tried not to sound too hopeful. "Which is?"

The doctor tapped on his chin. "His eyes fade in and out as if he were morphing from clay to paint."

"Meaning?"

"If humans have created multiple forms of us, we Artanians morph. I, for one, change from Impressionist paint to black and white photo or an occasional bronze when the mood suits me."

As if proving his point, Monet began to shimmer. The soft-brushed colors of his face faded, and a moment later a three-dimensional photograph stood in place of the Impressionist painting.

"I know," Bartholomew said. "But we can't do that."

Dr. Laennec placed a hand on Bartholomew's shoulder. "True, you humans have no such power. However, the Deliverers are usually immune to injuries such as these. Even when hurt, they have the healing magic."

"That is why I'm so worried. Whenever Alex and I traveled here before, we could heal just by imagining it. The goddess Isis taught us how on our first journey."

"You have good cause for concern. This is perplexing. Nothing like this has happened for centuries. But there may be some who have answers."

"Thinker?" Bartholomew ventured. He crossed his fingers and imagined Artania's leader giving him strength.

He needed someone to lean on right then.

Monet shimmered and morphed back to his painted form. "Yes, a message should be sent his way, I agree. But we also should consult the Silent Artists."

A weary Bartholomew sighed. The situation was one confusing mystery after another.

"The Silent Artists are...?"

"An ancient brotherhood of painters living in the heart of Paris, who can see beyond canvas," Dr. Laennec said.

"To the source of all creation—inspiration." Monet raised his painted hands.

"Which resides in the mind, of course," said Dr. Laennec.

Bartholomew gave a half-nod, pretending to understand what they were talking about.

"Okay, then what are we waiting for? Let's go."

Chapter 45

Gwen was too shocked to scream. The sensation of her body breaking into a million particles as it faded into the plaster was beyond anything she'd ever felt. It was as if every nerve, her heart, lungs, and all internal organs had just ceased to exist. In their place was a misty emptiness.

I am a ghost. Gwen flung her hands out, trying to reach for anything to keep from disappearing. But it didn't do any good. She was an amorphous comet shooting past stars. Without flame. Without form, without breath. Until she wasn't.

Her feet kicked on branches. Leaves scratched her arms. Gwen skidded backwards over a bush and thumped to the ground behind a patio table. She rolled sideways, knocking over a large trash can.

Brown paper bags, banana peels, half-eaten burgers, and milk cartons spilled onto the high school quad. A chewed apple rind rolled over the grass and landed at a pair of skater shod feet.

Those Vans looked familiar. She got up on all fours and gaped. No, it couldn't be.

"Gwen?" said the absolute last person she wanted to see.

Still on all fours, she slowly raised her head. Jose's windswept hair hung in a loose ponytail framing those high cheekbones like some friggin' Native American fashion model. The fog-filtered light of the sun was soft on his gorgeous face, now tilted in confusion.

"Umm...I, uh..."

Jose bent over. "What are you doing down there?"

"I, uh, fell?" Gwen stood up and brushed some grass and dirt off her enzyme-washed jeans.

After noticing a rip that hadn't been there before, she ran a finger over the jagged fabric.

Jose watched her with interest, and then glanced over at the tree with broken branches and the trail of leaves leading to the bench Gwen had landed behind.

"Were you climbing that tree?"

Deciding this was as good an explanation as any, Gwen nodded. "Yeah, thought it'd be fun. Guess it'd been so long I forgot how." She forced out a short laugh.

Standing taller, her boyfriend brought his fingers together in the shape of a pyramid.

"Buddha says we should not dwell in the past. We must shed it, as a snake sheds its skin."

There goes Mr. Wisdom again. Gwen thought but said, "Sure, I know. I was bored."

"Boredom is a state of mind. Karma, on the other hand, is what happens when you ditch English to climb trees. You fall from grace, literally."

"What do you mean ditched English?"

"I mean, as in absent. Not there. Lack of presence."

With a growing pit in her gut, Gwen said, "What time is it?"

"Don't you have your phone?"

"Battery's dead." Gwen lied.

Jose dug his 7 Plus out of his hoodie pocket and glanced down. "12:07."

"No way!" Gwen stared at him.

Jose held up his phone as proof.

An hour passed? But it only felt like a minute or two.

"Jose, Gwen!" called the waving Zach, from across the Quad, heading their way.

Gwen pushed one of the French fry trays aside with her shoe. The grassy courtyard was quickly filling with teens carrying backpacks, lunch bags, and trays.

Then she remembered. *Alex. Unconscious in a hospital bed.*

She turned to Jose with an apologetic smile. "I gotta go."

"You're just going to leave this?" He pointed at the trash that was strewn all over the grass.

"Can't explain now. See ya."

Jose leaned forward for a kiss, but Gwen ignored those pouty lips and brushed past him. Glancing around to get her bearings, she dashed toward the exit leading back toward the classrooms.

Her heart pounded as she crossed campus. Alex was hurt, bad. And stuck in that freaky art world where slimy monsters raised axes over your head and outlaws pointed arrows at your chest.

And what was up with Mr. Clean? She knew he was a little weird, trapped in that mansion with a cleaning-obsessed mom, but headbutting her? He usually welcomed help.

Maybe those monsters forced him to do it.

Sweat beaded on Gwen's upper lip as she quickened the pace, turning her power walk into a full-on jog. Panting, she ducked inside the hall and headed straight for the B-Pod restroom, where all this craziness began.

Thankfully, it was empty. Nevertheless, Gwen checked inside each of the stalls just to be sure. Then she approached the mirror where she'd seen the artist dude, Gauguin. Leaning over the sink, she stared into the glass.

"Hello?" she said.

Just a red-headed fourteen-year-old.

"Anyone in there?" She tapped on the glass. "Mr. Gauguin? B-3?"

Nothing.

Gwen knocked, gently at first. Then, using the side of her fist, banged on the mirror.

She thought she saw it shimmer. She stood back, but the vibrations had come from striking it.

"Bartholomew!" Gwen slapped the glass with both hands.

Nothing.

Pulling off the strapped-on backpack, Gwen grabbed it by the hip belt and swung. There was a loud thud but no portal, Bartholomew, or mustached Artanian.

Looking around desperately, she spied the stainless steel trash can near the sink and made a beeline for it. Curling her hands under the curved top, she tried to pry off the lid. Stuck.

She ran a hand over the cool metal until her fingers found a release button. She pressed it, removed the lid and began swinging it against the mirror.

"B-3! Thinker. Somebody!"

Just a normal mirror.

Shouting, she battered the glass once. "Take…" whacked it again, "me…" she lifted the lid over her head and brought it down on the sink with clang, "back!"

"Hey, hey. What's going on in here?" said a strong female voice.

Gwen barely heard, slamming the now-battered lid against the glass. "Open up!"

There was a tap on her shoulder. "Young lady, calm yourself."

Gwen turned and saw Officer Dirk, baton raised warily. "Relax. It's okay."

Groaning, Gwen hit her head against the sink. Now she was in for it.

"Rat farts."

Chapter 46

"We have to go in there?" Bartholomew gulped.

"Of course. It is the doorway to silence," Monet replied and reached into the neck of his shirt for a brass key on a chain.

The metal was oddly shaped, with a curled end that seemed to glow as it caught the light.

"But it's a-a—"

"Cemetery," Dr. Laennec said, finishing Bartholomew's thought.

Bartholomew stared at the wrought iron fence that surrounded the acres of headstones, mausoleums, and crypts. The sharp spikes on the black iron pointed upward, daring anyone to approach.

Glancing over his shoulder toward him, Monet fitted the key in the lock. "Art takes many forms in both life and death, Deliverer."

"Are there," he lowered his voice to a whisper, "ghosts here?"

"Not any more than on Earth," Dr. Laennec replied.

What kind of an answer is that?

The gate creaked open, and Bartholomew followed the two men inside. As soon as he passed the gate, he noticed a foul smell, like moldy earth or old wood. He really couldn't tell since he'd lived most of his life inside an antiseptic mansion. But it sure made him cover his face with a handkerchief.

The path was earthen at first, but soon widened into a cobble-stoned lane bordered by granite tombs. Many of these were as large as a child's playhouse, with gothic arches built into stone blocks, and were water-stained as if rainstorms had pelted them for centuries.

"This way." Monet turned toward a flight of stairs leading to a huge mausoleum.

As Bartholomew followed, he saw a marble woman in a long gown, face buried in her hands. Silent sobs wracked her body, but no tears moistened the long locks curling onto her lap. He started toward her, but Laennec pulled him back.

"She is the Mourner, the one who weeps unshed tears. It is forbidden to speak to her."

"Even for comfort?"

"Especially so. Her lament takes the pain of the millions, lessoning it. To interrupt her mourning would be to unleash tremendous grief on the world."

Fighting the urge to go up to the Mourner and pat her on the back, Bartholomew pulled out his hand sanitizer and rubbed a dollop in. Ahead was a temple-like monument with two tall pillars supporting a granite roof, where a heavy gray door with an iron ring in the center stood closed.

"Silent Ones, our need is great," Dr. Laennec called. "Please open your doorway and allow us pass."

State your plight so that we may determine if it is worthy.

Bartholomew gasped, stepping back. He reached up and touched his scalp. The words had echoed inside his head as if a woman was whispering into his ears.

Monet nudged the stunned Bartholomew. "Go ahead. Tell them what iz wrong."

"Me?"

Monet nodded.

Bartholomew approached the stone door, placed a hand on the granite wall, and put his mouth close to the crack between them.

"Hello!" he shouted. I am Bartholomew Borax the third! I am—"

You need not shout, said the voice in his head. *Stone does not block our hearing.*

"Oh. Okay. You probably have heard of my friend, Alex. He and I are those Deliverers you Artanians talk about in your Prophecy. We've been here a few times before, but lately things have been different."

We hear of doorways appearing and disappearing.

"Yes, exactly. And when the last one brought us here, Alex and I collided mid-air. Now he's unconscious and won't wake up."

And have you consulted a physician?

"I examined the boy myself and can find no cause for his continued coma," Dr. Laennec said.

Then you must enter.

Three seconds later, the door creaked and moaned before opening in a cloud of dust. A blinking Bartholomew sputtered and coughed twice.

Before him stood a tall figure in a long dark robe that covered her from head to foot. He couldn't make out her face since her hood was pulled forward. The robe itself appeared to be heavy wool like the ones monks or novices wore in centuries past, and was so dark he couldn't even make out any of the folds in the fabric.

Enter, the voice said.

Bartholomew glanced at the doctor, who gave him an encouraging nudge forward. He lurched forward, nearly tripping over his feet, which had grown to size ten seemingly overnight, and stumbled through the doorway.

The air was cool and damp as if the mausoleum had been closed to visitors for years. The granite walls inside were made of blocks carved with names and dates, many tinged with green mold. Bartholomew passed by several before he realized they were grave markers. Eyes wide, he halted.

A chill ran down his spine.

"Have you not been in tombs before?" Monet asked. "I heard you'd entered the Valley of the Kings and took Tutankhamen's place in his sarcophagus."

"Alex. Not me."

"But you were there?"

"Messing up," Bartholomew mumbled, remembering how he'd dropped the papyrus, nearly costing all the pharaohs their lives. *Because I was scared.*

The painted woman turned his way as her words filled his mind. *We learn as much from our errors as our successes.*

Bartholomew wished he agreed, but his mistakes were never erased. Unlike penciled sketches, his were tattooed on his life. Like that time he'd joined those bullies Ty and Con in seventh grade, and stole the answer key for math.

If I'd said no, Mother wouldn't have yanked me out of school. Now I'm trapped with Mr. White in that lonely room, day after day. And my only friend might be stuck in a coma forever. I'm such a screw-up.

The Silent Artist pulled her hood further down before leading them deeper into the cavernous tomb. Her rustling cloak echoed like hissing snakes through the deep tunnels surrounding them.

Dr. Laennec beckoned Bartholomew ahead so he could take up the rear with Monet. Lost in fretful musings about his best friend, Bartholomew barely spoke as he tiptoed after the mysterious woman.

Soon, the granite blocks faded into a tunnel of rough and pocked stone like the caverns he'd gotten lost in during his last journey into Artania. But while the Labyrinth had a confusing maze of forks and exits every few yards, this passageway was laid out in a more logical pattern, with channels leading right and left.

After walking for a while, Bartholomew started to wonder how far they'd have to go before this monk-like figure would help Alex.

"So are we going to a library or—"

He skidded to a halt, the last word stuck in his throat. He gaped, unable to move.

Just inches away stood a wall of skulls.

Chapter 47

Captain Sludge rocked back and forth on the rickety porch, chuckling as Crone told him what she'd seen in her cauldron.

"Unconscious, he is?"

"As lost to wakefulness as a larva before morphing to nymph," she said.

"Splendid. Can I invade his dreams?" Sludge licked his bulbous lips, imagining sending horrors into Alex's mind that he was powerless to wake from.

"Only I can twist the fog of his consciousness into nightmares. And even then, the nightmares are convoluted and brief. He is in Artania, after all."

"That idiotic healing magic?"

"Or I believe, the remnants of it. This is uncharted territory, even for one as old as I."

"What horrors will you send him?"

"If I shared everything with you, the knowledge might... alter you."

She means, my powers might exceed hers, Sludge thought, but said, "Ahh, your concern touches my black heart."

"Go ahead and joke, Pupae, but there is some knowledge that no Shadow Swine can possess. It is too dangerous. No, what I need from you is to continue to keep your axe strong with the trapped unicorn."

Sludge thought back to being inside Mount Minotaur and watching fires twist around the unicorn. How wondrous it had been to watch the tortured animal bolt from one fiery wall to the other.

But there was no escape.

Then when they were ready to strengthen the axe with fear magic, his dragon ally, Lucretia, brought down the blade to create a blooming explosion. Fiery embers had rained down, forcing shrieking nickers from the horned mare.

Music to his ears.

He sneered. "Goes without saying. But you can't leave me out of your schemes. I've worked too long and hard to get where I am."

The snaggle-toothed woman planted her granny boots on the floor and fixed him with an even stare.

"Can't I? Your knowledge might excel, but you are a nymph in comparison to me. Now you just do what you do best, and leave the rest to me, *little Pupae.*"

Sludge curled his claw-tipped fingers into fists to keep from retorting. She knew his height was an exchange for power. It had been her idea! For the first time in his life, he wanted to put a fist right in the center of that wrinkled walnut face. Nostrils flaring, he met her stare with his own blank expression.

He rocked once and rose from his chair. "If you must hold this over me like dream draining mist over a child, I needn't stay."

"Take your leave, then, Pupae. But don't forget, powers that are given can also be taken away."

Chapter 48

In his dream, Alex reached out into the darkness. Cold stone met his imagined hands. He groped along, patting the rocks until empty space loomed. Backed up, turned right. More rocky walls. This twisting tunnel was eerily familiar.

Through the fog of unconsciousness, he tried to remember. When had he been in shafts like these? He caressed the wall, nicking his palm on a sharp rock, and glanced down. Shimmering blood began to bead in his hand. He held it up like a glow stick to shed light on his surroundings.

He was inside a tunnel with an impossibly complex series of exits stretching all directions. Not just lateral, there were vertical and diagonal tubes leading up and down, like that insane painting he'd seen in the Santa Barbara Art Museum.

"Which way leads out?" said a crackly female voice.

Alex turned toward one tunnel.

"Are you sure?" the witch voice said.

He pivoted, crunching pebbles under foot. Waved his glimmering hand to and fro. Blood dripped off his hand and splattered onto the gravel ground. He watched them pool and expand like a bubbling spring. He stepped back to keep his feet dry, and hit a wall.

"Watch out, Deliverer. Dream minerals are sharp."

"Where are you? Come out and face me!" Alex cried.

"I am everywhere and nowhere, just like you. But feel free to search. The Labyrinth has many twists and turns. You will likely spend eternity lost in this puzzle of shrinking and expanding channels. Forever searching."

Just then, the walls began to shudder and shake. Alex glanced up and watched as every exit tunnel contracted. His head clouded and the walls closed in.

Chapter 49

Still motionless, Bartholomew felt the hair rise on his arms and scalp.

"What the dust bunnies?" he rasped, gaping at the wall of bones in front of him.

The hooded woman turned back. *Ahh. You see the Catacombs, where Paris deposited the dead from the overflowing cemeteries. It began after a wall in Les Innocents collapsed and rotting corpses spilled onto an adjoining property.*

"Rotting corpses? No, thank you." Crossing his arms, Bartholomew dug his heels into the gravel ground. "I'm not going in there."

You needn't worry. The decomposition has long passed.

"Absolutely not." He shook his head.

But to access the Deliverer's mind, we must surround ourselves in bone. The hooded woman blinked her clear brown eyes in confusion.

"I can't." Bartholomew had barely taken a step back, when he felt his arm caught in a tight grip.

Heart pounding, he glanced sideways to find Monet holding his elbow.

"I know it may seem frightening, but this underground depository is also true art. And what we need. Look at the display of bones."

The last thing Bartholomew wanted was to look back. He started to say no, but then he thought of Alex, unconscious and needing his help. Reluctantly, he lifted his gaze, trying to see art in death.

The wall ahead was at least eight-feet high, with long bones laid sideways. The old and yellowed bulging ends were piled atop the other and interspersed with white skulls every three to five feet. Eyeless sockets stared at him. But he forced himself to step closer.

Upon further inspection, Bartholomew realized that this wall was in front of another, leaving a foot-long space for a corridor. Further on, another bone cluster assembled in a barrel-shape with scalloped backs which had shining heads turned inward to the suffocating darkness.

A chill ran down Bartholomew's spine, and he shuddered. He couldn't decide which was worse—skeletal faces staring at him, unmoving, or the backs of heads ready to turn his way and screech their dismay at being disturbed.

Shivering, he rubbed his arms and shoulders.

Dr. Laennec took one of the torches from an iron bracket in the wall and approached his other side. He held out the burning rod and placed it in Bartholomew's hand.

"Fear can be channeled. Try looking at the flames."

Bartholomew clutched the wooden stave as if it were a shield protecting him from the surrounding ghosts.

"Ready now?" Monet asked.

Not trusting himself to speak, Bartholomew nodded. The flames flickered and cast strange shadows on the walls as the Silent Artist turned back toward the long tunnel ahead. He followed, the musty smell of earth and death filling his nostrils. Coughing, Bartholomew covered his face with a monogrammed handkerchief.

After a couple of minutes, they came to a dead end. In a corner niche, someone had carved a miniature fortress into the limestone. Tiny steps as wide as his thumb led to a curved wall with a knee-high arch in the center. If he'd been a mouse, he could have walked through it to the citadel etched into the wall. Then he'd scurry through the doorway and up the battlements to peek through the crenels between the merlons, before running inside the rectangular guard tower where he was safe from gaping skulls.

He looked at the Silent Artist, who now stood facing the fortress. She pulled a long paintbrush from some hidden pocket in her robe, and with the bristles traced a circle in the ground in front of the tiny stairs. The soil groaned and parted as a black hole opened in the gravel floor.

With a beckoning hand, the woman turned toward the round opening and slowly descended. When a tentative Bartholomew approached, he saw worn granite steps corkscrewing downward to a green water well. Torches were set in iron sconces at intervals, but he still kept his own clutched in his left hand, steadying his descent with his right.

"The Quarrymen's Footbath," Monet said, behind him. "Long ago, the catacombs were a limestone quarry, used as the building blocks for Paris. One day, workers uncovered this well and then used the water to make the cement they needed throughout the mines."

Now these pure waters hold answers. If our dipping brushes are true.

"Answers to what?" Bartholomew asked.

To that which you seek. The female voice replied before tip-toeing down the final steps to the pool below the twisting staircase.

In that moment every torch flickered and went out. Gasping, Bartholomew clung to the rocky wall, digging his fingers in the gaps between the limestone blocks. Long seconds passed in silence. He was about to cry out, when in a puff of blue and yellow smoke, every torch, including his own, burst into flames.

"Huh?" Bartholomew dropped the wooden stave and teetered, his feet slipping on the step's edge.

As the torch tap danced down the stairway, he thrust out his arms, scraping an elbow on the wall. He reached for a handhold, but gravity works the same in Artania as on Earth, and soon he was bumping down the stairs like a kid on a warped slide.

"Deliverer!" Monet cried, from above.

Five seconds later, Bartholomew was sitting, feet splayed out on the landing. A cloud of smoke and dust swirled around his aching body, but it was the fears of injury that whirled most in his mind. Since one side hurt more than the other, he first checked the right by patting his shoulder and arm, before moving downward to rub a hand over both legs. Repeating this on the left, he attempted to stand, but his ankle buckled under him. He fell back down with a thud, adding three more bruises to his sore tailbone.

Then the smoke cleared. Circling the well were two more Silent Artists, each wearing hooded robes like the woman who had led them here.

Dr. Laennec, please attend to the Deliverer.

Her silent message wasn't necessary. The doctor was already scrambling down the twisting stair, toward Bartholomew. When he reached the boy's side, he made a cursory exam and asked a few questions.

"It looks like you have a sprained ankle and, perhaps, wrist. Can you try the Healing Magic?"

Bartholomew took a deep breath, trying to imagine his body healed and whole. He felt a tingling sensation in his foot as if it was just waking from being asleep. With a wriggling of his toes, the prickling pins and needles moved upward. He waited.

Usually the Healing Magic brought relief in warm waves, but today sharp barbs accompanied every thought.

"I-I-can't," he managed to croak out, after another stinging shock shot up his leg.

A new voice, male and tortured, spoke in his mind. *Injury or not. We must proceed. Please rise.*

Swallowing hard, Bartholomew took Dr. Laennec's outstretched hand and stood. He tried putting weight on his injured leg, but the pain made him recoil. *Ow!* He clenched his jaw to keep from crying out. His throbbing leg dangled in the empty space beside the stair as he waited to see what the Silent Artists would do. A moment later, all three turned inward and pushed their cowls back.

We are ready. The trio bared faces that were each strangely beautiful.

Closest was a man made of painted dots, with gentle eyes, who reminded Bartholomew of Alex's dad. The woman next to him had hair with curling tendrils that was swept up in a loose chignon. Even though her mouth was a thin line, it wasn't tight like Mother's, but relaxed as if ready to smile at any moment.

The painted man with red hair and beard was the strangest of all. His tortured gaze was too intense for Bartholomew to meet, but the boy couldn't help staring at an ear that appeared and disappeared in flashes.

Greetings, Deliverer. Greetings, Dr. Laennec and Claude, said the trio inside his head.

Bartholomew's companions bowed their heads curtly, and he waved.

"Pleased to meet you." He waited for them to introduce themselves.

When none did, he continued, "Umm, you probably know by now that Alex is in trouble. Unconscious. And not waking."

One by one, the Silent Artists bent down and pushed their sleeves back, folded the rough fabric above their elbows. Curling their palms into bowls, they dipped their fingers in the well and submerged their hands up to the wrists. In unison, they inhaled a great breath and held it.

After several moments of silence, Bartholomew began to wonder if they'd ever start breathing again. He raised a confused brow and looked to Monet, who shrugged.

"Are you all okay? Can I..."

The Silent Artists exhaled as one. They lifted cupped hands overhead as the liquid spilled through their fingers, creating rivulets on the well's green surface. Water splashed up on their sandaled feet and darkened the hems of their cloaks.

The ripples on the well swelled to waves, undulating in currents that crashed on the walls. Heaving water rose higher, soaking the Silent Artists' skirts before submerging bent haunches, torsos, shoulders. And finally, heads.

The surf surged upward like a tsunami, filling the stairwell and rolling over Bartholomew and his friends. A second later, he was choking underwater.

"W-whaaat?" he gurgled, as bubbles bloomed.

Breathe the Healing Magic. You are a creator. Make it so.

Blinking in the churning waters, Bartholomew glanced up. He didn't know how, but torches still burned at intervals, allowing him to see Monet and the doctor's feet kicking far above. With them safe, Bartholomew curled into a ball, turning his thoughts inward as he imagined sweet oxygen filling his lungs.

And it was so.

Now let the waters heal your wounds so that we may continue.

The boy nodded and envisioned a strong, healthy body. Like before, cold prickles shot up his leg, but this time he imagined the surrounding waters as a warm bath soothing his ankle. A second later, the throbbing subsided. He repeated this with his wrist, but something like a force field around his arm blocked the mending.

He shook his head.

It is sufficient, the woman's voice soothed.

And the waters receded.

As the well drained, Bartholomew drifted down until he was standing between the woman and the red-headed man. He ran a hand over his head to brush back the water, but was surprised to find his hair and clothes perfectly dry. As was the circle of Silent Artists.

One by one, each laid a hand on the other's shoulder until the circle was complete. Then they stared into swirling waters as their voices chanted in Bartholomew's head.

> *But hope will lie in the hands of twins.*
> *Born on the cusp of the second millennium.*
> *Their battle will be long, with seven evils to undo.*
> *Scattered around will be seven clues.*
> *And many will perish before they are through.*
> *But our world will be saved if their art is true.*

"I know the Prophecy tells us to keep making true art," Bartholomew said, "but can it reveal what's wrong with Alex?"

There are many evils. Some understood. Others as mist.

"Mist?"

Alexander Devinci is lost somewhere between.

"What do you mean, between?"

He is neither of one world nor the other.

"He's not becoming a-a…"

Bartholomew couldn't bring himself to say Mudlark, one of the mindless slaves of the Shadow Swine.

No. As far as we know, humans are immune to Mudlark Maker's powers. Your kind cannot be swallowed and morphed into a demon servant of Lord Sickhert.

Bartholomew sighed. "If he's between worlds, how do we get him back?"

We know not. You must find a way into his thoughts, and guide him back to the Impressionist Republic.

"But how?"

"With our help," Monet said shuffling down.

"And the true art, of course." Dr. Laennec added.

Chapter 50

While waiting for Dad to arrive, Gwen wriggled in the hard wooden chair, trying to avoid eye contact with the school counselor, Mr. Cisneros. The man smoothed his thin goatee and moustache with one finger, eying her as if she were some sick kid he pitied.

Stop staring! I'm not crazy. Now, more than ever, she wished she had her skateboard. She'd kick off, launch over that huge desk, and crash through the window, onto the cement sidewalk. Then she'd fly through the streets, not stopping until she was safe at home in the foothills.

On the other side of the room stood Officer Amy Dirk, hands resting on her utility belt as if ready for action. If Gwen hadn't been so upset, she'd roll her eyes. Seriously, how much ever happened at this school? Half the kids arrived in Mercedes, and the other half in mom-mobiles so suburbia you'd think it was a TV sitcom.

"Perhaps you'd like to explain yourself before your father arrives. Why were you yelling and throwing things?" Mr. Cisneros leaned forward, his grey eyebrows drawn together with fatherly concern.

What could she say? *No reason. I was just hanging out in the girl's restroom with a painted man, when we were thrown into another world. Then I saw an unconscious Alex lying in a hospital bed and was about to check on him, when someone I thought was my bud decided to head butt me back to Santa Barbara High.*

Gwen stared at her skater shoes and shrugged.

There was a knock at the door, and Officer Dirk unlinked one thumb from her belt to reach for the handle. When she opened it, Gwen was shocked to see her white-faced dad, his tie askew and dress shirt half-tucked in.

Mitch Obranovich rushed into the room and went straight to Gwen. He bent down on one knee next to her chair.

"You okay, Tinker Bell?"

Gwen couldn't speak. Just nodded.

Dad stood. "So what's all this about?"

"Please have a seat, Mr. Obranovich," the school counselor said, indicating a chair next to Gwen.

Gwen could tell that the last thing Dad wanted to do was sit down. But he was a polite man—most of the time—and lowered himself onto the wooden chair without complaint.

Officer Dirk strolled up to Mr. Cisneros's desk and assumed her at-attention-with-both-hands-on-the-belt stance.

"We haven't met. I'm Hector Cisneros, the school counselor, and this is Officer Dirk." He extended a hand across the desk to shake.

"And?" Dad barely squeezed Mr. Cisneros's hand and ignored the officer.

Mr. Time Management liked to get to the point.

"Perhaps Officer Dirk can explain…"

She gave them all a curt nod. "When there was a report of shouts from B-Pod at 12:19, I proceeded to investigate. As soon as I entered the hallway, I could hear loud cries and crashes from the restroom. Keeping one hand on my baton, I slowly opened the *Girls* door. That's when I found the perpetrator screeching at the mirror and smashing a garbage can lid against the sink. As soon as I'd calmed her down, I brought her here."

"Where she came willingly and politely," Mr. Cisneros said.

Dad looked at Gwen and then back across the desk. His voice was barely a whisper when he asked, "What did Gwenny say?"

"Your daughter has not spoken a word since the incident. But I have seen things like this before. It could be drugs."

Dad gasped.

"I wouldn't take drugs like those burnouts in the parking lot!" Gwen turned to Dad, who was rubbing a hand over his short cropped hair. "Never. I swear."

"Look at me."

When Gwen did so, Dad surveyed her face, paying close attention to her eyes.

"Your eyes aren't bloodshot, and your pupils don't seem dilated."

"Not all drugs cause dilation," Officer Dirk said. "Oxycodone, heroin, and morphine for example, have been known to constrict the pupil."

"Heroin?" Dad gasped.

"No way, Dad." Gwen couldn't believe her father would even consider the possibility.

"The only real way to know is to get her drug tested," Officer Dirk said.

"What?" Dad said.

"Many parents find comfort in monthly drug tests," Mr. Cisneros replied. "Some can even be done at home."

"Really?"

"I can't believe you're even considering having me pee in a cup. Gross! Come on, Dad. You know me."

"What other explanation could there be? Why were you yelling?"

"I-I-I don't know. I was upset. It's just…"

"Upset by what?"

"I can't tell you." Gwen crossed her arms and clamped her mouth shut so tight it felt like her retainer was denting her tongue.

Gently, Mr. Cisneros said, "Has there been any change in the home life? Any reason for her to get upset?"

As a horrified Gwen listened, Dad explained how Mom had deserted the family years before, to become a model.

"You heard of Rochelle?"

"Who hasn't?" Mr. Cisneros said.

"Her mother. Supermodel in photos. Terrible model in real life."

Gwen cringed. When was this horror going to end? While she sat, silent, the three adults continued discussing the impacts abandonment can have on a teenager. How it can cause all kinds of dysfunctional behaviors ranging from drug abuse to sexual promiscuity to depression.

But I'm semi-normal. When I'm not being yanked into some crazy world.

"Shut up! My daughter is not—"

The room grew suddenly dark.

It wasn't the lights. They were still on. It was as if a thick fog had just rolled in off the bay, blocking out all light. But the sun had been shining brightly out on the quad. Not a cloud in sight.

They all grew silent.

Officer Dirk marched over to the window. "Oh, no. Looks like more fires."

The dry hills around Santa Barbara were often victim to raging fires. Fires that engulfed homes, oak forests, and shrubs in a matter of hours. The Obranoviches had even had to evacuate the previous summer when a huge one came too close to their home. They'd been lucky, but their neighbors lost everything.

Mr. Cisneros and Dad slowly rose from their seats and joined the officer at the window. No one spoke for long moments. As if night had suddenly fallen, the sky darkened. Gwen fought the urge to sidle up next to Dad.

"I don't think that's smoke," he said. "It's happening too fast."

"Gotta be," Mr. Cisneros replied.

"Do you smell anything? I don't."

"Whatever it is, I'd better investigate." Officer Dirk turned toward the exit and had only walked a few paces, when the dark mist snaking under the door stopped her dead in her tracks.

Black smog threaded through the cracks of the window and wound down the wall. Dad thrust out an arm, pushing Mr. Cisneros back. Gaping at the rising fog, the counselor gasped and raised both hands.

The dark mist covered the floor and began to rise like water in a bathtub. It swelled, splashing up their quivering bodies. Dad reached a hand toward Gwen.

And after calling her name, froze mid-air.

Chapter 51

A knot twisted in his gut as soon as Bartholomew saw Alex lying helpless in the cot on the far side of the hospital room. Nothing had changed in his absence. Moaning Parisians still begged for medicine or reached to the shelves above their beds for metal cups of water. Nurses in long black dresses, with their hair in buns, still mopped feverish brows with cool rags. And Alex was still as pale as bone.

Ignoring the other suffering patients, Bartholomew stiffly marched to Alex's bedside and stared into his tortured face. He rubbed the wrist he'd injured in the Quarrymen's Bath, wondering why the Healing Magic hadn't worked for either of them.

His best friend shuddered, eyes twitching in some sort of nightmare.

"I'm going to figure this out, Alex. You'll see. The true art will free you."

He knew it was a lie, but what could he do? His best friend was trapped somewhere between worlds and even the Silent Artists didn't know what to do.

"You think so, huh?" a nasal voice said, from behind.

Bartholomew turned toward the sound, surprised to see Paul Gauguin leering through hooded eyes.

"Huh?"

"You believe you actually have power?"

"I don't know. I just…the Silent Artists…Prophecy."

"Tales of the misinformed. Bedtime stories."

Bartholomew stared at him. "Stories? But the Prophecy is how Artania began. It tells of how the twins' cave painting started it all."

"That may be true, but what it foretells doesn't always happen like Thinker says. My interpretation of the words is a little different from our ineffective leader's."

Bartholomew crossed his arms. "Is that so? How would you interpret the final lines of the Prophecy?"

Gauguin sighed as if Bartholomew were an idiot. "Think about what the following lines might mean.

The Shadow Swine will make you live in fear.
Bringing death to those whom you hold so dear.
For they will open the doorway so wide.
That none of you will find a place to hide?"

"Thinker explained that Lord Sickhert's army would gain power and there'd be more losses here in Artania. But that Alex and I could help to slow it down and eventually stop it."

"Thinker says, Thinker says. Blah. Blah. Blah. His interpretation is so limited. However, I've come to construe these words in a different way."

"Like how?"

"Perhaps death should not be taken so literally. It could represent change, as I have proposed at many Salon lectures."

"What are you spewing now, Gauguin?" Monet said as he entered the room. "More about how we should replace our leader?"

Gauguin smoothed his bushy moustache with a finger. "He has had power for over a hundred years, yet still the Shadow

Swine grow in power. Look at what has happened to me. Thrust into Earth and back with no warning."

"And who would take his place? You?"

"If that responsibility were offered me, I would accept. It would be my honor to serve all Artanians."

"You think you sound so noble, but your words are as transparent as water in the Seine."

"Your interpretation, Monet. I only care that the Impressionist Republic remains intact. *I* do not let self-pity get the better of me. Or my land."

Bartholomew remembered how depressed Monet had been when they'd first met. He'd later read that the real Claude Monet had money problems when he was a young father. Even though he'd received some critical acclaim for a portrait of his wife, Camille, he was in debt and unable to support his family. Then he was evicted from his home and felt so hopeless that he threw himself into the River Seine.

He could relate.

"My namesake may have jumped, but he did not let the waters take him. Instead, he chose to swim."

"But the damage was already done, wasn't it? The ripples of despair spread and empowered our enemy." Gauguin pointed at Monet. "Your suicide attempt cost us an entire village."

"As you remind others at the Salon during your inciteful tirades!"

"Only telling the truth."

Bartholomew cleared his throat. "I'm sorry to interrupt, but shouldn't we be focused on Alex? He's the one who's in trouble here."

"Of course, of course, Deliverer," Gauguin said. "That is my point exactly. When I overheard your predicament, I thought of an idea that just might help."

Monet thrust his hands onto his hips. "I heard about the last Artanian you *helped*. He ended up here for a week."

"When one's manhood is put into question, he must defend it."

"By inciting violence? And injuring fellow Artanians?"

"An unfortunate accident. If he had kept his fists raised, his nose would not have been broken."

"Your idea?" Bartholomew was disgusted by Gauguin's excuses.

The man obviously used any means available to get what he wanted.

Gauguin smoothed his moustache with a finger again. "When I was chosen to be thrust into Earth, and met that sweet girl Gwen, I noticed a few things."

Bartholomew narrowed his eyes. No one called Gwen that. Alex called her tough, strong, and even annoying, but never sweet.

"What things?" Bartholomew asked.

"If Alexander is between worlds, I must find my way there."

"How?"

"What lies between Earth and Artania?"

Bartholomew considered. "Space. Most journeys are like a trip flying through galaxies."

"Then galaxies we become." Gaugin lifted his chin. "I will paint some for you."

Monet glared at him. "Stop lying to the boy. You have no more solutions than I."

"Your anger doesn't serve you, Claude."

"Not anger. Truth. I know what you're trying to do."

Gauguin gave him an innocent look that was about as convincing as Mother's had been when she'd lied about father's art.

"I am only trying to help the Deliverers," he said.

Claude Monet turned to Bartholomew. "Do not listen to him, young one. His only desire is power. And for that he needs a narrative, a story of heroics."

"I am greatly offended. Believe what you wish, but I do have Artania's best interests at heart."

Bartholomew glanced from artist to artist, wondering who to believe. Gauguin might be cocky and full of bravado, but he had helped rescue all those people down by the river. And for some reason had been sent to visit Gwen on Earth. On the other hand, Thinker's guidance had helped more times than he could count. Simply remembering his deep rich voice imparting words of wisdom had kept Bartholomew on the right path.

Until recently.

Was Gauguin right? Could Thinker's time be coming to an end? Maybe Artania needed more than the bronze statue could provide.

Bartholomew tucked Alex's woolen blanket in and smoothed the worn fabric.

"Wake up, please!"

Alex's ashen face remained unchanged.

Ignoring the arguing Gauguin and Monet, Bartholomew leaned closer to his best friend and whispered, "Don't worry. You're coming back to us. No matter what it takes, I'll find a way. You'll see."

He uttered more encouraging words, telling Alex how he would unlock this cage, and with the true art, would free Alex's mind. Bartholomew tried to sound confident, but he had no idea how to turn his words into action.

So he just kept whispering.

Chapter 52

Dream-Alex reached through the mist for something solid, but all he felt was cool fog coating his hand in water vapor. He glanced down. His feet seemed to be missing, lost under surging foam. This white sea rolled in all directions as far as he could see.

Where am I? He thought rubbing his forehead.

Nothing looked or felt familiar in this surreal place. He tried to recall a recent memory, but drew a blank. What had he just been doing?

A cold panic set in as he realized the harsh truth.

"Who am I?" he whispered.

A woman's ancient voice crackled from the mist. "You are a servant."

"Servant?"

"Yes, you serve he who disciplines the world."

"I do?"

"Yes, you help to keep children away from the dangers of idealism."

Alex nodded, but at the same time something felt off. Her voice and words were so unfamiliar.

He blinked. "What is this place?"

"Home."

Alex took a step back. Even though his mind was all a muddle, he didn't think he lived in a foggy wasteland where he couldn't see his feet.

"But where are the...?"

The old woman sounded like she was smiling. "The what?"

Alex opened and closed his mouth, trying to envision a home. But he couldn't picture, much less find the words for objects that seemed to be part of another life. A dream.

"Parts of a-a home" he finally sputtered.

"Why, everywhere, servant. And nowhere. Just look."

Alex turned right and left, seeing only white fog. Everything about this place felt wrong. He tried to think. The voice that came from the mist didn't make any sense.

Somewhere on the edge of his consciousness, different voices were speaking, comforting voices full of kindness and concern.

"...figure it out...true...soon," he thought he heard.

Had someone been shouting? Maybe they were the children he was supposed to help. He cocked an ear.

"Don't listen to them, servant. They are the enemy, bringing useless buoyance to the naïve."

"But to be buoyant is a good thing," Alex argued, as a blurry image started to form in his mind. "It's part of the-the-the..."
Why can't I find the words?

A louder voice burst through the mist. "Please!"

"Ignore that. It is just our foe trying to trick you."

Alex narrowed his eyes. "I don't know. It doesn't sound like a trick. More like someone in trouble."

"That's the oldest ruse of all! Pretend to call for help, get your enemy close, and snap, you have the hero trapped."

Alex considered what she'd said. "Maybe. But why say *please*? Wouldn't it make more sense to cry for help?"

"That is what makes it so tricky. But enough of this. I have a task for you."

"Yes?" Alex was relieved to have something else other than confusion to think about.

"I want you to move to your left." When Alex took a small step, she said, "More. Three more steps.

Alex bumped into something solid. He groped over the surface. It felt cold and hard.

"There, that's it. Now press against it."

Alex hesitated.

"Children need you. In this exact moment, suffering babes who could be choosing incorrectly. Now, push!"

He rocked back on one leg, raised both arms and leaned into the hard thing. He shoved.

There was a groan, and the next thing he knew he was in some sort of long tunnel. Here, the mist was thinner and strange lights flickered in the distance. The fog had sunk to the ground and he was facing a series of gray rectangles with pocked surfaces. The edges were irregular as if they'd been there a long time. He struggled to match a word with what he was seeing.

"W-wha-what is it called?"

There was a cackling, and he heard the woman say, "Wall, servant, wall. It is a wall. One you must follow, to help the suffering ones."

With a tentative nod, Alex began shuffling along this thing called *wall*, hoping to find answers at the end.

Chapter 53

"Thank you for coming so soon." Thinker nodded his appreciation at the gathered company standing around the green well. "As you know, we are faced with a grave situation."

The Deliverer remains suspended between worlds, said Mary Cassatt. *And even our silent entreaties are powerless to move him.*

"Oui." Monet turned toward the Silent Artist dressed in a long robe. "Although we brought zee other Deliverer here, he was unable to find a solution."

"That is why I have gathered you all, hoping your powers would combine with these waters. Perhaps the Quarrymen's Footbath will bring us clarity." Thinker nodded at the five Artanians encircling the well.

The worn granite steps corkscrewed up toward the catacombs, with the exit and light beyond reminding Thinker that young Alexander was trapped in darkness.

The hooded ones kept their heads bowed, while the other two looked at him with a mixture of confusion and concern.

All were needed in this quest. When young Alexander fell into a coma, the leader had consulted the Soothsayer Stone on Mount Olympus and ran a hand over the Prophecy etched into marble. After reading the words carved in that hemisphere, again and again, he came to realize why it looked incomplete.

The Soothsayer Stone was but half a circle. It stood ready to join with Earth's art, just as Alexander, Bartholomew, and Gwen had united to keep Artania strong. Two parts making one whole, like Thinker needed now.

The torches set in iron sconces around them flickered for a few moments.

The rosy-cheeked Renoir asked, "Why us?"

"I needed three Silent Artists joined with a pair of Impressionists who have been loyal during the rebellion."

"That Gauguin!" Renoir said. "Why must he lead a revolt when unity is what we need?"

Thinker shook his head. "I know not, but we must focus on helping young Alex right now."

Clutching his bushy brown beard, Monet pointed it at The Thinker. "True. But when one of our own starts fights with the faithful, it is difficult. Skirmishes have been breaking out all over Paris."

"Which saddens me greatly," Thinker said.

"Could the dissent be part of why the Deliverer won't wake?" Renoir asked.

"My bronze palm tells me little of late. When I look into it, mist and confusion cloud the images." Thinker glanced at the Silent Artists opposite, and raised his steely brows.

The long dark robes covering the three voiceless ones from head to foot, rustled as they pulled their raised hoods further forward. The trio linked arms and leaned toward each other while the green waters of the well in front of them splashed at their sandaled feet.

Their voices toned inside Thinker's mind. *An enigma exists. An anagram for which there is no cipher.*

"Then how do we find the key to unlock this mystery?"

The three pushed their cowls back, revealing two male and one female face. The redheaded man, whose ear appeared and disappeared in flashes with each glimmering spark of the nearby torches, gave Thinker a curt nod. His companion, a gentle-faced soul made of painted dots, followed suit. The woman, Mary Cassatt, gave him a piercing stare as she smoothed her hair, which was swept up in a loose chignon.

It was her voice he heard next. *The Deliverer must follow the clues.*

"Which ones?"

The redheaded man, who Thinker recognized as Van Gogh, clapped a hand to where his ear would have been.

Quarrels and disappearances change our world's energy.

"Oui, Vincent" Monet said with a nod. "Of which your creator knew all too well."

Renoir reached a kind hand toward the robed Van Gogh. "We know you carry the pain of that long past argument, but your vow of silence has sustained the Impressionist Republic for many years now. And for that we are most grateful."

Thinker agreed. Ever since Cassatt, Van Gogh, and Seurat had become Silent Artists, Paris had been safer. Shadow Swine attacks had decreased, going from an average of two a week to less than one a quarter.

Their sacrifice was great, and each had suffered so in his or her own way. Yet it was Van Gogh's story that pained Thinker's bronze heart most.

Many years before, the real Paul Gauguin and Vincent Van Gogh had spent a couple months as roommates, painting side by side in the French village of Arles. These nine weeks were a productive time, with the two creating more than fifty canvases between them. Van Gogh welcomed the company, but the two men often quarreled, as Gauguin had a short temper and little patience for Van Gogh's bouts of depression. One night, an argument culminated in Gauguin packing his bags and leaving.

Van Gogh cut off a portion of his ear a few hours later.

Of course, all that happens on Earth effects Artania, and this was no different. Soon, ripples of despair threatened to overcome the painted Van Gogh. He endured many days of agony before deciding to take a vow of silence and serve the Impressionist Republic, which he had been doing ever since.

Mary Cassatt's tender voice toned, *It is possible that all these events are related. The rebellion. Alexander's coma. Hygenette's increasing cleaning frenzies.*

Thinker hunched over, trying to picture the connection. "A Deliverer's mother combatting Artania can cause great havoc. Yet Hygenette has long tried to keep young Bartholomew from art."

"With little luck," Monet added.

"Yes, the Deliverer continues to create. Although sporadically, of late."

Van Gogh's tortured voice sounded in Thinker's mind. *That is unacceptable. The young one must seek the true art.*

The waters began to rise, splashing them all in a sweet-smelling liquid. The scent reminded Thinker of the rosewater his sculptor's mistress used in her claw-foot bathtub over a hundred years before. For a moment, he was back in Rodin's studio, the creator tugging and pressing at the clay that would eventually be his form. Thinker's eyes became misty with the memory.

The Silent Artists' lips were unmoving with the words, *Water, water rising high. Find what is hidden to open eyes.*

Thinker blinked as the splatters took shape on the limestone walls. Each dash of spray formed a letter on the pocked stone, until soon an entire line waited to be read.

Anagram is to analogy as decipher is to___?

"What does it mean?" Renoir asked.

Van Gogh fixed them all with an even stare. *It is for the Deliver to discover. Let him ponder the words. When the true art comes, clarity will be his.*

Chapter 54

"Zis way, young one." Monet led Bartholomew up the wooden staircase with an iron handrail.

Higher they went, passing floor after floor of the Parisian apartment building. With labored breaths, Bartholomew climbed towards the top floor. Although he was curious about Monet's garret studio, he asked no questions.

His head was too jumbled.

There had been a message from the Quarrymen's Bath. A cryptic analogy he'd been working on for days, that said, *Anagram is to analogy as decipher is to___?*

He'd come up with various solutions sitting there at Alex's side, but none felt quite right. So Monet proposed leaving the hospital for a while, saying that a change of scene might spark ideas.

"Trying to solve a puzzle while so near your unconscious friend makes it challenging to zink," he'd said.

That was all too true. Bartholomew was trying to hold it together, for Alex's sake. But now the coma had stretched into a week, and if anything, his best friend was worse than before. At first, Alex's eyes had fluttered when Bartholomew whispered reassuring words. But now both lids remained firmly shut, even if he shouted into his ear.

"Wake up! Please!" he'd cried, afraid that the Swineys were invading Alex's comatose dreams.

Bartholomew rubbed his own arms, shuddering to think what might be happening inside that cataleptic mind. He'd had his share of the nightmares and the horrors they could bring. One had him grasping Father's hands as the poor man struggled to escape drowning mud. Father choked and sputtered while Bartholomew fought to pull him free, but his dream arms dissolved before his eyes. He woke in a cold sweat.

If Swineys were in Alex's mind, twisting his dreams...Bartholomew shook his head. *Don't think about that. You have a puzzle to solve. Focus.*

Clenching his teeth, he marched up the final flight of stairs and waited for Monet to fumble for the key in his pocket. Once the door was opened, he followed the bushy-bearded artist into the attic studio on the fifth floor.

Here, the jumble of canvases stacked up against the wall were like old friends leaning against each other. Easels of various sizes stood over sad sketches strewn all over the wooden plank floor. Opposite the glowing iron stove and pipe chimney sat a paint-splattered bench containing assorted brushes, cans, palettes, and multi-colored jars.

Drying works of animated people hung from the sloped ceiling. The painted individuals inside the framed pictures overhead chattered amiably amongst themselves, but all the burbling jabber stopped when Bartholomew looked up.

Clapping in glee, one watercolor child with long blonde hair exclaimed, "A Deliverer! Hurray!"

The portrait of a man in a top hat waved and shouted a welcome before the young lady in a long white dress on the canvas next to him said, "Have you come to model, like me?"

With a wink, she turned right and left while lifting her chin, tilting her head, and placing one hand and then the other on each hip. When she finished affecting these poses, the pretty girl lifted her parasol and twirled it. As her linen dress fluttered inside the picture frame, Bartholomew thought how these portraits were like 3-D movies.

Artania never failed to amaze.

Monet shook his finger like Mr. White did when Bartholomew wasn't paying attention in class.

"No, he is not. Zee Deliverer is here to work. He has a cipher to solve. So if you would all be so kind as to keep zee noise to a dull roar, it would help our young artist to zink."

"I can be very quiet, like a mouse. Just watch." The painted child put a milky white finger to his pouty lips.

"It's no problem. I can focus with you all talking," Bartholomew said, embarrassed by the attention.

"No it iz not. Come over here, Deliverer," Monet said waving Bartholomew toward a little desk against the wall. Several fountain pens, an eye dropper, three ink wells, and a sheath of paper were arranged on top, obviously waiting for him to use.

Bartholomew took a deep breath and pulled out the ladder-backed chair. After plopping down, he picked up a pen, unscrewed it, and dipped an eyedropper with ink before inserting it into the pen's reservoir and squeezing the bulb. Now that his fountain pen was full, he smoothed out a sheath of paper and wrote.

Anagram is to analogy as decipher is to___?

He had read and reread these words so many times the last few days he could have recited them in his sleep. But he still thought writing them would help.

"Okay, anagram is to analogy, anagram is to analogy," he mused. "Well, an analogy is a similarity between two things that are not the same. Or a comparison between pairs of words based on similar characteristics, like *up is to down as cold is to hot.*"

"Are zee words in the puzzle opposites?" Monet asked.

Bartholomew shook his head. "No, but analogies don't have to be opposites. They can just as easily be relationships, like *cat is to kitten as dog is to puppy.*"

"I see. Or *sheep is to lamb.*"

"Yep. So now we need to think of anagrams. They are not the same. An anagram takes a word and rearranges the letters to make a new word or phrase. You can form all kinds of ideas just by reordering the letters."

"*Cat* and *act*, for example?" Monet said.

Bartholomew nodded. "To find the missing word in the puzzle, next we need to look at how an analogy and an anagram are related. What relationships do they have?"

"Zey are both used in language."

"True. But an analogy usually has just one answer, whereas an anagram can have many."

"Like what?" the portrait of the blonde boy called down. Then he covered his mouth. "Oops. Sowwy. I was supposed to be quiet."

Bartholomew gave him a reassuring smile. "It's okay. To answer your question, let's try making anagrams with your name. What is it?"

"Louis," the boy replied, slowly.

"All right, Louis. First, I write your name, like this. "Bartholomew scratched the letters out and held them up for the boy painting to see. "Then I try to mix up the letters to make new words." He tapped his chin, then tried to come up with as many anagrams as he could find.

Louis: Soilu, I soul, oil us.

"Oil us, that's funny. I'm a watercolor, not an oil."

"Well, they don't always make sense. But that does give me an idea. Maybe the puzzle is asking us to find an anagram of some word."

"You may have something zere," Monet said. "But which word?"

"It says, *Anagram is to analogy as decipher is to___*? Let's start there," Bartholomew suggested and wrote, *Decipher*. "Now we mix up the letters so they make sense. Backwards sometimes works. Rehpiced?" He shook his head.

"Can it be two words?" Monet said.

"Sure. As long as it's an anagram.

Hands behind his back, Monet began pacing from one end of the little attic studio to the other.

"How about cried hep, or chip deer?" he said.

"Well, hep isn't really a word, and chip deer sounds weird. How about chip reed, deep rich?"

"Creep hid?"

"Creep hid, hmm." Bartholomew thought that Swineys were creeps that hid in shadows.

They waited until humans were asleep to invade their dreams and turn them into nightmares where art was something to be feared instead of embraced. In some ways, that was like an anagram. They mixed up people's ideas like anagrams mixed up letters.

"Try it," Monet suggested.

"Okay." Bartholomew wrote the possible answer, then read, "Anagram is to analogy as decipher is to creep hid."

"That sounds funny," Louis said, from overhead.

Bartholomew let out a long sigh. "I agree. So maybe the answer isn't an anagram for decipher. If not, what the dust bunnies is it?"

Monet shrugged.

Bartholomew pulled a new sheath of paper from the stack and wrote, *Deliverer, Shadow Swine, Thinker, Alexander, Dream, Impressionism.* He paused and tilted his head, trying to come up with more words related to Artania.

Monet came up behind him, looked over his hunched shoulders. "You are going to make anagrams for all of those?"

Bartholomew sighed. "You might as well sit down, Mr. Monet. I think we're going to be here a while."

Chapter 55

"Dad?" Gwen whispered, staring at her father frozen mid-step, a few paces away.

She called toward the others. "Officer Dirk? Mr. Cisneros?"

The dark mist rose, drifting in from the doorway until it covered the adults' shins. It looked like they had been wading in an inky pool, when someone took their photo, fixing them at strange angles to one another.

Gwen drew her feet up on the chair and hugged her knees, just clearing the dark fog. She considered hopping down and heading towards Dad, but decided against it, afraid she'd end up just as motionless as he was.

Her father's lips were pulled back over his teeth, his mouth trapped forming her name. One strong arm was suspended in air, reaching toward her, his only child, as unblinking eyes stared past.

Gwen hugged her knees tighter, pulling deeper into herself. Perhaps if she waited, this crazy fog would go away and everything would return to normal.

She counted. "Fifty-seven, fifty-eight…three-hundred four, three-hundred five…" At six hundred, she lost her place.

All the while, no one moved a millimeter.

Gwen looked into Mitch Obranovich's strong face, searching for some sign of change. But he was an entrapped statue and she had no idea how to free him.

Slowly she glanced around, squinting in the dim light while willing herself to stay calm. "Okay, Gwen, assess the situation." She recited the words Dad had drilled into her since she was little. "Here, we have some freaky mist in the counselor's office. It filled the sky, then creeped inside, freezing people in place like that Statue Maker game I used to play when I was little.

"But what we don't know is how far it goes. Is it just this room, or the whole school? All of Santa Barbara? The entire Earth?"

She pondered for a moment, before deciding to test a theory. Making sure to stay above the rolling smog, she took off one shoe and loosened the laces. Next, she grabbed the toe side so the strings dangled below, slowly lowering them until the frayed ends touched the cloudy surface.

They didn't freeze.

She let her arm sink lower. Her shoelaces swayed freely, unlike Officer Dirk's microphone, which was fixed mid-swing, one hand reaching for it.

"Okay. So far so good. Maybe this is one of those weird Artania events," she said wondering whether she should try her fingers and see if they moved or not.

As Gwen put her shoe back on, she thought back to the year before when they'd found a bunch of frozen Knights. When B-3 approached, he had almost ended up as a kidsicle, too, and after Alex pulled him back, he'd said that the freezing began with his fingertips before moving up his arms to the rest of his body.

Gwen took a deep breath and plunged her hand into the fog. Green eyes wide, she tried wriggling her fingers. She thought she felt a cold tingling and jerked away. A growing pit in her gut, she stared at her hand and tried curling it into a fist.

It moved. The cold was just her imagination.

"Good. Now for the next step. I'm going to figure this out, Dad. You'll see." She tightened the laces on her Vans.

Gripping both sides of the wooden chair, she leapt to the floor. When she landed, she almost expected to end up like Dad and stared at her body waiting to see if that would happen. After a few moments with no prickling sensation, she ventured a step toward her father. Another.

"Can you hear me?" she asked the motionless face.

She reached out a tentative hand. "Dad?"

Gwen brushed her fingers over his freshly shaven face, but even his warm skin didn't move under her touch. She tried to adjust his collar, but it was as stiff as stone. Interlacing her fingers between his, she clutched at his rigid palm.

He didn't squeeze her back.

"Daddy?"

She hadn't called him *Daddy* since she was seven.

Heart racing, she dashed to the window. Figurine people in various positions were arranged like toys over the blanket of fog that covered the ground. Friends she'd had since first grade were as motionless as Gwen's discarded dolls, making the entire campus look like a claymation movie on pause.

How far did this motionlessness go?

Gwen gulped and slowly glanced up.

A blue sheriff helicopter hung in the midday sky, its stock-still blades defying gravity and all logic. Further on, a cloud of blackbirds that had taken to flight were now were suspended on silent wings. And down the hill, palm trees waited mid-sway for a time when their fronds could fly free.

The only thing that moved was the dark fog rolling over it all.

Gwen's knees buckled under her and she clutched the window-sill. She dug her nails in until one bent back and began to bleed. After popping a finger in her mouth, Gwen tilted her other hand back and forth as the eerie shadows played tricks on her skin.

Gwen thought back to her first journey into Artania, two years before. She'd asked if people would worry if she were gone too long.

"No, they won't, because time is frozen on Earth while we're here," Bartholomew had said.

Alex had added, "We're in another dimension that comes from people's art, but it's connected to Earth. Humans' creative energy keeps this place alive."

"Has Artania frozen time, or what?" Gwen pondered for a moment. "But if I can move…"

Fear flooded through her, an Arctic wave passing through her veins. After spinning on her heels, she faced Mr. Cisneros, whose face was stuck in a perplexed frown.

"Move!" She struck out at his face, her open palm slapping his cheek.

Her hand recoiled as if he were made of ice.She stared uncertainly at the frozen figures in the room, praying for change. Her heart beat out the moments, but nothing stirred in this silence, where the only sound was her shallow breath.

She flew to the door and yanked it open before bounding down the hallway calling, "Someone, anyone! Are you there?"

Chapter 56

Sludge held his battle axe over the warped cauldron as sickly sweet mist filled his piggish nostrils. He was about to lower it into the bubbling brew, but paused.

"No tricks this time, Crone."

For once, she didn't reply right away, but kept stirring as that long ladle circled, once, twice, three times.

"Crone?"

She lifted her gaze from the mixture, leaning on the ladle to straighten her slouched back.

"The human has exhausted my ruses, Pupae."

He pulled his axe back and furrowed his hairless brows. Crone was usually as spry as a nymph, but today she seemed weary. Slack-jawed, she stood next to the pot, leaning on the long ladle as if it were a cane. Breathing slowly, it looked as if she barely had the energy to stay on that stool.

"Are you sick? We could do this later."

Crone's demeanor immediately changed. "I am fine. Worry about yourself, Pupae. Let's get on with it."

With a shrug, Sludge eased his hatchet nearer as the Crone raised a ladleful in her gnarled hands. Once his blade was directly under the wooden spoon, she tilted it and the steaming potion dribbled over the metal.

An image of the unconscious Deliverer appeared on the surface of the liquid. Alexander was groping along a maze of misty walls, his face twisted in confusion.

Glorious.

"Let me send him a nightmare, Crone. One that will have him forever screaming."

"No. The coma is too precarious. Even as we speak, the other Deliverer draws close to an answer."

"I thought you said nothing could wake Alexander."

"What you heard is not what I said. You have always had selective hearing."

"Then what's happening?"

"The Borax boy seeks the anagram that could undo all."

Sludge remembered the Crone mentioning something about Bartholomew trying to decipher a code. But he'd dismissed it, sure that whatever the idiot human was doing would be ineffective.

"If he finds the key" Sludge began.

"Our efforts will be thwarted, yes," Crone said.

"Then you must let me invade Alex's mind. I will create a nightmare that will stop all art in him. He will never lift another paintbrush again!"

Crone sighed. "You still do not understand. Only I can invade."

Sludge clutched his axe handle so tight his claw-tipped fingers dug into the wood.

"That's just your ego. If you put it aside for five minutes, I could do much better."

"I would welcome the assistance, Pupae, but it is not possible."

"Stop calling me that! I am a grown Shadow Swine, not a nymph newly emerged from Swallow Hole Swamp." He lifted his battle axe as if ready to strike.

Crone narrowed her chestnut eyes and shook her head. "What? You would strike me down now? After all I have given you."

Sludge's brutish arm twitched, and he growled through clenched teeth. He breathed heavily, his nostrils flaring. It would be so easy. Just a swipe and she would be gone. Then he could take her place, grasping powers to rival Lord Sickhert's.

But then he considered. Might there be an ounce of truth in her words? She had guided him his entire life. He would be less powerful, but much taller, without her help.

Sludge swung, his battle axe slicing the air. Crone cried out and staggered back, falling from the stool.

He stood over her splayed body and sneered. She wasn't so powerful, after all.

"Let this be a lesson to you, Crone. I *will* take my leave now, bruising nothing but your backside. But denigrate me again, and I will not be so merciful."

Chapter 57

"Are these connected, and do any of them solve the riddle?" Bartholomew glanced down at the sheathes of paper scattered around him. *Alexander: ax learned, DNA earl ex, axe lane. Shadow: sad who, how sad. Borax: ax bro, ax orb. Nightmare: arming the, grim neath, hating rem, her taming, hermit nag. Silent Artist: listen traits, strait, enlist its art, it star...*"

For hours he'd worked on making lists of anagrams to solve the puzzle sent from the Quarrymen's Bath. *Anagram is to analogy as decipher is to___ ?* He'd written so many possible solutions that his hand was beginning to cramp and his head felt fuzzy. Stifling a yawn, he rubbed his right hand.

"Perhaps zere are repeated words or ideas," Monet suggested.

"You might have something there," Bartholomew said tapping his chin.

He scanned the anagram list for any repetitions, and began to circle them.

Alexander: ax learned, DNA earl ex, axe lane. Shadow: sad who, how sad. Borax: ax bro, ax rob, ax orb.

"An axe. Hmm," Monet said.

"Captain Sludge has one. I saw it at the Halloween party. Scary looking thing."

"Are zere are more about weapons?"

Bartholomew continued his search. *Nightmare: arming the, grim neath, hating rem, her taming, hermit nag, gate hr. min.*

"Maybe we're getting somewhere," he said. "The Shadow Swine are arming themselves with some kind of axe, a weapon."

"Look zere, next to *nightmare.* It says, *hating rem.* REM is zee time of sleep when humans dream."

"Yes." Bartholomew nodded. "It also says *grim neath* and *gate, hr. min.* Could it be that there is something terrible beneath that's causing REM to be hated?"

"We all know zat the Shadow Swine make nightmares. And they live below. So zat makes sense. But *gate, hr. min?* What gate, and how is time of zee essence?"

Monet just might have something. Bartholomew lifted a finger before shuffling through his notes. When he found the page he'd been thinking of, he held it up. *True Art: a turret, rare tut, rat true, rate rut, rut tear.*

"Look. Rut is repeated twice."

"Then we must seek a gate zat is also a hole. But we have already been to zee catacombs and sought answers in the Quarrymen's Bath."

"You know, that was a gate for Artanians, not Shadow Swine. They make their own tunnels to the surface. We need to look for one of those."

"But they close their doorways after they capture our people. We cannot use them."

Bartholomew considered for a moment. For some reason, the words *rut tear* seemed to pop out at him. His mind still hadn't completely cleared, so he read them several times.

"Rut tear, rut tear. Hmm. Tearing into a rut. Digging deeper." He snapped his fingers. "That's it! We have to find a used tunnel and dig into it."

"No use. Many have tried after zere loved ones were pulled away. No matter how much zey dug, no doorway was found."

"But were any of them a Deliverer?"

Monet ran the back of his hand over his bushy brown beard. "Not as far as I know."

"Then it's time to try. Let's go to where you last saw an Artanian disappear."

A half-hour later, Bartholomew and Monet were standing inside the charred remains of the café that Thinker and Monet had escaped from when Swineys invaded.

"The barkeep disappeared in zat place." Monet pointed into a corner.

There, behind a scorched bar was a pile of rubble.

Bartholomew tried not to imagine how the painted man now suffered. Once pulled below, Artanians were taken to Mudlark Maker and thrown into its mouth. There, the monster swallowed, then morphed the painted beings until finally they were regurgitated as zombie-like slaves of Lord Sickhert.

Horrible.

Bartholomew lowered the easel from his shoulder and extended the three legs so it would stand.

"Why haven't they fixed this place up since the fire?"

"Superstition. Fear zat the Swineys will return."

Monet propped the canvas he'd been carrying up onto the easel, and then showed Bartholomew the drawers which housed paints, palettes, and brushes.

Bartholomew thanked him and stared at the pile of rubble in the corner.

The blonde boy closed his eyes and pictured a tunnel with a rickety ladder beneath the floor. It would lead from Subterranea, up to this burned out café, and have the perfect acoustics to echo his every word. The wooden rung would be weak, further irritating the evil captain with every step.

By the time Captain Sludge reached the top, he'd be so incensed he wouldn't be thinking straight. There, Bartholomew would be waiting with some kind of weapon.

If he could think of one in time.

After envisioning the entire shaft, Bartholomew picked up a jar of paint and poured a tablespoon on the palette. He repeated this with another, and two more until he had just the right colors to make his doorway.

He took a deep breath and held it until an inspiring image like white clouds dappled with sunlight filled his lungs. As soon as the picture was clear in his mind, he seized a paint brush. He held his hand aloft for a microsecond, before attacking the canvas. Each stroke swept ever faster, until soon even lightning bolts would have had trouble keeping pace.

In five seconds, it was done.

Bartholomew shoved the painting of a tunnel on top of the rubble pile, and stood back, waiting for the Creation Magic to begin. Monet glanced his way, eyebrows raised.

"Wait and watch," Bartholomew said.

A moment later, there was rumbling below them and the ground began to shake. Bartholomew widened his stance for balance just before the floor shuddered. Then he heard a groaning, like megaliths parting. A cloud of dust rose near the painting, darkening every corner of the small café. Bartholomew blinked in the quiet.

When it cleared, he could see that a dark shaft had taken the place of his painting. After moving forward until he could peer inside, he bent over the newly formed hole.

"Careful, Deliverer," Monet warned.

With a dismissive brush of his hand, Bartholomew dropped to one knee and called down into the pit.

"Hey! Captain Sludge. It's Bartholomew. Remember me? I'm the Deliverer you thought you could beat!"

He turned back, raising his eyebrows and grinning at Monet. Then he lied, "You think you have the upper hand? Think again! I know all about your axe and plans. I have the key, Sludge!"

Bartholomew paused and listened for the inevitable growling approach. When his ears met silence, he began a new series of taunts.

"Do you hear me? I'm coming. And this time, my art will melt your—"

He was about to say *jackboots*, when the tingling began. He reached out for something to grab a hold of, but there was nothing but rubble. He grasped a handful of pebbles and watched them spill from his fading fingers. Clinking, they rolled and tumbled down the long black hole.

"Deliverer?"

"Nooo!" Bartholomew stared into Monet's shocked face.

Then the burned-out café disappeared from view.

Chapter 58

Gwen rushed down the hallway. "Is anyone there! Ms. Leed? Teachers? Guys?"

But her words didn't even echo in the hollow silence.

She ran faster, poking her head inside classes and restrooms, down corridors and around corners. Nothing but dark smog rolling away, dissipating until by the time she reached the end of the hall, all the smoky mist was gone.

Fingers crossed that this meant everyone would begin moving, she bulldozed through the double doors, to the grassy area near the quad.

And stopped dead in her tracks.

The courtyard was scattered with statue people in positions that no sculptor would ever try. One boy was suspended two feet off the ground, his heels together in some sort of celebratory leap. Another's open hands were in front of his chest, a football mere inches from his grasp. Lacey Zamora, ever the brat, was holding a water bottle over one of the Book Arm Girls, a frozen stream perched to pour all over her hair. All crazy, but she could handle it... sort of.

Until she saw Jose staring into his phone.

Her boyfriend's long lashes cast shadows on his copper skin. Any other time, Gwen would have gotten butterflies looking at that chiseled face. But today the pained look in his dark brown eyes was a knife in her gut.

She walked around behind him to see what on his phone. The text drove the blade deeper. *Your chica was freakin. Campus cop found her screaming and breaking stuff in the cesso. Full on Halloween IV. She been blazing or what?*

She rested a hand on his shoulder. "I'm so sorry, babe. Crazy stuff's happening, and I don't know how to stop it."

Swallowing hard to blink back the tears, she stroked Jose's stony shoulder, wishing she knew what to do.

Just then lightning crackled in the silence, followed by the low rumbling of thunder and a warm breeze on her face. As her braids bobbed, Gwen gaped at the skater logo on her tee, rippling over skin.

"What the—?"

The ground shuddered. Gwen stumbled, trying to lean over and shield Jose's body with her own. Arms outstretched, she waited, nose twitching furiously.

There was a *pop!* followed by a hollow *thud*.

A second later, a familiar voice shouted, "Please, no!"

"B-3?" She straightened up.

Mr. Clean's head pivoted slowly toward her. "Gwen, what are you doing here?"

"I could ask you the same thing."

He cocked his head, glanced around. "This isn't my room."

"School." She raised both hands. "Cha!"

"Not again." He groaned.

"Yep. More materializing in crazy places. But this time it's different. Look around." She pointed at Jose and Lacey.

Bartholomew's gaze followed her motions. His mouth opened and closed.

Then he stumbled back. "That's not—"

"Imaginable, likely, conceivable, freakin' possible?"

He nodded.

"Well, maybe not, but it's happening. Along with vanishing acts that'd make Houdini jealous, the world is frozen. And I need you and Alex to fix it." Then Gwen remembered her bud in the hospital. "How is Mr. Hero, anyhow? I saw him full-on zonked."

Bartholomew explained that when a mid-air collision had knocked Alex unconscious, he and Monet took him to the Parisian hospital, but even doctors couldn't rouse him from the coma. Puzzled, they met with special Artanians called the Silent Artists, who told them that Alex was trapped between worlds and wouldn't wake up until the true art freed him.

"Then make some true art, stupid head."

"It's not that simple. It has to be specific to the task. The Prophecy says, *Their battle will be long, with seven evils to undo. Scattered around will be seven clues.*"

"So?"

"Every time we encounter an evil, we have to follow the clues before we create the true art that stops it. I was in the middle of trying out a possible solution, when I disappeared." Mr. Clean paused. "But I was yanked back to Earth before I could see if it worked."

Gwen thought back to her previous journeys into Artania. Her buds had made some freaky things out of dirt, rocks, and sticks. But it wasn't until they molded something that could change someone's heart that the *task* was considered complete and they could go home.

"What'd you try?" she said.

"Oh, I painted a tunnel to Subterranea. I wanted to bait Sludge by shouting insults down the hole."

"Bold." Gwen nodded her props.

"Perhaps. Or reckless. Now there's an opening between the underground Subterranea and Artania." He paused. "I think. I don't know if the hole disappeared when I returned to Earth, or not. Hope so."

"Well, why don't we tackle this freak show, and you can worry about that hole endangering Artania whenever you get jerked back."

The Richie nodded.

Gwen rubbed her hands together. "O-kay then. Where do we start?"

"This has never happened before. I don't know."

"Think."

"Well, I am aware of Earth's time stopping when we venture into Artania, but I've never seen it because it begins again when we return."

She jerked her thumb toward Jose. "Not this time."

"Have you looked around? Is it everywhere?"

"I don't know if it's all over the world. But if helicopters and birds are stopped mid-flight, I think it's pretty widespread."

Looking up at the motionless clouds, Bartholomew nodded. "So you and I are the only ones who can move?"

"Looks like it. And the super freaky thing is, people don't even feel like people. They're as hard as that marble statue David."

"Really?" Bartholomew poked at Jose's long ponytail.

Not a single hair moved.

"See?"

"If I can't move anything, how can I create something to fix this?"

"Hell if I know! You're the artist—use that magic of yours to paint or sculpt something."

"I could try. Do you know where an art class might be?"

Chapter 59

"This is Alex's fifth period," Gwen said before entering the classroom.

Bartholomew glanced longingly at the assortment of paintings, sketches, and collages arranged around the room. What he wouldn't give to take this class. He had always dreamed of openly creating with other kids instead of sketching in secret or hiding in his underground studio to sculpt. He often imagined sitting in a class just like this one, talking theory, perspective, and composition under the guidance of a kind master like Leonardo. It wasn't until sixth grade, when Mother finally allowed him to go to school, that he was able to talk openly about his work.

That's when he met Alex and realized they shared a common destiny. For over a year, he'd been relatively free. Until seventh grade and that stupid stealing incident. Ever since, he'd been trapped inside that mansion with the fingernail-obsessed Mr. White.

"Hate being homeschooled," he mumbled.

"What?"

"Nothing. Let's look around. I need blank paper, brushes, and some paint."

Gwen started rummaging through the shelves built into the nearest wall, while Bartholomew set up an easel next to the window.

"How's this?" She held up a sketch pad.

"Fine. Clip it to the easel, and I'll get out the rest." He searched around until he found a palette tray, a few tubes of paint, and a roll-up canvas bag full of brushes.

"What's the plan?"

"Hmm, not sure. It seems that Artania doesn't know that you and I are here. It's like the controls are confused."

"So create something to un-confuse them."

"I suppose. But I don't get it. I thought Thinker had powers to prevent anything like this from happening."

"Maybe he's not as strong as you thought."

"Perhaps." Bartholomew picked up a tube of Burnt Sienna and squeezed.

Nothing happened. He squeezed harder. The tube didn't even dimple. Biting his lower lip, Bartholomew grasped it in both hands and tried constricting his muscles.

"Maybe that one's old and dried up," Gwen said. "Try another."

With a nod, Bartholomew pinched Titanium White. Hard as stone. Cobalt Blue. Unyielding.

"They're as solid as statues."

"No," Gwen argued grabbing a tube. "It has to work."

After sweeping one tube onto the floor she stomped on it. Once, twice, three times. When she stepped back, they both leaned over.

Bartholomew shook his head. "Not even a dent."

Gwen blanched. "Does that mean that we're trapped?"

"Looks like it. And for now, I'm fresh out of ideas." Bartholomew sighed and rested one thigh against a desk.

"Don't tell me you're giving up." She crossed her arms.

Bartholomew shrugged.

"You have to do something."

"Like what? Wave a magic wand and force paint out of the tubes? They're petrified, and there's nothing I can do but wait."

"So you're quitting on me? On the world. On Artania?" She stomped a foot and glared at him. "On Alex?"

"I'll try later. When things move."

"What if they never do? What if we're stuck like this forever? Did you ever think of that, Mister I Can't Try?"

Bartholomew chewed on his lower lip. "I try. Sometimes."

Gwen stepped up closer to him, shaking a finger in his face. "No, you don't. This is what you always do. Every time the going gets rough, you start a pity party and give up."

"Maybe there's no point."

"Quitter." She jabbed her finger into his chest.

"Be quiet."

"Who's gonna make me? You?"

When she poked her finger at him this time, Bartholomew saw red and slapped it away.

"Jerk!" Raising both hands, Gwen shoved him against the desk.

He stumbled and bounced off, landing on all fours with a thud. A corner of Cobalt Blue pressed into his index finger, cutting it open. As if from a distance, he could hear himself cry out.

Sucking air back into his lungs, he rolled over, gaping at his bleeding finger. Mother's voice filled his mind. *Filth. Get rid of it.* He glanced around for something to wipe it on. When he saw the paper clipped to the easel, he stood and smeared his hand over the paper.

"Dude, sorry, you o—" Gwen narrowed her eyes. "Did you hear that?"

Bartholomew cocked an ear. "I didn't hear anything." He blotted his hand on the paper.

"There it goes again!"

Clicking came from the other side of the room.

"Look, the clock!" she said.

The classroom clock's second hand moved twice. And stopped.

Gwen rushed to the window. "I don't know, but I think the helicopter moved."

Bartholomew stepped up next to Gwen and surveyed the sky. It did look like the helicopter was in a different place. And was he mistaken, or had a cloud changed shape? He watched, but long moments passed with no movement. He felt his finger get wet before a drop of blood rolled off his nail, onto the sill.

"Eww," Gwen said staring at the droplet.

Click. Click.

"There it goes again! I think your wound is causing it."

"Huh?"

"Your cut. Your cut! It's making time start."

Bartholomew raised his eyebrows, thinking.

A few seconds later, he said, "I get it. My blood is like paint."

"Now you can make something."

"With...with...blood?" Bartholomew gulped.

"Don't you dare go into Mr. Clean mode now. Suck it up and do something."

Bartholomew clenched his jaw. "All right. Let me think. The last clue I had was an analogy. It said, *Anagram is to analogy as decipher is to blank.* So I made lots of anagrams related to Artania, and came up with painting a doorway to the Shadow Swine's home."

"Then what happened?"

"As soon as the painting was complete, the Creation Magic morphed it into a real tunnel. Next, I shouted down the hole, hoping Captain Sludge would hear and maybe do something to wake Alex up." Bartholomew chewed on his lower lip. "But if it worked, is anyone's guess."

"Anagrams, huh?"

"You know, mixing up letters from words?"

"I know what an anagram is, Mr. Clean. What I'm thinking is that we should try a few out. Let's focus on *time* and what anagrams it has."

Bartholomew liked the direction Gwen was going with this.

He thought a moment. "Mix up *time,* and you get...hmm. *Mite?* No, that's a little bug. Not related to art at all. *Emit? It me? It me!* That's it! Time is what *I* will emit."

"Huh?"

"What represents time?"

"A clock."

"True, but I don't think I could show it moving."

"How about that sand-filled thingy? What do you call it?"

"An hourglass. Good idea." Bartholomew stepped up to the easel.

After closing one eye, he pressed the bleeding digit at the top and let a few drips fill the paper. Then, with his opposite hand, grasped the index finger and drew two curved shapes.

Tick-tock. Tick-tock.

"It's working. Draw more!"

He closed in the top and the bottom, then tapped his finger inside both ends of the hourglass to make sand.

A breeze blew back the blinds.

"More! Go faster."

Brushing his finger down, he painted sands of time pouring from the top into the bottom.

And the world began.

Chapter 60

When a couple chatting kids entered the classroom, Gwen stopped high-fiving B-3 to turn their way. She gaped, thinking how surreal it was to see people moving again.

She almost hugged Mr. Clean, when it hit her.

"Oh, no, school counselor, Officer Dirk...Dad!" She slapped her forehead.

"What?" Bartholomew asked.

"Dude, gotta go. There's going to be a freakout in Mr. Cisneros's office."

"You disappearing mid-conversation? That's an understatement."

She rested a hand on his shoulder. "You okay? Can you find your way home?"

"Of course. Go."

He was in the middle of waving her away, when his body began to shimmer. It brightened for a moment, then *pop*, disappeared. After everything she'd seen in the last few hours, this barely fazed Gwen. She did glance over to see if the kids entering had noticed, but they were so engrossed in some YouTube video that they never saw B-3.

Gwen dashed out the door and raced down the hallway, darting in and out of kids checking phones while drifting to class.

"Sorry! Excuse me. Gotta get past."

When she arrived at the counselor's door, she skidded inside, colliding with Officer Dirk, who was staring at her walkie talkie. With a harrumph, the officer stumbled back and raised her hands. Her microphone fell and then started to do a Slinky dance, bouncing up and down.

On the other side of the room, Dad stood, blinking. "Gwenny? How did you—"

"Sorry. I got scared by the smoke."

"Smoke? What smoke, miss?" Officer Dirk asked before sliding her walkie talkie back into her belt holster.

"You know, the smoke outside. Just a minute ago."

The three adults all stepped toward the window and stared out.

"I don't see anything," Dad said.

"Well, it's gone now, but it was there. Don't you remember?"

"See what I mean Mr. Obranovich?" said Counselor Cisneros.

Gwen realized that the moments leading up to a frozen world had somehow been erased from the adults' minds. They seemed to only remember what happened before the smoke appeared. So the lie she'd been composing while dashing across campus wouldn't fly.

Gwen's father bobbed his head up and down before beckoning Gwen closer with a curled index finger. When she shuffled up to him, he grasped her shoulders and examined her eyes.

"I'm okay. Really."

"Perhaps the counselor is right. I'm taking you to see Dr. Brandt." He turned to Mr. Cisneros and held out a hand. "Thank you for letting me know about this, *ahem*, incident. And taking care of my daughter."

"Certainly. I sincerely hope that family physician can help." Mr. Cisneros shook Dad's hand.

"Officer Dirk." Dad nodded at the campus police as he led Gwen out the door.

And the redhead shuffled behind, trying to think of a way to convince the doctor she wasn't on drugs.

Chapter 61

Bartholomew landed on his rear, blinking. *What is going on?*

A second ago, he'd been waving goodbye to Gwen, and now he was back in Artania.

He put his bleeding finger in his mouth. Wishing he'd remembered hand sanitizer, he glanced around.

And squeaked.

This time, he hadn't ended up in Monet's attic apartment. Or on the banks of the River Seine. He wasn't even in the forest. This time, Bartholomew was smack dab back in the middle of the cemetery.

Just a few feet from that sad statue of the Mourner.

The marble woman kept her sobbing face buried in one hand, while the other wrapped tendrils around a finger. She twisted the grey locks until her finger was matted with stony hair, then unwound the tangled knots before starting all over again.

Watching her drove a knife into Bartholomew's heart. He thought how much the Mourner was like Mother, suffering endlessly as she sought to purify the world. Of course, Mother's idea of purity was scrubbing, bathing, and sanitizing, while the Mourner helped lessen the Artanians' grief.

Bartholomew drew his brows together and rubbed the back of his neck. Why were they trapped in looping cries. The statue's silent, and Hygenette's loud and protesting? Those mind prisons wouldn't let anyone in.

"I'm so sorry," Bartholomew said, unsure if he was addressing the statue or his distant mother.

He thought back to all the times he'd watched Mother panic. She'd mumble, "Germs, filth, mud," while staring at some imagined disease. Shaking, she'd pale ever whiter until all blood drained from her face. He tried to talk her down so many times while she was swooning, but it never worked. Once a panic attack began, her only reprieve was retreating to a bath heaped in bubbles.

"All that pain," he whispered, trying to tear his gaze from the tortured statue in front of him.

The Mourner's shoulders shook as she buried her face in both hands. Mother might have had long tresses like these long ago. Instead of the perfect bun that kept her platinum blonde hair pulled tight. He imagined it flowing free as she giggled about some joke Father might have told.

If he hadn't hit his head on that boulder before falling face down in muddy water.

Bartholomew shook his head as memories flashed. Alex unconscious, face twisting in nightmares. Mother's vacant stare as she muttered about filth. Gwen quivering beneath Captain Sludge's axe. And this poor little statue sobbing unshed tears.

He couldn't take it anymore.

"They shouldn't have to suffer!" Bartholomew shouted shaking a fist at the sky.

He rushed over to the Mourner and placed an arm over her shoulders. In that moment, he felt like he was soothing Mother, finally giving her the comfort she'd needed all these years.

"Hey, it's okay. Don't cry." He patted her on the back.

The marble statue uncovered her face to reveal hauntingly beautiful features that immediately enraptured Bartholomew. Her pale lids were closed at first, as if locked in place. But as he continued to watch her face, something seemed to unbolt from deep inside.

Millimeter by millimeter, the Mourner lifted her lids until eyes as white as bone regarded him. With a slow blink, these colorless orbs locked him into a gaze, pulling him closer.

His voice sounded far away. "It's all right. I—"

There was rumbling from behind him, and he heard silent shouts. *No, Deliverer! You don't know what you're unleashing on the world!*

The Silent Artists had appeared behind him, all three trying to unfasten his hand from around her shoulder.

Van Gogh tugged his arm. *Don't!*

"Leave me alone! I'm helping her." Bartholomew hugged the marble statue tighter.

You must not. Mary Cassatt implored. *She bears our pain and lessons it. Your interruption is unleashing tremendous grief in our world. For millions.*

"I don't believe you."

It's true. Van Gogh said, from inside Bartholomew's head. *She grieves so the rest of us don't have to.*

Bartholomew rubbed the Mourner's shoulder again, and then looked into those colorless eyes.

His lower lip trembled. "It's okay now. I'm here. You don't have to suffer any more."

Yet suffer she must, said the Silent Artists.

"But it's not right."

Right or not, it is the way of our world. Van Gogh tapped the side of his head, where his ear appeared and disappeared. *And it keeps sorrow at bay.*

"Just look at her tortured face!"

She is aware of what she does for the rest of us. It is her choice. Mary Cassatt tried to pry Bartholomew's finger's loose from the Mourner's shoulder.

A low whimper came from off in the distance. Followed by another.

Let her go before it's too late!

"No. It shouldn't be!" Bartholomew wrapped both arms around the Mourner.

More wails pealed like distant church bells ringing lament. A creaking sound from an opposing mausoleum made Bartholomew look up. There, a sobbing Greek carving pried himself off the wall before falling into a crouched position and quivering with sobs. Next, a granite angel began flapping her wings as if trying to escape a predatory bird. She ascended a few feet, then went limp and crashed into a headstone. A moment later, statues of writers, artists, and musicians rolled off their crypts and curled into fetal positions.

Only the Mourner can stop this. Release her! The Silent Artists shouted, in his mind.

Desperate cries filled the air, but Bartholomew held the Mourner fast.

"There, there. I have you."

Van Gogh grabbed him around the waist, while Seurat and Mary Cassatt each grabbed an arm. Bartholomew clung to the marble woman and struggled to hold on, but they were too strong. A second later, he was looking up at the Mourner's placid face.

While all around, Artanians wept.

Chapter 62

Thinker was trying to calm the unruly crowd, when it happened.

An hour before, during one of his *It's Time for a Change* speeches, Gauguin had convinced a group of fifty or so rebellious Parisians to march down the Champs-Elysees, toward the huge triumphal arch at the other end. Waving French flags and anti-Thinker banners in the streets, the crowd grew, swelling to hundreds by the time Gauguin led them to the Arc de Triomphe.

Once there, Gauguin started riling up the mob with chants of, "Down with Thinker! Down with Thinker!"

Monitoring the events in his steely palm, from a nearby café, Thinker had considered letting this all play out. He assumed that the throngs would have their say and then go home. But when things escalated into brawls and broken windows, he decided to head down the Champs-Elysees to intervene.

When he arrived at the Arc de Triomphe and saw fists flying, he called, "Friends, violence is not the answer. Please stop." He reached toward the audience as if inviting embrace.

"All you want is control! Gauguin bellowed.

"Untrue. I desire freedom for all Artanians. But not at the cost of injury. I'm afraid that—"

Gauguin cut him off. "See, friends? He is afraid!"

"I only fear for your safety. You could…"

Thinker's words were drowned out by the crowd's angry cries. He trailed off trying to find the right phrase to calm the crowd. He curled his bronze hand into a fist and pressed it against his forehead, boring it into each metal crease.

That was when every riotous shout ceased. For long moments, there was absolute silence. Thinker raised his head and stared at the gathered company. Painted hands that a moment ago had been poised to slap, were now hanging limply at sides. Sculpted mouths went from gnashing teeth to slack jaws. Stomping feet quieted into shakes and quivers.

Then men and women fell over like tipping dominoes and dropped to their sides in fetal positions. Many lay there wreathing, or stared at some imagined horror. Some hid their faces in the crook of their arms, while others tore at their hair or clothing.

And then the sobbing began. A dirge of lament unlike anything Thinker had ever heard. Voices so pained it sounded like every Artanian's heart had entered into atrial fibrillation. Even Gauguin dropped to one knee, mumbling apologies to the long-lost wife and children his creator had abandoned long ago.

"I am sorry, Mette. I miss the *bebes...*"

Then, Thinker felt a sharp pain, as if someone had just driven a rapier into his chest. He gasped at the sudden sting, barely steadying his stance before the ache could overwhelm him.

Even before becoming this world's leader, Thinker had felt its suffering, yet still he willingly took on Artania's burdens, no matter the cost. That choice would forever leave him hunched over.

But this was different.

This was more than heaviness. This was a weight so oppressive he was afraid his bronze knees would buckle beneath him. Gravity increased a hundred-fold as if the sky had turned to lead and was pressing his head and shoulders down.

Thinker was confused at first. What could cause such torrential pain? Lord Sickhert was powerful, but he couldn't unleash sorrow storms in Artania. And while young Alex still lie unconscious, the other Deliverer was seeking answers.

Could Bartholomew have been that naïve?

The bronze leader stared at the scores of suffering people all around. And then he knew.

Thinker heaved a sigh. "Oh, young Bartholomew, what have you done?

Chapter 63

Bartholomew covered his ears. Didn't help. Pressed harder. No change. Drove his thumbs into the meaty tragus until they were inside each canal. But no amount of pressure could muffle the sound of crying Artanians.

He dreaded the unescapable answer, but still asked. "What's happening?"

You know full well. Mary Cassatt's voice toned in his mind. *The Mourner unleashed the pain she had been carrying for all of us.*

Yes, now our sorrows are ten-fold, Seurat said.

Face blanching, Bartholomew glanced at the man painted in tiny dots.

"But I don't feel anything," he lied as pangs of guilt wrenched his gut.

That is because you are human. Shaking her head, Mary Cassatt turned away and knelt beside the curled-up Van Gogh.

Only now did Bartholomew notice that the painter had dropped to all fours and pulled his woolen cowl up over his head. The man was rocking back and forth and moaning low like an injured animal.

"What's wrong with him?"

The real Vincent Van Gogh long suffered from depression, Seurat explained. *As did his creation. But the Mourner was there to make his load lighter. Her constant vigilance helped him to function normally.*

Mary Cassatt nodded. *He still had mood swings, but they no longer overwhelmed him. When you comforted the Mourner, her support ceased.*

Bartholomew slumped his shoulders. "But I just wanted to help. She looked so sad. It seemed wrong to let her stay that way." He stepped closer to the rocking man. "Hey, Mr. Van Gogh, I—"

There was a sudden explosion of thoughts from the man. Van Gogh clutched his monk's habit at the neck, baring his chest, before lifting his head to stare, unseeing, at the sky.

Sunflowers. Stacks of wheat. My brother. Ear. Listen. Gauguin leaving. Angry with me. Alone. Sheaves of Wheat. Alone. Self-portrait. Self-portrait. Starry night. Stars. Silent Artists. Silent. Mourner. Pain. Pain.

The onslaught of chaotic thoughts sent Bartholomew reeling back, his face contorted in the confused jumble.

"What? I don't understand."

Anagram is to analogy as decipher is to____? Anagram is to analogy as decipher is to?

"I don't know! I've tried a hundred different solutions, and none worked."

Mary Cassatt smoothed her loose chignon and fixed Bartholomew with an even stare.

Anagram is to analogy as decipher is to?

"I have no idea." Bartholomew wished he could just run away. *Let someone else fix this. Like Alex. If he were awake, he'd know what to do.*

The dots making up Seurat's painted face broadened and narrowed. *What does it mean to decipher young one?*

Bartholomew shrugged.

Young one?

"It means, solve. Crack. Figure out." He sighed. "As if a definition will help now."

Yes? Go on. Seurat rolled his hand in a circle.

"It also means *decode.*" He paused, struck by the word. "Decode. Is that what I'm supposed to do, decode the anagrams?"

Seurat nodded as Van Gogh's tortured voice sounded in Bartholomew's mind. *Silent Artist. Silent Artist.*

"I tried anagrams for those, but they didn't make any sense."

Mary Cassatt's silent voice was hopeful. *Do you recall them?*

"Hmm. Let's see. I got *listen traits,* and *artist inlet.* What else? *Inlet strait, astern sit til.*"

Van Gogh rocked back and forth. *Starry night. Stars. Silent Artists. Stars. Café. Silent Artists.*

Watching him made the twisting pit in the bottom of Bartholomew's stomach grow. He rubbed it.

Did any solutions relate to artistic journeys? Seurat asked.

Bartholomew chewed on his lower lip. "Not that I recall. Unless *enlist its art* or *inset starlit* sound familiar."

Van Gogh nodded once. *Stars. Cafe.*

What about those? Do they seem significant? Seurat jerked a dotted thumb at Van Gogh.

Bartholomew recalled that two of Vincent Van Gogh's most famous pieces were *Starry Night* and *Café Terrace and Night.* Each had swirling stars painted in deep blue skies over French streets. One of a distant village, and the other of a café up close.

"Actually, come to think of it, the burned-out café was familiar. It struck me as strange when I saw it. I mean, why would the Shadow Swine attack a café with Thinker in it? He's too powerful."

Cassatt adjusted her monk's habit. *Now you are getting somewhere.*

Bartholomew thought for a moment, trying to put the jumbled puzzle pieces together.

"Because the café was the same one from Van Gogh's famous painting! And he is a Silent Artist."

A beautiful place once, said Van Gogh.

"Okay, so if the best anagram for Silent Artist is *enlist its art,* I think I know what that means. But…" Bartholomew was unwilling to say what he knew he must do.

Van Gogh seemed calmer with the next words. *I have but one ear, yet still I listen. Why with your two do you not?*

"I listen."

Do you? Or are you deaf to that which you do not want to hear?

Bartholomew picked at some dried blood under his fingernail. In a low voice he said, "But Alex isn't here to help me."

I think he is. You have only to listen and his voice will sound.

Bartholomew looked at each Silent Artist in turn, and nodded. He didn't really believe them, but what choice did he have?

Chapter 64

"You can do this. You can do this." Bartholomew tried to drown out the anguished cries coming from every building, house, and cathedral along the Parisian street.

He'd messed up things before, but this really took the prize. If someone had been giving out blunder awards, he'd have a gold medal right now, to match all the imaginary medals for gaffes, missteps, errors, and poor calculations.

Back when he'd first traveled to Artania, when he was eleven, he'd blown it multiple times, and it had almost cost them an entire nation. Cringing, he recalled being faced with his chance to save a captive pharaoh.

"Let him go," he had said, his wobbly hand raising a sword.

But the Shadow Swine had only burst into laughter.

The taller one pushed Bartholomew's chest. "Make me."

The other creature shoved his right shoulder. Bartholomew took a deep breath and waved his sword again, but the Swineys simply exchanged amused looks with their yellow eyes.

Trembling, Bartholomew swung, but the sword whistled past its head. He adjusted his grip and jabbed at the other. His thrust fell short. He shifted his weight to his hind leg for leverage. Before Bartholomew could ready another jab, the Swiney thrust his knife into the pharaoh's chest. The Egyptian king began to fade, his life force ebbing like fiery embers immersed in the sea. The last to disappear was his eyes. Sad, tortured eyes.

A low moan came from behind a shuttered window. Bartholomew winced. An Artanian inside that house was sobbing, overwhelmed with pain the Mourner had just unleashed.

"I am such a screwup, ruining everything," Bartholomew said.

He almost stopped right there in the middle of the cobblestone street. Who was he kidding? He'd never be able to go down *there* and face *them.* Not without Alex.

Alex, his best friend. The brave one. The guy who always put everyone else first. Whether he was skateboarding up a vert ramp or facing that evil Captain Sludge, Alex just ran head-on into the fray without any concern for his own well-being. Never hesitated.

Not like me. I flinch at the sound of my own feet. Bartholomew looked down at his oversized feet and kicked a pebble.

Whirling in guilt, he was surprised to find himself facing the burned-out café, which was unchanged since he'd come here with Monet to create a tunnel. The peeling paint still crinkled, while smoke shadows tinted the walls. The smell of charred wood assaulted his nostrils and he wished, once again, that he had a bottle of hand sanitizer to mask it.

Burnt holes in the awning filtered the fading sun. When one shard of light hit the cobblestone patio, Bartholomew thought it'd pierce the granite. Or him. He sidestepped it before approaching the doorway.

Would the tunnel and ladder still be there? Monet said it was the last time he looked. Afraid that the Shadow Swine had discovered his opening, Bartholomew tried not to imagine an axe-wielding Swiney cresting the floor, ready to strike him down.

He swallowed hard and opened the scorched door. Inside, the overturned chairs and soot-covered tables rested at odd angles on the blackened floor. Glass crunched under his feet as he stepped toward the corner where his painting of a tunnel with a long ladder leaned against a pile of rubble.

Bartholomew curled his hands into fists and stopped, afraid of what he might find.

I can't.

Seriously, B-3? I'm in a coma and you can't take three little steps? he imagined Alex saying.

He closed his eyes and shuffled forward, inhaled, took one step and paused before forcing his foot to lift again. He cocked an ear. No rattling Swiney snuffles. He opened his eyes and looked down.

The dim light from distant torches told him the coast was clear. For now.

After turning around backwards, Bartholomew grasped the wooden ladder and slipped through the hole in the floor. Not wanting to take a header, he clenched the rungs as he descended. When the wood creaked under his weight, he hugged the rails, praying it would hold.

He waited long moments, fully expecting the rickety wood to crack and break. The wall in front of him was choppy and irregular. He'd painted it that way to unnerve Sludge, hoping to daze the captain as he ascended the weak ladder. Bartholomew hadn't planned on using it himself.

If the rungs split, he'd fall a hundred feet into the abyss.

While clenching his jaw, he descended further. Soon he was in a cave with limy sandstone walls. A few stalactites hung menacingly from the ceiling some twenty feet above. Half a dozen stalagmites grew on the floor. Like a ticking clock, water dripped rhythmically from the rocky formations above to the ones below, leaving ghostly deposits of calcite. They reminded Bartholomew of sobbing Artanians as if the dripping water was tears from all those suffering creations above him.

"Focus," he said glancing around the cavern., saw five exits. "Dust bunnies!" he rasped, unsure of which direction to go.

He leaned against the wall and hit his head against the rough surface. *Ouch.* He rubbed it.

Where had that ibis god Thoth led them when they'd come here in sixth grade?

"Up? Left?" Bartholomew tapped his chin, trying to remember. "Right? Oh, yeah, Thoth said, 'Downward we must go."

"Okay, which way is down?" Bartholomew mused glancing from one exit tunnel to the next.

With only distant torches for light, he could barely see twenty feet inside each lava tube tunnel, much less tell which one went down. He hated to waste time, but the only way to check was by process of elimination. He'd have to check them all, one by one.

Chapter 65

From his underground home, Captain Sludge watched mist rise from the River of Lies. Seething, he opened and closed his gnarled hands several times. When viscous slime speckled his face, he narrowed his yellow eyes.

"Try to trick me, will you? Idiot Deliverer. I'll show you."

With an angry bob of his porcine head, he picked up a rock and threw it in the bubbling waters. Concentric circles expanded in the warm river, releasing pockets of steam.

He'd been addressing the troops, when Bartholomew's words echoed up the canyon. Sludge had just begun a rant on how they'd better shape up, or face torture in the Correction Chamber, when the boy's squeaky voice interrupted him.

"I'm coming, so you better watch out!"

When two privates snickered, he'd slapped them to the ground, then ordered the rest of the battalion to scatter into the tunnels to investigate. The boy hadn't been discovered any-where, but Corporal Stench reported that there was a new exit tunnel leading up to Paris.

"I try to close, sir, but the shaft remained."

Sludge had nodded, realizing that only Bartholomew could have made such an exit. That's when he'd gone over the River of Lies to think.

Captain Sludge ran a hand up his bony forehead, spreading the slime over his now-wilting spikes. As he straightened one and then another, a plan took shape in his twisted mind.

"Humans. They think they're so smart, but they're idiots. All of them."

As a cruel smile curled at the corners of his bulbous lips, Captain Sludge clapped three times. Within moments he could hear the sound of his corporals, Stench and Gunge, marching over the rocky cavern's floor.

"Sir?" they said, in unison, quick-stepping into a salute.

"Mudlark Maker is hungry. Go to the prisons and retrieve the barkeep you captured in the café."

Stench gave his captain a slow nod and raised his hairless brows lecherously.

"May we stay and watch?" Gunge asked rubbing his claw-tipped hands together.

Sludge considered. Mudlark Maker transforming an Artanian into a Shadow Swine slave was a cruel process. First, Captain Sludge or another high-ranking officer tapped the ground with an axe to make a glorious mouth appear. Next, Mudlark Maker smacked its bulbous lips and sprouted tentacle-like arms as the soil became a legless creature with long twisted hair and a huge cavernous mouth.

But the fun didn't end there. Oh, no. While the Artanian quivered in terror, Sludge shoved him towards the mud creature. The boggy arms then snatched the prisoner from the air and popped him into a great mouth before swallowing loud enough to shake the walls. Finally, with a huge belch and a spray of steam, Mudlark Maker spewed out the Artanian.

And a mindless slave joined the Shadow Swine ranks.

"Perhaps I'll let you stay when I meet you there," Sludge replied. "That is, if you can keep your mouths shut about the doorway to Subterranea." He paused and gave them warning glances. "Lord Sickhert cannot know that humans have carved a shaft into our home.

"We stay quiet," Stench said.

"As silent as a Mudlark mouse." Grunge bobbed his head.

"Then go quickly, before I change my mind."

The corporals turned on booted feet and quick-stepped toward the prisons.

Sludge watched them go, then rasped, "Come quickly, Deliverer. I am in the mood for battle."

Chapter 66

Bartholomew glanced around. Things were beginning to look familiar. Although the scattered torches along the access tunnels provided dim light, he still recognized some of the rocky walls. After finally finding the correct exit an hour before, he'd followed the long tunnel that sloped downward. Soon, the rough sandstone wall changed to the glassy obsidian of a lava tube. Then he reached the place with the hole in the floor and knew exactly where he was.

Directly above the stalagmite forest. Right where he and Alex had been three years before.

Good. Those rocky formations will be the perfect place to hide and listen to what the Shadow Swine are up to.

Bartholomew hung his head over the opening and peered down. He was suspended over one end of an enormous cavern with a stalagmite forest as thick as Alex's messy curls directly below. At the far end, in the glow of multiple torches, was a wooden platform.

"But no Swineys this time."

Bartholomew was both relieved that he could slip through the hole in the floor unnoticed, and annoyed that he still didn't know where the Shadow Swine were or what they were doing.

Once he shimmied down the ladder, he dropped into an immediate crouch. He might not have seen any of those cruel creatures, but he wasn't taking any chances.

He cocked an ear. No voices echoed off the huge cavern walls. Nor did a single footfall reverberate. The coast was clear. But now which way?

The last time he was here, there'd been a large gathering of Shadow Swine around the platform at the far end of the football-field sized floor. Then, along with scores of Egyptian gods and goddesses, he and Alex had gone into battle mode, creating animals, skateboards, and very cool swords.

Bartholomew froze. Just what the dust bunnies could he create to battle an army? He was all alone. One boy against thousands.

Deciding he'd at least need some sort of weapon, Bartholomew thought back to the Persian scimitar he'd made three years before. The razor-edged blade was a crescent moon and the grip fit perfectly in his hand.

"It's better than nothing." He snapped off a thin stalactite from a rocky outcropping.

He set the long piece on the ground and began rolling it between his palms. Flatten and sharpen. Smooth and shape. His hands became a blur as he went faster and faster. Three breaths and it was done. Bartholomew ran his fingers over the flat of the curved blade. Its silver shone in the faint torchlight of the cavern.

This felt all too familiar. Not for the first time, Bartholomew wondered how many times he was going to have to return here. It seemed like he'd just defeat the Shadow Swine in some drawn-out battle before it would start all over again.

He clutched the hilt of the sword and chewed on his lip. Remembering Mudlark Maker, he shuddered. *I can't do this again. Not one kid alone against zombie-like slaves, Swineys, and that sleeping mud monster by the platform.*

Bartholomew glanced up at the exit hole overhead, wanting more than anything to scramble back up the ladder and run back to the Impressionist Republic.

Come on, B-3. Don't wuss out no, he imagined his best friend saying.

Alex was still unconscious and maybe trapped in some Shadow Swine nightmare, while Artanians sobbed.

Gripping his sword tighter, Bartholomew forced his feet toward the nearest stalagmite, which reminded him of a tree in a Dr. Seuss picture book. The impossible column was at least ten-feet high, with knots of what appeared to be fossilized wood in lopsided lumps.

Flattening his back against the bumpy stalagmite, he scanned the cavern for movement. When he saw none, Bartholomew dashed toward a short squat formation ahead, where he crouched and listened.

What was that? He cupped a hand around his ear.

He strained to listen, but it was near impossible over the pounding of his heart. He took several slow breaths, waiting for that I'm-sure-an-alien-is-ready-to-burst-from-my-chest feeling to subside. After what seemed like years, his ears could finally hear more than the drumming in his ribcage. There was a swishing sound, but no marching jackboots or monstrous feet pounded over the ground. He wondered what the dust bunnies it could be.

"Go," he whispered, willing himself toward the next stalagmite.

Then another, repeating his listening, looking, and crouching movements until he reached the edge of the Stalagmite Forest. Here, he leaned up against a tall pillar where the stalactites overhead met their cousins on the floor and tried to locate Swineys.

He'd been sure that Captain Sludge would be around here somewhere. At least that's where they'd encountered him three years before. He knew little of this underground place, how big it was, if they had houses down here, or schools or anything. Did Shadow Swine even have mothers? Or childhoods, for that matter? Maybe they just appeared fully grown and disgusting, ready to invade people's dreams.

The swishing sound repeated.

That's when he remembered that muddy creature who lived next to the platform. Bartholomew shuddered, recalling the last time he'd seen Mudlark Maker. Sludge had been torturing Pharaoh Ramses by dangling him over the monster's huge mouth, lowering and raising the poor king like a yoyo. The sounds reminded him of Mudlark Maker's huge tongue flicking over the pharaoh's feet.

"So you're waiting for a snack, huh? I'll give you something to chew on." Bartholomew stabbed the air with his scimitar.

He took a deep breath and ran toward the platform.

Chapter 67

The roars reverberated throughout the cavernous Subterranea. Each howl echoed through lava tube tunnels, up the sulfuric River of Lies, and over the cavern floor.

When it vibrated Captain Sludge's bat-like ears, he tugged on the tingling lobules.

"What?" he murmured, stopping mid-stride.

The howls sounded nothing like the daily cries of a disobedient private being punished in the Correction Chamber— too low and loud—nor did it resemble a captured Artanian. They always blubbered while begging for mercy. It was more like...

"No!" he cried quickening his pace to a trot. His jackboots pounded the sandy soil, but the bellowing grew until the tunnel walls shuddered and shook.

When he reached the great cavern, Sludge skidded to a halt. Just a few yards away, Mudlark Maker's enormous mouth grinded a champing rhythm of gulping sobs. Its stretched arms, so glorious with muscles bulging every time they'd squeezed a struggling Artanian, quivered and tremored. Then it rubbed its bald scalp.

Bald? What, in Sickhert's realm?

Strands of Mudlark Maker's wondrous dreadlocks were strewn on the ground at odd angles. The dark braids spread over the soil like black snakes on sand. If Sludge had been trying to create a terrifying nightmare, this is what it would have looked like.

"Cap'n, what is it?" Corporal Gunge said, from behind.

Sludge turned to see Gunge and Stench quick-stepping toward him. The Artanian barkeep he'd ordered them to retrieve trailed them like a dog, a rough rope tied round his waist. When the French barkeep slowed, Stench savagely jerked on his end.

Sludge nodded his approval. "Mudlark Maker has been attacked."

Gunge glanced around furtively. "How that be?"

"I don't know. You tell me."

"Sir, we've looked everywhere," Stench replied. "No sign of Artanian or human."

"Artanian?"

"I know nothzing of zis. How could I?" the barkeep replied, weakly.

Sludge walked over to the still-howling monster nearby. He pulled his battle axe from the folds of his long cloak and tapped the creature with the butt end.

"Mudlark Maker, arise."

"Ouches! Oooh! Owie."

"Arise, I say," Sludge said, louder.

"I am…I am…owie, hoo." Mudlark Maker burst into a new round of wracking sobs.

That's when Sludge noticed the gaping wound on the monster's cheek.

"Someone stabbed Mudlark Maker?" Stench gasped.

Sludge narrowed his yellow eyes and scanned the huge cavern for signs of movement.

"Whoever it is cannot have gone far. You two, search the side tunnels, but hand the Artanian over to me. In order to heal, Mudlark Maker needs to eat."

"But sir, you said—"

Sludge knew how much Stench wanted to watch Mudlark Maker feed, but he didn't give a rap about the corporal's disappointment.

He pointed at the far wall. "I gave you an order. Now give me that leash and go!"

Head hanging, Stench handed over the rope. With a salute, the corporal turned on his heel and marched toward the nearest exit tunnel, shooting one sad look over his shoulder before disappearing into the shadows. Gunge followed suit, heading in the opposite direction.

Sludge jerked on the rope. "Come on, Artanian scum. Mudlark Maker is hungry."

Chapter 68

While plugging his ears, Bartholomew curled into a tighter ball. That poor man was being dragged overhead, his feet scraping over the platform planks as he struggled against Captain Sludge's cruel pulling. The Artanian uttered one desperate cry, and Bartholomew's chest constricted. He knew what those sounds meant. Soon the man would be thrown into the open mouth of the still-sobbing Mudlark Maker.

His sword lay on the ground beside him, waiting to be picked up, but Bartholomew refused to look at it. It was safer to stay hidden there under the wooden platform.

Do something, B-3! Don't just crouch there and hided like some sort of freakin' rabbit, he imagined Alex saying.

But Sludge is too strong.

Wuss.

I can't do it. Not without you.

Then he remembered his conversation with Vincent Van Gogh.

"I have but one ear, yet still I listen. Why with your two do you not?"

"I listen."

"Do you? Or are you deaf to that which you do not want to hear?"

"But Alex isn't here."

"I think he is. You have only to listen, and his voice will sound."

Bartholomew was sure Alex's strong, clear voice came next.

I am here, B-3.

He blinked. Van Gogh was right—Alex was here. He'd never really left.

Bartholomew nodded and turned his focus inward, envisioning the form. Five-ten. One hundred forty-six pounds. Cocky grin. Mop of curly hair. Shoulders a little broader and more muscular than his own.

Bartholomew patted the soil, searching the ground for a wet patch. Then he plunged his fingers into the mud, and scooped up a handful and plopped it at his side. Trying to stay quiet, he dug in again, getting a larger scoop before adding it to the pile. He repeated this multiple times, until his ever-growing clump was boy-sized.

Now it was time to mold the clay into shape. He kneeled and grasped his sword in both hands, using the flat of the blade to spread the out wet soil. Once it was the desired length, he leaned back and narrowed his eyes. Next he began pressing and pulling the soft dough.

Once he'd fashioned a rough form, Bartholomew ran a hand over the ground touching different stones as if searching for a good skipping rock. When he found a couple foot-sized ones, he set them into place.

"Arise, Mudlark Maker. Arise," Captain Sludge chanted overhead.

Bartholomew didn't know if he'd be able to call upon the Creation Magic. He was afraid that being alone might prevent the true art from becoming, but he drew his brows together, trying to fight through.

Thump. Scrape. A man's cry.

Bartholomew swallowed hard, willing the Creation Magic to accelerate time. Everything around him blurred as his hands tugged, twisted, and flattened. A leg appeared. And then another. Feet. A life-sized head. A sun-burned nose emerged. Then an arched brow. Power coursed through Bartholomew's fingers as he sculpted at the speed of light.

One final pinch, and the sculpture shimmered. Then hair sprouted out of its head, followed by clothing all over its body. Two soft eyes looked up at him, and Bartholomew got a lump in his throat. He tried to swallow, but his dry mouth made him choke. He pressed his Adam's apple to keep from coughing.

When he'd finally composed himself, he whispered, "Crawl over there." He pointed backwards. "As soon as you're a few feet behind the platform, start jogging toward the exit tunnel."

He whispered a few more instructions as the sculpture nodded in understanding. Bartholomew crossed his fingers and then picked up his sword, hoping his trick would work.

Chapter 69

Sludge had just dragged the Artanian barkeep to the edge of the platform, when he heard the crash. He turned around and peered through the cloud of dust near an exit tunnel behind him.

A familiar hand waved.

Sludge blinked. "It can't be."

The boy waved again and shook his hips in mockery.

"What! Awake? How did that happen?"

Forgetting the rope attached to the barkeep, Sludge started dashing across the platform until the taut line stopped him halfway. With a growl, he yanked savagely on the rope, dragging that idiot Artanian back over the wooden platform and down the stairs. The sound of his body bumping down each step was satisfying, but did little to cool his anger.

He tied his end of the rope to the stair rail and began jogging toward the boy, who now had his thumbs in his ears and was making donkey ears with his hands.

"Aargh!" Sludge ran faster.

Then the boy disappeared into the exit tunnel.

Captain Sludge ran as fast as his jack-booted feet would allow, but by the time he arrived there was no sign of the mocking boy.

"Crone, I told you to include me, but you wouldn't listen. Now we have a Deliverer loose in Subterranea," he growled, shaking a fist.

He began searching one tunnel and then another, but even after several minutes didn't find a single footprint. Alexander had disappeared.

"A farce!" Sludge raised his arms. "Well, I'm sick of being the Crone's buffoon."

Deciding it was time he took over, Sludge pivoted on one foot. He knew Crone was supposed to be meeting with the Mud Princess, so he squared his malformed shoulders and marched double-quick toward Swallow Hole Swamp.

Once he reached the misty waters where Shadow Swine hatchlings grew, he ducked behind some irregularly shaped boulders and glanced around. With nothing but pupae bumping against each other in the waters, it was safe to steal closer to the shack beyond the shore.

Okay, Crone. Time for me to turn this floundering circus into a worthy performance.

With a final glance over his shoulder, Sludge tiptoed up to the shack's dilapidated porch and tried the knob.

"Locked. Of course."

He pulled out the key he'd made after a recent visit. When Crone was in the kitchen making worm tea, he'd grabbed the key on the wall and pressed it into a block of clay in his pocket. Later he'd taken it to an Artanian blacksmith he could trust, who forged a new one.

"Now I'll have a look in those cauldrons of yours, you old witch." He inserted the key in the lock.

Once inside, he turned right. He knew exactly which room he wanted. While each held a single boiling pot in a unique shape, some as round as the ones the Wayward Sisters used in *Macbeth*, with others forged like serpents or krakens, the one he wanted was misshapen and warped.

This kettle held answers.

The view through the round door looked almost the same as it had days earlier when he'd stood there with the Crone. A three-legged cauldron with a long ladle inside still rested atop a fire pit, flames licking the bent and twisted iron.

Here, he'd watched the Deliverer groping along in confusion, enjoying every glorious twitch on Alex's pained face. But the Crone hadn't let him create any nightmares in this bubbling brew. And now Alexander was roaming free in Subterranea.

"Shut me out, will you? We'll see about that." Sludge stepped closer to the kettle.

The boiling surface was misty at first. No images. Not even the slightest hint of a human or Artanian. But as Captain Sludge looked deeper, a faint outline began to appear.

He leaned in closer. The hazy form took shape with lumps under a blanket, arms and legs splayed out in a prone position, and a curly head.

"The Deliverer sleeping? But I just saw him...how can that be?" Sludge gasped and stumbled back.

What was going on? Had Alexander been here and then gone back to unconsciousness? Or was the cauldron less powerful than Crone had led him to believe, only displaying what had already passed?

Either way, he had slogged through much to get here and wasn't about to waste this opportunity. When he first set out, he'd hoped to gain some leverage against Crone, or at least find answers to her cryptic dialogue. But never in his wildest dreams had he imagined uncovering a possible doorway into Alexander's comatose mind.

"I think I'll craft you a nightmare, Deliverer. What horrors should I send your way?" He rubbed his hands together. "You've always worried about that disgustingly kind mother of yours. How about I make her so angry that you beg for forgiveness. Maybe I'll make her pocked with disease. No, not frightening enough. Crying out in pain?" He paused a moment, considering. "I know, I'll turn her skin so pale you'll think her dead."

Sludge took a deep breath and blew a long stream of black mist over the simmering liquid. The dark smoke entered each gurgling bubble before rising on the steam. He smiled and blew more.

The hazy image of Alex rose higher over the kettle as a female form took shape in the boiling waters. A moment later, it ascended and Cyndi Devinci's face materialized in the air. Licking his lips lasciviously, Sludge blew harder and both images sharpened.

"Pain, sickness, suffering," Sludge chanted, between panting blows.

The image of Alex's mother opened her mouth in a silent scream and clutched her gut.

"You don't know what you're doing. Stop!" an ancient voice cried, from the doorway.

Sludge shook his head. "Shut up, Crone."

"This will end all. Cease!"

"No. I'm fixing your mess." He blew again.

Arms extended, the Alexander image rose from the bed and reached for his now doubled-over mother.

The Crone came up behind him and yanked on his long black cloak. "Stop!"

One of the ascending bubbles grew, encasing boy and mother.

Sludge smiled and pointed. "Watch as I craft a nightmare to end all nightmares."

He loosened another smoky snake from between his serrated teeth. Instead of turning Cyndi's face paler, the misty droplets fused into an arrow that pointed at the bubble.

Sludge narrowed his yellow eyes. He'd never seen that before.

Pop! Everything disappeared.

Sludge ran a claw-tipped hand over where the image should be.

Crone slapped him. "Oh, you stupid pupae! You've sent him home."

Chapter 70

"Alexander Charles, where have you been?" Mom rose from the couch. "The school called."

Alex blinked and looked around. He had no idea. Just a moment ago, he'd been in the halls talking with Gwen about…something he couldn't remember. Then he was flying through clouds. Or was he? He ran a hand over his scalp. No lump where he imagined one should be.

"I-I, uhm, don't…"

"Honey?"

Cyndi Devinci's hand came halfway toward his forehead, before Alex ducked sideways.

"I'm fine. Don't worry."

Giving him a sideways glance, she crossed her arms over her huge belly. "Then why did you skip class?"

Alex tried to think up some kind of lie, but drew a blank. His head felt fuzzy. He opened and closed his mouth.

"Alex?"

"It's just…." He shook his head. *I'm in trouble now.*

Just then his cell rang. *Saved by the bell.* He pressed the answer button and gave Mom a sheepish grin.

"Hello?"

"Did Mr. Clean do it? Are you back in one piece?" Gwen's breathless voice said, from the other end.

"Huh?" Alex turned away from his glaring mother.

"Are you okay? We were so worried."

"I-I have a headache."

It wasn't a lie. His head was pounding.

"No wonder. We thought you'd never wake up."

"Yet here I am." *What the heck was Gwen talking about?*

"Where are you?"

"Home." Alex rubbed his temples.

While Gwen began babbling something about a frozen Earth, Mom reached around and placed the back of her hand on his forehead.

"You feel warm," she whispered. Then louder, said, "Alex, get off the phone."

Gwen kept chattering. "It's been half-pipe crazy. You unconscious. Mr. Clean freakin... I've got so much to tell you."

Mom thrust her hands into her hips. "Alex. Now."

"I gotta go. See you later." He pressed *End*.

"You think so, huh? You are not going anywhere for a while. Headache or no headache, you should not have just left school."

Alex groaned. Now he was grounded and he didn't even know why.

Chapter 71

Bartholomew was crouching outside the dilapidated shack with the boy sculpture, when he heard the screeching.

"You've sent him home!"

His heart skipped a beat. After going after Mudlark Maker, Bartholomew had molded a statue to trick Captain Sludge into thinking Alex had woken up and was on the attack. His hope was that the confused Swiney would then lead him to whoever or whatever was keeping his best friend in a coma.

It just might have worked. When he'd seen the sculpted boy, the grumbling captain had stomped out of the huge cavern in pursuit. Anticipating this, Bartholomew had ordered the Alex-sculpture to circle back and join him a few minutes later, and then he'd untied the barkeep and gave him directions back to Artania.

"Merci, Deliverer," said the quivering Artanian, shaking his hand.

"No problem. Now go." Bartholomew replied shooing him toward the exit.

With the barkeep safely on his way, Bartholomew could begin trailing Sludge through the underground maze of tunnels and caverns. As he shadowed the captain, Bartholomew was careful to drop scattered stones, like breadcrumbs, for his Alex-sculpture to follow.

Soon he found himself next to a bubbling swamp, where he stopped and waited for his molded creation to catch up. On the shore, warped stalagmites bent their stony heads toward the misty swamp, while large egg-shaped creatures that reminded him of mosquito larvae bobbed in the waters. He caught a whiff of a rotten egg smell and wrinkled his nose against the stench right before he heard footsteps behind.

When the molded boy appeared, Bartholomew forget that it was a sculpture and almost leapt up to give his best friend a celebratory hug. Then he noticed that the eyes had a strange shine to them, and he shook his head.

After staring in silence at his friend's doppelganger while recalling things they'd shared, the lump in Bartholomew's throat forced him to look away. Poor Alex, lying in that hospital day after day, trapped in an unconsciousness that left him susceptible to all kinds of nightmare invasions.

Bartholomew chewed on his lower lip, his eyes rim with tears. *All because I didn't control my fall. Messing up. Always messing up.*

Swallowing hard, Bartholomew jerked his chin at the sculpture and the two of them moved forward, skirting the brackish waters until a dilapidated shack came into view. Was Sludge in there? He'd seen the captain round the lake, but had lost him a few moments before when the captain had glanced back, forcing Bartholomew to duck behind a boulder.

He had to know.

"You stay here and keep a lookout," he said to the clay Alex, before dashing up the rocky path toward the little shack.

Inside, muffled angry voices argued about something indiscernible. Bartholomew couldn't really hear what was going on, but with them distracted, now would be a good time to enter. Fists curled, he set his shoulders and tiptoed onto one of the rickety steps. It creaked, and holding his breath, he froze and cocked an ear.

The arguing didn't stop.

Lightening his steps, Bartholomew approached the entry. The front door was ajar as if someone—he prayed was Sludge—had entered in a hurry. After flattening his back against the outside wall, he craned his neck to peer inside.

Dark.

Bartholomew crouched on all fours and cocked an ear again. Now he could hear a woman's rusty voice lambasting someone.

"...such an idiot! Everything was perfect until you got involved...stupid pupae!"

"But I saw him—"

"But nothing..."

Not daring to breathe, Bartholomew began crawling through the doorway. It was so dark inside he couldn't make out much at first, but once his eyes had adjusted to the dim light, he paused, confused.

From the outside, the shack looked small, with perhaps two bedrooms at the most, but this was obviously an illusion. The entry was as big as the Borax mansion's, but Mother wouldn't like this place much, with spiderwebs dangling in every corner, warped floors, and peeling paint on the walls. In the kitchen to his right, a pot belly stove topped with a rusty pan faced a pine table and three-legged stool. He turned to look straight ahead, where a long hallway with steam curling under the countless doors carpeted the wooden floor.

The shouts appeared to be coming from that direction.

Go, B-3, he imagined Alex saying.

He blew out a slow breath and crept toward the hallway, which seemed to stretch ahead like something from Alice in Wonderland. Inch by inch he crawled, praying no Mad Hatter or Cheshire Cat would open one of those doors.

After a few feet, he paused, straining to listen for the source of the arguing voices. It seemed as if they were coming from a room about five doors down.

What now?

You know the answer to that, B-3, he imagined Alex saying. *Keep going.*

What does it look like I'm doing? Taking a nap? he almost retorted, before catching himself and continuing to crawl forward.

When he got to where the shouts were the loudest, he put an ear up to the door. Definitely Sludge. He'd know that raspy voice anywhere.

Bartholomew swallowed the dry pit in his throat and took a moment to collect his thoughts. Since the arguing duo might come out any second, hiding in the adjacent room where he could listen and hopefully uncover something to help Alex wake from his coma seemed best. He tried the levered handle, and finding it unlocked, ducked inside.

He scanned the room, relieved to find it empty. Almost. In the center was a boiling cauldron atop a brick-lined fire pit. Flames licked at its black sides as the brew inside bubbled and popped.

Curious, he stepped closer and gasped.

Images of Gwen and her dad from inside her house floated in the simmering pot. They were deep into a heated conversation, and it looked like Gwen had been crying.

"Messing with my friends." Bartholomew shook his head.

Although he knew he should have been listening to Sludge in the next room, it made him so angry he got lost in a fantasy of bursting into that house and telling Mr. Obranovich the truth. Once her dad was convinced about Artania, he and Gwen would join Alex in a quest to save Artania.

And everyone would be so thankful.

He was so caught up in his daydream that he didn't notice how the voices next door had quieted. Then the bang of the adjacent door hitting a wall brought him back to reality.

Oh, no! he mouthed, hitting himself in the forehead. *They're leaving!*

Then the levered door handle began to twist. While Bartholomew gaped, it tilted downward as if in slow motion. Wrenching his head right and left, Bartholomew searched for a place to hide.

There was none.

But the huge cauldron.

He ducked down behind it just as arguing voices entered the room.

"I told you, I have it under control," said an old woman's voice. "The girl Gwen is so distracted with the events I put into place, she will not be a problem. And if you hadn't been so rash, and trusted me, you'd realize that."

"But I saw him."

"A hallucination."

"I don't hallucinate."

"You did today."

Bartholomew heard Captain Sludge growl.

"Now look." The woman said, drawing closer.

Now Bartholomew was face to face with a little bald woman, so wrinkled her face could have been a raisin. He gasped, his eyes wider than Sludge's hulking form behind her.

"You!" Sludge pulled the battle axe from his cloak.

Reacting on instinct, Bartholomew head-butted the raisin lady, which sent her reeling backwards against Sludge. The monster began to stagger and wobble.

With them stumbling over each other, Bartholomew darted past and made it through the hall, out the door, down the rickety steps, and over the gravel path in about three seconds flat.

"Run!" he shouted, when he reached the boulder.

Two boys, one real and the other clay, raced for the nearest tunnel.

Chapter 72

"How many times do I have to say I'm sorry?" Dad asked as he pulled up to the curb.

"Whatever," Gwen said. "I just wish you would have believed in me."

"Tinker Bell—"

"Thanks for the ride."

She'd heard that apology more times than she could count, over the last few hours, but it didn't change anything. Mitch Obranovich had still forced her to go to the doctor, where she suffered the humiliation of peeing in a cup, baring her veins, and having a tongue-clucking nurse suck out her blood. All to check for drugs.

Unforgivable.

She jumped out of the SUV and slammed the door. She was fuming, but remembered enough of Alex's text to put on a mask of worry before ringing the Devinci bell.

"I'm sorry, Gwen," said the hugely pregnant Cyndi Devinci, as she opened the door. "Alex is grounded. He can't have visitors."

"I know, Mrs. Devinci. And I wouldn't have come by if it wasn't important. I have to talk to him. Mr. Clean is in trouble. Real trouble."

"Bartholomew?"

Gwen nodded. "You know how it is for him, locked up in that mansion. He's been super bummed out lately. And now…" She trailed off.

"His mother just called looking for him."

"My dad got a call, too. That's when I thought about Alex. Since he's the Richie's, I mean, Bartholomew's best friend, maybe he knows how to find him."

"I already asked, and Alex said he had no idea." Cyndi crossed her arms over her belly. "Are you sure that's all there is?"

"Honest." Gwen held up her hand like someone taking the witness stand.

Alex's mom gave her a doubting look. Gwen felt like a jerk looking back with a fake smile. Cyndi Devinci had always been so nice to her, offering some new concoction from her kitchen while asking how she was, all motherly and stuff. Gwen's nose twitched as she fought to keep smiling. *That sweet lady. I'm such a slime ball.*

After long moments, Cyndi said, "Okay. Just for a little while."

A minute later, when Gwen could finally breathe, she collapsed into a paint-splattered lawn chair in the garage studio. Across from her, Alex stopped rubbing his fluffy Australian Shepherd's ears, and raised an eyebrow.

"Don't like lying to your mom," Gwen said.

Alex nodded. "Kind of comes with the territory. Can't exactly tell her that Bartholomew's trapped in an art-made dimension."

"Cha."

Through texts, she'd already filled Alex in on all the craziness that'd gone down. From Earth being frozen to Bartholomew arriving and making a painting of an hourglass to restart time, and then how he'd disappeared again.

"Although, I can't help but think that if he weren't so self-obsessed, that this might not be happening," Alex said.

"I don't agree. Even though things were full on freaky, he wasn't focused on himself. All he could talk about was you."

269

"So? That doesn't mean he did jack." He ran a hand over Rembrandt's silver and tan coat.

"Don't you realize that Mr. Clean was working his butt off to wake you up? So the least you can do—"

"Okay, okay, I get it." Alex held up a hand to stop the impending lecture. "Still, you got to admit that this is all so bizarre. Everything is so different from years past. Popping in and out alone. Earth time all screwy while we're there. I don't know what's up."

Gwen thought for a moment. "Hey, Alex, I know you thought you were powerless to enter and exit Artania, but what if that's changed? What if you *can* go there at will?"

"How?"

"I don't know. Think."

Alex tapped his chin and got that cute look he had when he was focusing on a problem. Gwen couldn't help but smile.

"Well, the last couple times I appeared, I was with you or Bartholomew. But B-3 was alone."

"What were you doing?"

"Once, I was running away from Sludge. And last time, you and I were chatting. Remember?"

"Yeah, I thought you ditched me. Ticked me off."

"I didn't do it on purpose!"

"Okay, okay, whatever. Right now let's try to recreate the last time you left."

Alex stared off into space and made a face as if trying to re-enact the last time he transported. He stuck his lower lip out in a funny expression that made Gwen giggle.

"What?"

"You look ridiculous." Gwen covered her mouth.

"Lot of help you are." Alex crossed his arms. "I don't think this is working, anyhow."

Gwen slumped down in the chair and started picking at some of the dried paint on the seat.

"Poor B-3. Alone out there. No friends. Not even a friggin' blue jewel to guide him."

"Blue jewel?" Alex repeated.

"Yeah, remember how it led us onto a rainbow the first time I went with you guys?"

"And it was on the bottom of the pool the third—"

"So maybe if you created it—"

"The doorway would open!" Alex whooped before dashing towards the jars of paint in the cabinet. "Rembrandt, fetch brushes. It's time to paint."

While Gwen watched open-jawed, the Australian Shepherd jogged over to cabinet and gently picked up a few brushes in his muzzle, and then trotted back to deposit them under the nearby easel. He repeated this twice before finally biting down on a corner of the drop cloth beneath them and pulling it taut.

"Good boy," Alex said, as if it were perfectly normal to have a dog fetch art supplies and smooth a drop cloth.

He mixed up a few bluish colors on his palette, then closed one eye, held up a thumb and passed it in front of the easel.

Gwen started to ask what he was doing, but Alex shushed her with a flick of his wrist. Then he dipped a brush into the palette and slapped a swatch of bright blue on the canvas. About thirty minutes later, Alex had a decent replica of the blue jewel.

He stood back nodding his head. "Now what?"

"Cross your fingers, find a four-leafed clover, and hang a horseshoe over the easel," Gwen shrugged, "cause I'm all out of ideas."

Chapter 73

While waiting for the Creation Magic to morph the canvas, Alex stared intently at the painted jewel. Five seconds passed...ten, twenty, a minute. He didn't really believe that something created on Earth could become real, like in Artania, but he still narrowed his eyes to intensify his gaze and concentrate more energy.

Another minute passed. Gwen grabbed his shoulder and squeezed. His strained eyes started to water yet still nothing happened.

Oh, well. It was worth a try. He turned to Gwen, shrugged, and began to apologize.

She pointed behind him. "Look!"

The gem in the center of the canvas was quivering. Alex glanced down at Rembrandt, sure the dog's wagging tail was banging against the easel legs again. But the Australian Shepherd had slinked away and was cowering behind Gwen as if afraid the easel would grow teeth and bite him.

Alex leaned closer. The blue jewel throbbed for a moment like his hopeful heart beating faster in his chest. Then he saw it move an inch to the left. Pulsing, it grew by a third and brightened to sky blue.

Gwen stepped up next to him and punched him in the shoulder. "Dude, it's working."

The ever-brighter gem began a slow spin. Then expanded more and whirled faster, shooting rays of azure, sapphire, and cerulean blue in all directions.

Alex reached a tentative hand toward the painting.

Pop!

He closed his eyes, and when he opened them again found himself facing the same café where he'd fought flames months before with Thinker. Gwen clung to his arm, gaping at the charred building.

"I thought those rainbow rides were freaky, but that trip was beyond bizarre." She shook her head.

Alex nodded and looked around. The two of them were standing on a cobblestone road, and it appeared to be late afternoon. The sun was low in the sky, and long shadows reached their dark arms over the buildings. But the street was as empty as tomb.

The burned-out café hadn't been repaired, which struck him as odd since Artanians were usually industrious, working hard to keep the light of creation shining. Black splotches still stained the walls. The round tables and soot-covered chairs were left overturned, and even the scorched awning continued fluttering in the breeze. No one had bothered to scrape the peeling paint from the doors, or even sweep up the shattered glass on the ground.

"Why haven't they fixed this?" Alex asked.

Gwen shrugged. "Who knows anything about this crazy place?" She turned north and south. "Where is everyone?"

From off in the distance, Alex thought he heard people sobbing, as if a choir were humming a sorrowful song.

"Heck if I know," he replied. "And do you hear that?"

"I know. Like a huge funeral, where everyone's crying."

"Never heard anything like it. Weird. Let's go inside." He then explained that Shadow Swine had started a fire there months before.

Gwen's face blanched. "Those slime monsters? In there?"

"I'm sure they're long gone. And you're with me, a Chosen Deliverer." Alex puffed up his chest like superhero.

"As if more air in your lungs is going to help you fight those gross things." Gwen rolled her eyes.

"It'll be fine. Come on."

Inside, shattered glass globes still hung from the chandeliers, while chairs and ash-covered tables remained on the blackened floor. The glass crunched under their feet as they paced from one end of the room to the other. Then Alex saw a painting propped up against a pile of rubble.

"That is Bartholomew's work. I'd recognize his style anywhere." He picked up the painting of the café interior with a hole in the floor.

Gwen pointed at the ladder jutting out of the shaft in front of them. "And it looks like it caused that magic art thing to happen." She paused. "You don't think Mr. Clean went down *there* where those"—she gulped—"monsters live?"

Alex's reply was cut short by gasps echoing from the dark hole. He paused, staring as a bald head topped the ladder. Fearing it was a Swiney, he leaped back, thrusting a protective arm in front of Gwen.

A painted man climbed up the ladder and kissed the floor. "Home! *Je t'aime. Je t'aime!*"

Alex was about to ask the Frenchman who he was, when a familiar sweep of blonde hair topped the rise next.

"Run!" Bartholomew cried pulled the Frenchman to his feet. Tugging on the man's arm, he pivoted, then froze.

"You? But I left you in Subterranea."

"Huh?" Alex said.

"How did you get ahead of me?"

"Ahead?"

"I thought you had to stay below and return to mud. That the creation magic would fade up here." Bartholomew glanced past Alex, at Gwen.

His eyes grew wider than that hole in the floor.

She waved.

"Gwen?"

"That's me."

"Where'd you come from?"

Gwen backhanded Alex. "From this dude's garage."

"You mean"—Bartholomew gulped—"you're not a sculpture?"

Alex pulled on his collar and peeked inside his t-shirt. "Appears not."

Bartholomew rushed Alex and wrapped his arms around his chest. He leaned back in a waggling bear hug that lifted Alex off the ground.

"You're okay! And awake. You're awake!"

Alex chuckled. "Not for long if you don't stop squeezing me."

Bartholomew set Alex down and pat his shoulders. "Are you truly real?"

"Of course. Why wouldn't I be?"

"Well, after I made a sword, poked Mudlark Maker, cut off its hair to bait Sludge, and hid under the platform, I realized I needed an ally to trick the captain, so—"

"Hey, what? You attacked that mud monster? By yourself?"

"Uh-huh." Bartholomew nodded and went on to explain how he'd gone into Subterranea with two goals—wake Alex, and stop the grief he'd unleashed when he comforted the Mourner statue. "One worked, but the other? I don't know."

As if in terrible pain, the Frenchman clutched at his heart and staggered toward the doorway. Before getting there, he slid down the wall and slumped down in the soot. He pulled his legs up toward his chest and buried his face in his knees, rocking back and forth. A sob escaped his throat.

"I think that's your answer." Alex jerked a thumb toward the painted man. "You can hear crying all up the street."

Gwen nodded. "We wondered what it was."

"I didn't mean to." Bartholomew stared at his shoes. "I was trying to help."

As usual. "Explain," Alex said. "You say this statue took on everyone's sadness?"

"I guess she suffered so others wouldn't have to."

Alex tapped on his chin. "Where is she?"

"You're not going to like it."

There was one place Alex always avoided. A place of the worst nightmares. The place Mom almost went to.

"You don't mean the...?" He paused, unable to say the word.

"Yes, the cemetery."

Alex shook his head. "No way. I can't"

"Then more Artanians will end up like him." Bartholomew pointed at the painted man still rocking back and forth on the floor.

Alex's gaze swept over the painted man. Only the true art could turn that tortured face back into the thankful Frenchman who'd kissed the ground moments before.

Our world will be saved if their art is true.

Alex let out a long sigh. "Let's go."

Chapter 74

"This way." Bartholomew pushed on the wrought iron gate. The hinges creaked morosely, a bitter reminder of the pain he'd unleashed. Why did he ignore Monet's warning against comforting the Mourner? If he'd only listened, Artanians would be celebrating the return of one of their own right now. They'd be skipping and dancing with the rescued barkeep, while he and Alex worked to create the true art the Impressionist Republic needed to stop the growing white.

"Creepy." Gwen tilted her head at the acres of headstones, mausoleums, and crypts inside the cemetery.

"No argument there," Alex said sidling a little closer to her.

Without a word, Bartholomew led them past water-stained tombs skirting the gravel path. All around, carved effigies shed long tears and sobbing statuettes curled into fetal positions. After seeing yet another grabbing at her hair like a child during a nightmare, the pit deepened to a sharp pain in his gut and he averted his gaze.

But he couldn't shut out the grief that had pelted his ears for the last fifteen minutes.

Bartholomew shot his friend a sideways glance. Alex hadn't said anything to him during the entire trek.

Probably thinks I'm a screw-up. And he's right.

Alex trudged beside Gwen, his jaw set in grim determination. One protective hand rested on her back like a shield deflecting the overwhelming sadness everywhere.

Focused on the task. Like always.

When they reached the marble woman in a long gown, her face was no longer buried in her hands. Instead, the Mourner tilted her chin back and forth, her expression as emotionless as the gravel under Bartholomew's feet. Alex started toward her, but Bartholomew pulled him back.

"Let me try. Maybe she'll listen to me."

He stepped up to the Mourner, looked into her bone-white eyes, and began to speak to her in low tones. Asking, begging, imploring her to take back the grieving Artanians' the suffering.

But she didn't seem to hear or understand. She just kept staring straight ahead, tipping her head from one side to the other.

"I don't think it's working," Alex said.

"But it has to."

"She's like a baby seeing the world for the first time," Gwen said.

"Maybe we should sculpt a copy of her," Bartholomew suggested. "To take her place."

But when the boys tried to dig their hands into the soil, it was as hard as mausoleum stone. Bartholomew slumped his shoulders.

Alex wasn't giving up so easily. "How about we go to Monet's studio and paint one?"

"Too far," Bartholomew said.

"So? He has supplies there."

"I can't explain it, but I think whatever we do has to happen here."

"Then come up with an idea, Mr. I Can't Do Jack. You got us into this mess, now get us out of it!"

Bartholomew stared at the nearby a statue of a little girl who clutched at a short dress while her tears dampened the ground. The dark patch grew like a lengthening shadow at day's end. He started toward her, but halted and kicked at a pebble. The child was just one of the hundreds sobbing in the cemetery.

Gwen, who had been watching all of this quietly, folded her hands together and began humming.

Bartholomew ignored her at first, but when she switched to song, he was drawn to her beautiful voice.

> "*Hush, little baby, don't say a word.*
> *Mama's going to buy you a mockingbird.*
> *And if that mockingbird don't sing,*
> *Mama's going to buy you a diamond ring.*"

The little girl wiped away a tear with the back of her hand and took a step closer to Gwen, who stopped and gave the little girl a gentle smile.

"Keep going," Bartholomew said. "I think it's helping her."

Gwen gave him a doubtful look.

"I think B-3's right," Alex said. "Go on."

Gwen shrugged and continued.

> "*And if that diamond ring is brass,*
> *Mama's going to buy you a looking glass.*
> *And if that looking glass gets broke,*
> *Mama's going to buy you a billy goat.*"

Two more statues stopped crying and came closer.

Alex whispered into Bartholomew's ear. "Music. That's it."

"Like when we made that hypnotizing painting."

Bartholomew nodded, remembering how a couple of years back their creation had entranced a fish in league with the Shadow Swine.

He thought for a moment. "Could something like that help?"

"Well, music does soothe. And it also inspires."

"It makes people want to move," Gwen offered.

"And it is shared," Alex said.

Bartholomew bobbed his head. *Sharing. Soothing. Moving. What do they have in common?*

"Yes!" Bartholomew raised his palm toward Alex.

Alex stared at the waiting high-five like he was crazy. "What?"

"Gwen, you keep singing. We have work to do." Bartholomew grabbed Alex's arm and tugged. "Come on!"

Bartholomew jogged up the steps of the temple-like monument he'd entered earlier with Monet. When he approached the heavy stone door with an iron ring in the center, he pushed. It was locked.

"Silent Ones! It's Bartholomew, with Alex. Can you open the door?" He crossed his fingers.

Nothing happened.

"Hello? I have an idea to fix all this sadness."

"Let us in. Please!" Alex added.

Bartholomew was about to start pounding on the door, when it groaned open in a cloud of dust.

Chapter 75

Alex shoved his hands deeper in his pant pockets and blinked. Before him stood a painted figure wearing a heavy robe that covered her from head to foot. Since her wool hood was raised and pulled forward, he couldn't make out her face, but he had the feeling that it was kind.

Greetings, a female voice said, in his mind.

Alex glanced around, confused.

"They're Silent Artists," Bartholomew explained. "They speak with thoughts instead of words. That one is Mary, Mary Cassatt."

Alex tilted his head. "Hi."

Welcome. Please enter. The Silent Artist swept a hand towards the dark tunnel behind her.

Alex set his jaw and stepped over the threshold, toward a granite wall carved with names and dates. God, he hated cemeteries. They were ugly and stunk like mold and rotten leaves.

The painted woman turned his way as her words filled his mind. *I am much relieved to see you returned.*

"I don't really remember, but thanks." Alex followed Mary Cassatt deeper into the dark shaft and tried not to think about Mom's heart attack.

That day she clutched at her throat, gasping for breath, and almost ended up in a place like this. To Alex, this underground space with names and dates etched in granite was an empire of death. Rather than a place to create true art, he saw a vast disorienting labyrinth of tunnels and skeletons, with eyeless rows of skulls arranged in weird patterns of long bones. And the smell! Cold rot and mildew filled his nostrils. Alex squeezed his nose but couldn't escape the stench.

When the three of them passed an urn in front of yet another wall of skulls, Bartholomew outlined his plan. Alex nodded, trying to visualize the sculpture they were about to make. But between hollow sockets staring at him and a dizzying maze of bone-lined tunnels, it was hard to think of anything but that day.

Mom was clutching at her blouse, her jaw open wide. She sputtered and gasped, seeming to fight for breath.

"Mom! Mom! What's wrong?"

Her hands shot to her throat. No sound came out. She mouthed his name.

The dish slipped from his hand and shattered into a thousand pieces. He wanted to go to her but couldn't move, frozen and trapped as if at the end of a long tunnel.

Mom again reached for his hand as she desperately sucked for air. Then her head slumped.

In that moment, a funeral flashed in Alex's mind. He'd seen Mom laying in a coffin, hands folded over her chest, with a sprig of violets in her cold white hands.

Later, in the hospital, clutching a wilting bunch of her favorite flowers, with Mom an alien of tubes and wires, he'd crawled onto the bed as narrow as a coffin, and rested his head on her shoulder. The beeping machine stopped, and he nearly fell off the bed. A nightmare moment.

Shifting his weight, Alex dropped the flowers and opened his mouth to cry out. The violet petals scattered on the gray floor like a forgotten funeral bouquet over a flat headstone. He had just begun to sob, when a nurse entered to replace the cord he'd knocked lose.

That visit had haunted him for weeks, making him hate cemeteries ever since.

"This is where I thought it'd work best," Bartholomew said, when they came to a dead end with a waist-high niche.

Alex barely registered his friend's words.

"What do you think?" Bartholomew asked.

"Huh?"

Bartholomew pointed at a miniature castle carved into the stone wall. Here, tiny steps led to rectangular towers barely inches high.

Alex knelt in the open space in front of the battlements and nodded slowly. "I think I see it."

Bartholomew bent opposite him and drove his hands into the ground. Then he scooped up a handful of soil moistened by damp air and began digging. He tossed up some for Alex to pile into two mounds, a large one about knee-high, and a smaller ball-sized lump of clay. Next, they separated the earth into clusters and began to pull apart the small clumps. Little by little, they stretched and took shape.

While mirror images of an orchestra flashed in their minds, Alex moved his hands faster and faster. As their sculptures grew, the boys worked as one, molding, forming, pressing, and hewing. And in three breaths, it was done.

Alex waited for the Creation Magic to do everything else. He looked expectantly at the completed sculptures, but they didn't move.

He furrowed his brow. Usually their creations came to life the instant they were complete. He adjusted one tiny hand, and then sat back on his haunches.

Nothing happened.

He looked from Bartholomew to Mary Cassatt, and shrugged.

Do you recall the anagrams? Although her voice rang in Alex's mind, she was obviously addressing B-3.

"Yes, the anagram for Silent Artist was *enlist its art.* Like I've done these past few weeks."

Perhaps. But Artanians still suffer. Van Gogh most of all.

"I know. You don't have to tell me again and again. What do you think I'm doing here?" Bartholomew flapped a hand at the tiny sculptures on the ground.

There is another anagram. The one we need. Solve it.

Bartholomew shrugged like he didn't know, but Alex had a feeling he did.

"Dude, what is she talking about?"

"I don't know."

He has the knowledge, but refuses to access it.

Chapter 76

Why were they all staring at him? He'd done his part. Woken Alex up, taken him to the Mourner, and created what felt like true art with his fellow Deliverer.

Think. Mary Cassatt gave him an even stare. *Which anagram will remove their pain?*

"I have no idea."

"Come on, B-3. Don't quit again," Alex said.

Bartholomew crossed his arms. "What do you mean, *again*?"

"Every time the going gets rough, you give up, then pull away."

"But I've been by your side or working to wake you up for weeks!"

"Yeah, but before that you went inside yourself. Shut me out. Like you always do."

The comment stopped Bartholomew. Wearing a mask of fake smiles was what kept him from being a burden. Although the loneliness had been so overwhelming that his only respite was sleep, he couldn't tell Alex. His best friend had enough to worry about.

His voice was barely audible when he said, "I didn't go anywhere. I was right here."

"Seriously? You've been locked away all year, hardly talking to me or anyone else. Heck, you barely created like three sculptures!"

"It was Mother. She—"

"Bull! That's just an excuse. Something else is up. What is it?"

Then, like too much moisture heating an air pocket inside a clay sculpture cooking in his kiln, the pressure expanded. With nowhere for the steam to escape, it all exploded.

"Mr. Hero wouldn't want to hear about my *crap*. He'd tell me to suck it up."

"Sometimes, yeah."

Bartholomew made a mocking face. "Be what you were born to be, Bartholomew. Great like me."

"You have to admit, you do wallow in pity parties."

"The perfect Deliverer. Always doing the right thing."

"Well, it is our job to save *them*." Alex jerked a thumb toward the gathered Artanians.

"As if I don't know that? I think about it all the time. Along with..."

"Along with what? Tell me. I am still your friend."

"Are you?" Bartholomew searched Alex's face for signs of sarcasm.

"Of course, dum-dum."

The anagram? Mary Cassatt said.

Bartholomew chewed his lower lip and lifted one shoulder.

"Come on, Bartholomew," Alex urged.

"Another is *artist listen*," he whispered. "But no one wants to listen to my problems."

"That's not true. People care about you."

"Really?"

"No, I hate you. That's why I sneak past security to hang out in your hidden studio, punch slime monsters in the face, and urge you to create. But I sure as slime can't help if you don't confide in me."

Bartholomew felt a lump in his throat. "It's all been so hard. The loneliness... sometimes I don't know if I can take it."

"I know, bud. You haven't had it easy. Living in that mansion would drive anyone nutters." Alex slapped him with the back of his hand. "So stop trying to do it all alone."

Bartholomew hit his forehead with the back of his hand. "That's why the creation magic isn't working. Of course! The anagrams are *enlist its art* and *listen artist* because we need to enlist others' help. We listen to them, and they listen to us!"

I knew you would find the key. Mary Cassatt bent her head as she smoothed her long monk's robe.

From down the tunnel came the sound of shuffling feet, followed by a muffled melody. Bartholomew wasn't sure, but he thought he heard more than Gwen's voice this time.

A moment later, she appeared around the bend, her smiling mouth open in song. Trailing behind her was the little girl statue they'd seen in the cemetery above. Next came a granite angel blowing into a flute. At the rear, twin girls walked hand in hand, echoing the last words of Gwen's every line.

"*Mama's gonna buy you a horse and cart.*"

"*Cart.*"

"*And if that horse and cart fall down.*"

"*Down.*"

"*You'll still be the sweetest baby in town.*"

"*Town,*" Bartholomew joined in, and there was rumbling at his feet.

Then came a tinny sound, like a pocket doll playing violin.

"They're moving!" Alex cried as a high-pitched flute joined the strings.

Bartholomew bent on one knee, his mouth agape, as the tiny musicians he and Alex had just sculpted took up their instruments. The ankle-high woman in a long gown lifted her violin bow. A drummer boy raised his toothpick-sized sticks, and the flautist put her miniscule lips to a flute. Then they looked up at Gwen.

She gave them a gentle smile and nodded. The minute conductor in a coat and tails gave his baton a single wave, and the band started to play. Gwen joined in a moment later, starting her lullaby from the beginning.

Soon more shuffling feet approached, adding a new host of voices to the melody. Monet slung an arm over Renoir's shoulder while singing off-key. The painted Frenchman they'd left back at the café appeared holding a rosy-cheeked woman's hand. As soon as they took their places behind Renoir, they added their voices to the song. Next, Seurat came up next to Alex, the painted dots that made up his face twinkling.

Then Van Gogh approached, swaying in time to the music. Bartholomew's heart grew lighter than a cicada when he saw that all traces of pain were gone from him and that his ear had grown back. The *Starry Night* painter even smiled while his silent song filled everyone's mind.

More painted, sculpted, and molded singers joined his new friends in the catacombs. Bartholomew had started to tap one foot, when he saw four skeletons approach. He grabbed Alex's arm and squeaked.

Using scattered leg bones as mallets, three of the four became walking xylophones before their eyes. The bubbling sounds of femurs running up and down their ribs rattled in the dank air. Meanwhile, the fourth fleshless musician grinded his white jaw and crooned like a cabaret showman.

Alex and Bartholomew exchanged a stupefied glance.

Then came the Mourner, her marble arms lifted in boundless joy. Her feet barely touched the ground as she glided up to Bartholomew and took her hands in his. In place of the tears she'd shed for untold years were glowing eyes which looked into his with newfound joy.

"You have removed my torturous existence, given me new life. Thank you."

"But it was at such a cost. I—"

Bartholomew's words were cut hit short by a backhanded slap. His mouth flapped.

Alex hit him again. "Say you're welcome."

Bartholomew did so as the entire cavern filled with voices lifted in song.

Chapter 77

Gwen glanced over at the beaming Alex, who was playfully punching Bartholomew in the arm. And Mr. Clean actually punched back.

Good for you, B-3. She grinned.

Before she could start another verse, a hush fell over the crowd. Then everyone started to move back. Even though these catacombs were wall to wall with people, they parted like a comb through freshly washed hair.

The approaching bronze statue was hunched over like she'd seen before, but today his shuffle was different. How? If Gwen had to define it, she'd say he wasn't so caught up in worry. Today he strode along like a dude that'd just nailed an ollie on his skateboard.

For the first time, Thinker seemed light and free.

Brushing her shoulder kindly with a steely hand as he passed, Thinker strolled over to the playful boys. When he took his place between them, he bent over to peer at the tiny symphony in front of the doll-sized castle. The teeny woman in a long dress plucked her violin once, followed by a short blast from the chubby tuba player. After nodding his approval, Thinker stood back up and addressed the crowd.

"Friends of clay, paint, granite, and bronze. Rejoice! Artania is safe once again."

The skeletons paradiddled a drumroll over their ribs, bones jangling and clanking.

Then the crooner raised his gangly arms overhead and warbled, "Taa daa!"

With a deep chuckle, Thinker laid a hand on Alex's shoulder. "Give thanks, for the Deliverer has woken from his unexplained slumber."

"Finally," Gwen said, as her bud gave the crowd a half wave.

"That which was unleashed is now restrained. Our grief has subsided. The salty rivers have receded, and sobs became songs."

The little symphony played three sweet notes and the Mourner echoed them. When the crowd came back with same tones, Gwen got chills up her arm.

"Young Deliverers, you have changed Artania forever. Never again will one of our own hold the pain for all. A good lesson. One you should share."

B-3's face reddened as he exchanged a glance with Alex.

"Go on. Tell us what you learned."

"To work together," Alex said.

"And listen." Bartholomew lifted his gaze.

His clear blue eyes were all watery when he stared at Alex.

"To confide in your friends if it gets too tough."

"Yes, young one. Loneliness only increases when we isolate our feelings."

The three painted beings in monk's habits stepped up.

Mary Cassatt nodded. *Recall the anagrams and apply them to your unique friendship.*

Gwen got a lump in her throat when she saw both of her buds nodding in agreement.

Chapter 78

Alex could tell B-3 was embarrassed by all this. That guy hated being the center of attention.

"Please recite the anagrams you deciphered, Bartholomew," Thinker said.

With red creeping up his cheeks, he cleared his throat. "Well, when Gwen and I were stuck in time and nothing moved, I got *emit* and *it me.* Then I painted an hourglass with the blood from my cut finger."

"Gross." Alex feigned a shudder.

Thinker gave him a warning look, and then said to B-3, "Go on."

"Later, I tried anagrams for Silent Artists to get *enlist its art.* For true art there was *rut tear.* That's what gave me the idea of painting an opening into Subterranea."

"Which was literally a rut." Alex drummed "Shave and a Haircut" on his thighs.

"That a young Deliverer will be tossed into if he doesn't take this more seriously." Thinker thrusted his hands into his hips.

"Okay, I'll stop joking around." Alex turned away, curled his lip, and crossed his eyes at Gwen.

"Thank you." Thinker paused and addressed Bartholomew. "If you put all of these deciphered anagrams together, what do you have?"

"Enlist and emit. Join others to make art."

"That is the essence of creation, young one. Not in a vacuum, but as part of humanity. You must continue to enlist the help of your fellow Deliverer to emit the art within."

Alex turned around. "He's right, B-3."

"And you, Alexander, must learn to accept your fellow Deliverer as he is, without judgement."

"But…" Alex knew Thinker was right.

He did criticize B-3, expecting his buddy to suck it up and act strong. Bartholomew had hinted at depression several times, but Alex always cut him off before he could finish.

His cheeks grew hot and he stared at his shoes.

"Young one?"

Thinker's words made Alex's collar suddenly feel too tight.

He tugged on it. "I'll try, Thinker."

"Then it is time for a new song, one of joy and celebration. Gwendolyn?"

Gwen got a deer in the headlights look.

She leaned close and whispered, in Alex's ear, "What should I sing? I don't know what to pick."

Alex thought of the playlist on his cell phone. Did he have any celebration songs? Probably not. He looked to Bartholomew, who was grinning ear to ear.

"*In the morning. In the evening. Ain't we got fun?*" B-3 warbled, off-key. He raised his hands and shook them before pointing hammily at Gwen.

"*Not much money, but honey, ain't we got fun?*" she sang, picking up where B-3 left off.

B-3's voice cracked. "*In the winter, in the summer, don't we have fun?*"

"*Times are bad and getting badder. Still we have fun!*" the Mourner chirruped, as the tiny symphony began to fill the underground tunnels with the happy tune.

Alex shook his head in amazement. Still, this dark catacomb was not the place to celebrate.

"Let's get out of here." He grabbed Gwen's hand and twirled her around before shouting, "To the streets!"

Barely a second ticked by before everyone turned toward the exit. Thinker nodded and scooped up the conductor and drummer the boys had just sculpted. Next, the Silent Artists and Renoir and Monet knelt and extended their hands so the rest of the tiny symphony could go for a ride. A moment later, miniature cellists, violinists, flautists, and clarinet players were all perched on the strangest assortment of shoulders Alex had ever seen.

Thinker raised his hands to the ceiling, where one palm held the conductor waving his baton, and the other held the drummer beating a tiny bass drum.

"*The rents unpaid dear. We haven't a bus. But smiles were made, dear, for people like us!*" Gwen, Bartholomew, and the creations sang, as Alex tapped his feet to the tune.

When Artania's leader began marching forward, the Silent Artists and Monet fell in behind. Soon Renoir, skeletons, statues, and painted beings were parading along the catacombs. A few minutes later, the singing and dancing crowd pranced past the cemetery gates and was bopping through the streets.

"*In the meantime. In between time. Ain't we got fun!*"

More and more Artanians joined in until a cavalcade of horse-drawn carriages, twirling ballerinas, and top-hatted Parisians filled every street. And more. Over the River Seine, past the Arc de Triomphe, and right up to Van Gogh's burned-out café, the Impressionist Republic sang of joy.

When the song was at its height, Alex started to feel tingling in his toes. He looked down and noticed that his feet were fading. He glanced over to see B-3 and Gwen staring at their own vanishing feet, and knew what that meant.

"… *We are Artanians, and ain't we got fun,*" rang in his ears, as Artania disappeared once again.

Chapter 79

It had been three weeks since Bartholomew returned home, and things were pretty much back to normal. If you call having an army of maids scrubbing each corner of your home while your mother sniffs everywhere for germs and toxic gasses, normal.

"Whatever," Bartholomew said, after Mother ordered him back to take his third shower that day.

He rolled his eyes and set a foot on the bottom tread of the winding staircase. Then the phone on the glass side table rang.

"Borax residence," Mr. White said, after picking up the gleaming chrome landline.

His ear to the speaker, he nodded several times.

"Yes, I see. I will relay the message. Thank you." He hung up and turned to Bartholomew. "Alexander has just called to inform you that he now has a baby sister. He is at hospital with his family."

"I'm going."

"Bartholomew you need another bath," Hygenette Borax said.

"Nope. My best friend just became a brother, and I'm going to congratulate him. You can either send for the limo, or I'll walk. But you are *not* stopping me."

Drawing her pale brows together, Hygenette opened her mouth once, twice. Then, as if realizing she'd been beat, clamped it shut. She picked up the bell on a side table and rang for the chauffer.

Thirty minutes later, Bartholomew was in the doorway of a hospital room. Gwen and Jose were already inside, holding hands opposite Alex, who stood arm-in-arm with his dad, Charlie. Cyndi Devinci was propped up on pillows, holding a little bundle all wrapped up in a pink blanket.

When Bartholomew saw the look on Alex's face, he got a lump in his throat—and a tingling feeling in his chest.

Not now! He backed up toward the elevator.

He'd need somewhere to hide fast, or risk being seen in a disappearing act. He pivoted and jogged down the hall and pushed the button.

"What's up, B-3?" Alex asked from the doorway.

Gaping, Bartholomew twisted his hands back and forth in front of his face. They were still solid. He wasn't fading away, yet still his heart tingled. He put a hand over his chest and realized what it was.

Love for the little girl.

"It's a wonderful feeling, huh? Perfection personified."

Bartholomew swallowed hard and nodded.

"Come on, B-3." Alex waved him back.

Tentatively, Bartholomew stepped into the room and cleared his throat.

"Congratulations," he whispered, staring at the angelic baby girl.

"Thank you, Bartholomew." Cyndi smiled, then said to Alex, "Are you ready to hold your little sister?"

Alex slipped a hand under the pink blanket and put her head in the crook of his arm. His eyes brimmed with tears as he gazed at her lovingly.

Bartholomew had thought he would be jealous when the baby came, but now that she was here, he realized how silly that was.

The tingling in his heart hadn't been Artania yanking him away, but love increasing as if he, too, had just become a big brother.

"She's beautiful," he said.

Alex bent closer and gave her the softest Eskimo kiss. "Perfect."

"So what's her name?" Gwen asked.

"Yeah, Mom, what is it?"

"Her name is Destiny," Cyndi said.

"Because it seems like we were destined to have two kids. Huh, babe?" Charlie said.

Alex winked at Bartholomew. "What'd I tell you? Perfect."

Bartholomew couldn't help but agree.

Chapter 80

Sludge poked the misty image with a clawed finger and watched it dissipate.

"Smile and rejoice now, humans. But you will soon discover that we can invade dreams, no matter how tiny."

"Or young." The wrinkled Crone cackled.

And Sludge joined in, imagining the nightmares he would soon create.

For years to come.

THE END

Dear reader,

We hope you enjoyed reading *Artania - Portal Rift*. Please take a moment to leave a review in Amazon, even if it's a short one. Your opinion is important to us.

Discover more books by Laurie Woodward at https://www.nextchapter.pub/authors/laurie-woodward-childrens-fiction-author

Want to know when one of our books is free or discounted for Kindle? Join the newsletter at http://eepurl.com/bqqB3H

Best regards,
Laurie Woodward and the Next Chapter Team

You might also like:

Bigfoot Boy Lost on Earth by Kenna McKinnon

To read the first chapter for free, head to:
https://www.nextchapter.pub/books/bigfoot-boy-lost-on-earth

About the Author

Laurie Woodward is a school teacher and the author of the fantasy books: *The Artania Chronicles*. Her *Artania: The Pharaohs' Cry* is the first children's book in the series. Laurie is also a collaborator on the award-winning Dean and JoJo anti-bullying DVD *Resolutions*. The European published version of Dean and JoJo for which she was the ghost writer was translated by Jochen Lehner who has also translated books for the Dalai Lama and Deepak Chopra, In addition to writing, Ms. Woodward is an award winning peace consultant who helps other educators teach children how to stop bullying, avoid arguments, and maintain healthy friendships. Laurie writes her novels in the coastal towns of California.

Why do I write? I get to be a kid again. And this time the bully loses while the quiet kid wins. Also, I get to have awesome battles with wings and swords, while riding a skateboard.

Why did I write Artania? Several years ago when education changed to stress test score results over everything else, I began to think of art as a living part of children that was being crushed. But I have watched children create and discover the wonder inside. To me, Shadow Swine represent bullies who subdue that most beautiful part of children.

"Our world will be saved when their art is true," the Artanian Prophecy says. Every year I tell my students how every sketch, painting, or sculpture instantaneously becomes a living being in

Artania. Then I stand back as they hurriedly scribble a creature, hold it up, and ask, "Was this just born?"

"It sure was," I reply with a smile. "You just made magic."

And for that cool moment, they believe.

Artania Series

- Artania I - The Pharaohs' Cry

- Artania II - The Kidnapped Smile

- Artania III - Dragon Sky

- Artania IV - Portal Rift

Lightning Source UK Ltd.
Milton Keynes UK
UKHW021057021120
372650UK00004B/827